PRAISE FOR C

ANOTHER JUDAS

A PAV MCNEIL THRILLER
BOOK TWO

C. J. EMERSON

Arrowhead Publishing

ISBN 978-1-7391269-1-9

For all my Family
Canine, Feline, Bovine, Galliform and Human

CHAPTER
ONE

They used to leave time for the scars to heal, but not these days. More like open sores now, bleeding or weeping and staining the back of her dress. Not enough girls, they tell her, too many customers. What else can we do?

Eva hears the key turn outside, locking them in for the next few hours. It will be light soon. There used to be three of them in this room, but it's been more than a week since they've seen the Thai girl, with her skin like burnished copper. No one asks where she's gone, no one needs to; that isn't the way things work here.

She glances at Mira, already lying on her mattress, staring at the ceiling. Her friend hadn't looked over when she'd come in, nor said anything. If she has a voice, no one's heard it except perhaps a customer, forcing some animal noise from her as he reaches his crescendo. Eva sits on the edge of the bed and strokes Mira's hair, singing a remembered lullaby even though she doesn't know if any of the words are understood, stopping only when the younger girl's eyes close at last and her breathing becomes slow and regular.

When she's sure that the corridor outside is silent, the girl feels in a crack under the skirting board and pulls out the coin she stole from a customer last month, hiding it inside her body until she was safely back in the room. She needs a tool, and this is the best she can manage. Using the edge of the coin, she begins to scratch away at the nicotine-stained layers of paint that glue together the sash window and its frame. Every night, every hour she has spare, she scrapes away another few millimetres, making sure to clear the dust when she's finished so as to leave no sign.

It's hard this morning, her hand is shaking so. The last customer had been new; most were regulars and she knew what to expect, but this one was strong and silent, making no sound as the cane bit into her flesh. She didn't know what he wanted, to hear her cry out or not. Always give them what they need, the Thai girl had told her, help them to finish quickly. It's easier that way.

She tries the window again. This time there's movement, and her scratching becomes frantic as she works to break through the painted seal. She tries to lift the heavy frame, but it still seems stuck fast. Try again, she tells herself, trying not to think about what she'll do if the mechanism is broken, or something else is stopping it from rising. She uses all her strength, and suddenly the window comes free with a rattle of pulleys and moves up maybe half a metre. Cool early morning air pours into the room, displacing the stench of her soiled body; it's the first time she's smelled the outside since she was delivered here. Two months ago, three – she's long since lost track of time.

She looks over at the bed; Mira has stirred but not woken, and there are no sounds from the rest of the house;

with luck, nobody heard the window opening. For the first time since she climbed into the van that drove her halfway across Europe, there's no one to stop her. The window opens onto the flat roof of the kitchen extension, no more than a metre down, and she sits on the sill, swings her legs round and drops as lightly as she can. Still no sounds from inside the house.

They'd taken most of her clothes away when she arrived, and given her two dresses, identical except for the colour, cut low on her breasts. One red, the other blue, the one she's wearing this morning. That and a pair of flat sandals she wears around the house when she isn't working. She hadn't realised before how thin the dress is; the chill breeze cuts through to her skin as if she were naked, and she begins to shiver; best get moving. The next part will be more difficult; three metres, she guesses, from the roof to the ground.

She thinks of going back for the sheet from her bed, but what would she tie it to? No, she has to take a chance. She crawls across the rough felt to the edge of the roof and looks down; three metres seems much further looking down than it would looking up.

The drainpipe, of course. That's what rats use, she thinks, and is she any better than a rat? She tests it carefully, pushing it out from the wall, but the pipe seems firm enough. The distant noise of a plane makes her look up at the brightening sky; there's no more time to waste. She clutches the small crucifix around her neck – the only jewellery they allowed her to keep – and says a short prayer to the Holy Mother, the way the priest taught her when she was still a child. Back home. Then, without allowing herself to think, she holds onto the drainpipe and slithers down.

Within a few seconds, she loses her grip and falls,

landing on her feet and then toppling backwards. What are a few more bruises? But worse is the noise she's made, an involuntary cry as she hits the ground. A light comes on in the kitchen as she gets to her feet, and Eva scurries to the narrow side entrance separating this house from its neighbour. In the distance, muted on the other side of the wooden door blocking the passageway, are the first cars of the city rush hour.

Someone must be listening to her prayers. The door is bolted, but from her side; whoever fitted it originally wanted to keep intruders out, not keep prisoners in. She slides the bolts back, not caring about the noise any more, and runs into the street, turning right towards the main road a few hundred metres away. There are people there, ordinary people. Safety, if only she can reach them and lose herself in the crowds, to protect her from the footsteps she can hear gaining on her. The man behind is calling the name they gave her when she arrived, the name that sunk its tendrils into her like ivy – *'Eva, don't be a fool'* – but the Holy Mother has given her wings, she's skimming the ground, no one can catch her now. Her eyes are streaming with tears, blurring the world as she reaches the corner of the street and carries on running, straight into the path of an early morning van.

CHAPTER
TWO

D etective Inspector Parvati McNeil sat studying the mound in the middle of her small living room, and despaired. The top that made her look like a lap dancer, a skirt she might have worn at fifteen but not at thirty-four. The cartoon birthday card that only a man would find amusing. A pair of his ghastly underpants that once sat in the laundry basket for at least six months because she refused to do his washing. His Arsenal mug. The huge, art-grained black-and-white photograph of them smiling against a backdrop of mountains in Val d'Isere on her first - and last - skiing holiday. They'd signed it as if it were valuable – Ash and Pav, a golden couple. You had to laugh.

And there was more. On the dressing table upstairs was a bottle of ridiculously priced perfume, the one he'd bought her at the airport on the way back from Chiang Mai last year – but no, that could stay. She was nothing if not pragmatic, and there was no need to be too rigorous about these things. She had considered sending back the keys to the Porsche Cayman standing outside her small cottage, but how did bastards ever learn if they weren't made to pay for their mistakes? By keeping the car, she was performing a service to society, even though driving it always felt like an outside bet. The paint job on one side was a shade too light and the nearside wing mirror had a tendency to droop in warm weather. She imagined him buying an insurance write-off and having it fixed up in some dodgy body-shop, before passing it on as a gift. Second hand, third class. Just like Ash.

She checked her watch – 5.12 a.m., when normal people were still asleep – and then looked back at the small heap on the carpet; not much of a legacy for a relationship that had lasted, on and off, for nearly three years. She still couldn't believe that she'd wasted so much time on a man, of all things, a rebound and a half.

Pav scrolled through the gallery of photos on her phone, going back in time until she found Jess, the broken sparrow she'd rescued from a psychopath and then fallen in love with. Two years, that was all the time they'd spent together, until Jess decided to sell her farmhouse with all its memories and move to her father's palazzo in Venice.

Pav looked around her own cottage, no more than a couple of miles from where she and Jess had shared a life. Stupid, really, hanging on. She should have made a clean break and moved away, but the village had become home and she didn't have the energy to start over again. *There must be something wrong with me*, she thought. First Annie left to live in New York, then Jess deserted her. Perhaps Ash was an attempt to try something different. Hadn't worked, so no change there.

He'd seemed cute the first time she saw him, for a man, the friend of the brother of a friend. Didn't seem quite so short, back then, and still had hair. Not the world's greatest lover, but that was ok - preferable, even - and she never told him whose face she saw during his short, fumbling attempts. When Ma was first diagnosed, he was brilliant; came to the hospital and the clinics, played the clown to lift her spirits – he was the only person who could, back then; make her laugh.

The photo felt heavy in its metal frame; how many times had she studied it, looking for signs? Funny how we put on masks for the camera, she thought. She'd suspected, even then, that the relationship was a dead end, but it was so easy to pretend they were having good times. Looking at the two of them, she remembered that day a couple of winters ago; Ash had taken her up to the Tête de Solaise and she'd exhausted herself snowploughing under a blistering blue sky, on snow as sharp as diamonds. That was the holiday when she first started finding blood on his pillow-case in the mornings.

Nosebleeds, he'd said, nothing to worry about. And she hadn't, until the blood carried on after they got home and Ash started looking away when she asked what was wrong.

Thinking about it now, that's what upset her the most, the way he took her for a fool. All she'd wanted was honesty, an admission that his septum was being eaten away by the lines of coke he thought she didn't know about. She'd told him – my job's on the line here if they find I'm tied up with an addict – and he'd promised to stop, but what was a promise worth from a man with a habit? That was the breaker; she couldn't remember the last time she'd seen the Ash that talked at normal speed, the one that was able to listen, the one that could sleep at night instead of during the day. The one that seemed to care.

And now, at last, she'd thrown the bastard out. Another failed experiment, metaphorically speaking; he'd never deigned to live with her, not in London and certainly not here. '*How can you survive in that shit hole?*' he'd said the first time he came round to the cottage. '*Sell it to one of the local muppets and move back to civilisation.*' She should had chucked him then, with his high-rise apartment in Docklands and his whore-house furniture and the late night porn sessions on his laptop, sitting next to shelves of novels by Camus and Sartre. Better late than never.

She found a carrier bag and gathered up the detritus on the floor. The bin men were coming later; these outdated gewgaws could go with the kitchen scraps and the dust from the hoover and end up in a landfill restaurant for seagulls, slowly rotting. A bit like Ash. Even so, leaving the bag outside by the side of the lane wasn't easy. Back inside nothing had changed, not really, but somehow the cottage felt hollow, as if she'd thrown out a part of herself with all the memories.

Pav checked her watch again; five minutes had passed, but it was still too early to leave for work. She turned on the radio for company, made a mug of coffee, slumped on the small settee, and stared at the wall.

SHE PULLED into her car parking space at 6:50 a.m., outside the low-rise building that shared the site with a BT computer centre. An anonymous, unthreatening place if it weren't for the razor wire around the perimeter. Better safe than sorry, she'd been told when she started work here just over two years ago, transferring from the National Crime Agency to the local Regional Organised Crime Unit. She recognised the only other cars; Finn's Discovery, Amir's ancient MR2, Rachel's yellow Clio and Harry's unlabelled creation that looked as though it had been knocked up in a Mumbai backstreet. The A-team, but for how much longer?

Although the sky was clear, the breeze coming up from the estuary carried a chill. A late summer storm, perhaps, blowing its way in across the Atlantic. It would be warmer inside the sealed building with its recycled air; the mere thought made her nose itch with the veiled threat of a cold. She jogged across to the entrance and swiped her way in with her ID card, wishing that Starbucks was open this early so that she could have picked up a decent espresso on the way in. *What is it with me*, she thought, *holding meetings like this at seven o'clock in the morning? Unresolved masochism?* At least today she was awake, which had to be a first.

She made do with a coffee from the machine in the corridor, then went straight to the meeting room. The others were already there, looking no happier than she felt. Finn was talking quietly on his mobile in the far corner of the room, but he broke off when she walked in.

'Say hi to Sarah for me,' Pav called. 'I'm surprised she let you out so early.'

His pale face coloured under the thatch of black, wiry hair and he shrugged his cereal box shoulders. 'Did I have a choice?' he asked, but with a smile in his voice.

They arranged themselves around one end of the long table. 'I'll come straight to the point,' Pav said. 'Operation Hexameter's been on the sick list for some time; that's old news. The initial intelligence looked promising; a new human trafficking operation, bringing in teenagers for the sex industry in Wales and the southwest. A little hard evidence to back up the rumours, and we could have taken it to the next stage, but it still feels like we're operating in the dark. Now we're six months down the road with nothing to show for it. It's okay Harry, I know how much work you've all put in, but budgets are being squeezed and we can't afford to keep resources tied up with no results. The monthly priorities meeting took place yesterday and they've decided to cut our funding unless we come up with something concrete in the next week.'

She looked around the table. None of this was a surprise, and their faces showed the blank resignation of defeat. She hated this part of the job, leading them into surrender. Part of the price to pay for her promotion to DI; ROCU might not be part of the regular police, but she still carried her rank.

'We have one last chance, so I'm looking for ideas. Finn, what do you say?'

No, this wasn't easy. At first the case had looked exciting, the sort of thing she'd worked on ever since she joined the long since defunct NCIS, then the Serious Organised Crime Agency, and now ROCU, the Regional Organised Crime Agency. But like so many leads, she'd soon realised that it was a house of cards built on the flakiest of gossip and hearsay. Shutting down the operation without a result went against all her instincts, and she wanted to give the team one last shot.

'We're wasting our time,' Finn said apologetically. Her DS - solid, married, but barely able to hide the schoolboy crush he had on her. 'We haven't found any trace of the people doing the trafficking, let alone any of the victims. Every lead we've followed up either goes nowhere or is low-grade police work. I say we cut our losses. Pull the plug now, reassign us to something decent.'

She listened to the others repeating his sentiments. Perhaps, after all, this was a day for the clearing the decks all round; first a redundant boyfriend, now a redundant case.

'Okay,' she said. 'It seems we're all in agreement. The three of you can go – Finn, will you hang on for a bit?' She waited until the room was clear except for the two of them.

'We'll look like fools if this trafficking ring turns out to be real, and the case was shelved because we failed,' she said.

'There's only so much we can do with the resources we have. I don't want to spend my time chasing rainbows.'

'But we can't just walk away. Someone has to tie up the loose ends and square away the paperwork.'

'No! Please boss, not me. How about Amir - he's good on this sort of shit. He'll have it all tied up before we've even left the building.'

Pav watched the colour flood his face again. He'd climb Everest in a gorilla suit if she asked him to, and then jump off with a smile on his face.

'That's why I'm giving you the job, Finn, you'll do it properly, won't leave any skeletons rattling around to bite us on the arse later. On that note, there's an interview to be done this morning, a long shot on something Harry picked up. The chances of it leading anywhere are close to nil but we have to go through the motions.'

'I'll do it if you want, but why not let Harry?'

'For your ears only, but Harry's leaving us as of today. Decided our lifestyle isn't for him; we agreed to keep it quiet until now. Don't worry, I'll do the interview and you can start clearing away the paperwork.'

AN HOUR AND A HALF LATER, she walked back from the small park where she'd met the source. A waste of time, just as she'd predicted; no wonder Harry was leaving if this third hand gossip was the sort of information he was working with. She turned down the next side street towards her car, parked a few hundred metres away, and didn't hear the footsteps until a teenage girl pushed past, black hair skimming the back of a thin summer dress, running towards the junction with the main road. People didn't move fast around there, especially on a day like this; a sullen early morning rush hour in a part of the Uskmouth inner-city that hadn't yet made up its mind about gentrification. The girl stumbled, then righted herself against a crumbling garden wall and glanced back towards the sound of heavier footsteps.

Pav twisted around; a slight man with a face like a moonscape was almost level with her. He looked as though he'd run out of the house halfway through getting dressed. The belt of his trousers was flapping loose, with a shirt unbuttoned over a grey vest. He shouted something incomprehensible at the girl; Pav couldn't understand the words, but anyone running for her life wouldn't want that man to get within reach.

The girl was only a few feet from the junction, with her arms held out as if they were wings. She didn't even pause or turn her head as she swayed around a woman navigating a double buggy, pushed off from the kerb and ran into the road. The squeal of tyres cut through the hum of traffic as a van skidded into view, too fast for the morning, sliding towards the girl who stopped at last like a deer caught in headlights. Someone in the crowd screamed as the buggy woman took a couple of steps towards the girl, grabbed her arm, and tried to pull her to safety.

So close. The van hit the girl a glancing blow, tumbling her and the woman to the ground. No time to think; Pav kicked herself into action and hit a personal best as she covered the hundred yards to the scene of the accident. The man with the flapping belt was already lumbering back; as she ran by, he stared at her with a pinched look of derision and leant into her as if by accident, causing her to stumble across the kerb and into the road before she regained her balance.

There was no time to stop and swear; the woman with the pushchair was upright again, but the girl lay crumpled on the tarmac, with a splash of blood on her thigh where the dress had ridden up. The girl rolled over as Pav reached her, got to her knees, and then managed to stand, swaying slightly. A few people slowed down to watch, but the drama had played out too much to keep them. No-one was dead and the embryo crowd was already melting back into the flow of the pavement. Pav looked for the van; it had pulled in on the other side of the junction but drove off as soon as the girl was upright.

The woman tried to quieten her twins, crying from their buggy, and looked over at the girl. 'You okay, lovely? You should watch where you're going.' She turned to stare at Pav. 'Friend of yours, is she? I got to go, see, late already. You should tell her to take more care.'

Before Pav could say anything, the woman moved off, leaving her and the girl alone by the side of the road like pieces of jetsam from the tide of traffic and people.

'My car's just down the street,' she said. 'We should get that seen to.'

But the girl pulled away as Pav tried to take her arm. 'No hospital. Fine, all fine. I go now.' Her voice was deeper than expected, as if the words had rough edges, with an accent that Pav couldn't place. The girl's face looked narrow and underfed, making it hard to guess her age. Anything from fourteen to seventeen; who could tell with teenagers? But even in the open air, she had a smell about her that was only too recognisable; the smell of houses where clothes were barely ever washed and the floors were never cleaned. The smell of overused bedrooms.

The girl clutched a crucifix hanging from a silver chain around her neck, rubbing the small figure as if to release a protective genie; Pav remembered the man with the flapping belt. 'Are you sure you're all right?' she asked. There was fear in the girl's dark eyes; she'd seen that look often enough.

'I go – please!' The traffic lights were green, but before Pav could do anything the sobbing girl darted across the road, holding her thigh and dodging the cars, and made off down one of the side streets leading to the river.

Pav watched her disappear. The girl seemed shaken and scraped but not badly injured, so why get involved? If she wasted much more time, she'd be late for the monthly inter-agency liaison committee with the local CID, and relations were already strained enough without them thinking she was showing disrespect again. Go now and there would still be time to pick up a decent espresso before the meeting; after that she'd be lucky to find time for lunch.

By the time the traffic stopped again, the girl was nowhere to be seen; Pav glanced back at her parked car, swore quietly and then turned and jogged across the junction. In spite of the girl's injury, she must have been moving quickly; the street into which she'd turned was almost deserted and Pav slowed down. The girl could be in any one of the houses; maybe this was a fool's errand after all.

One final check up and down the street, but still nothing. She started to walk back to the corner, but as soon as her back was turned she heard shouting from a corner shop a few hundred yards behind. Pav swivelled round; the girl limped out from the shop doorway but clipped one of the boxes of fruit and vegetables balanced on old milk crates on the pavement. It must have been her injured leg – she crumpled to the ground and the apple she was holding fell from her hand and rolled into the gutter.

AFTER THE COMMITTEE meeting - a waste of time, as usual - Pav cut across town to Uskmouth General Hospital. Through the glass-panelled corridor outside A&E, the girl was nursing a mug of tea; she seemed even younger here under the artificial lights, a scraggy, unbrushed creature of sharp angles, although Pav still couldn't guess her age. She knew that one only too well; it wasn't so long since bar staff stopped asking her for ID, even though it had been fourteen years since she took a joint first in Maths and Computer Science.

With a slight change of focus, her own reflection looked back at her from the tinted glass, almost a stranger. Parvati McNeil – Pav to her friends – the same height as the girl, five foot six inches give or take, with blue-black hair scragged back in a ponytail. She'd cut it short again now Ash was off the scene, the way she preferred it. A figure that she called lean, but some people called stringy; partly genetic, partly her addiction to karate - Wado Ryu, the way of peace - and running. God knows she tried hard enough to build up the subcutaneous fat with red wine and chips, but the curves refused to come. She comforted herself with the thought that maybe they were waiting for something.

Another reflection in the glass was standing next to her. Pauline Treadaway, the eternal optimist of Uskmouth Social Services, wearing a small cheesecloth tent over Primark jeans that were at least two sizes too small.

'Has she said anything yet?' Pav asked.

Pauline shook her head. 'We know she understands what we say, but I'm jiggered if we can get her to talk. What do you think?'

'She said a few words after she was hit by the van. English, but a strong accent, and I don't mean the Valleys. East European probably.'

'You're the linguist. Anyway, we'll find out eventually,' said Pauline. 'My money's on Ukrainian or Bulgarian, one of these asylum seekers. I wanted an interpreter but guess what, no one is available at the moment. Maybe it's best to give her a day or so to settle down, then perhaps we'll get some sense out of her and find out who did this.'

'What did the doctor say?'

'Are you sure you want to know?' Pauline sighed. 'For a start she's malnourished, probably hasn't eaten a decent meal in months. After the doc gave a provisional okay, we brought up a burger and chips from the canteen – didn't last ten seconds. As for the accident – she has multiple bruising on her right-hand side, all down her arms and legs, and a gash on her thigh. Painful but not too serious; lucky that van wasn't going any faster.'

'You said something about her back.'

Pauline handed her a large yellow envelope. 'Take a look at these.'

Pav studied the photos, one by one, their flash-lit intrusions turning the girl into something inhuman. She shuffled the images, but with all the different shapes of broken flesh it was hard to decipher what she was seeing; there was a thigh, that was an arm, and this – this was her back, crisscrossed with scars and open wounds that seemed angry and infected.

Pav looked back through the glass; the girl hadn't

moved, still perched on the edge of the narrow chair, still studying the pattern of the floor tiles.

'Any idea how she got those?'

'According to the doctor she's definitely had sex in the last twelve hours,' said Pauline, 'and by the look of the scars on her back, I wouldn't think it was consensual.'

'So there's no name, no address, no nationality, no age,' Pav said. 'Over sixteen and you have no reason to hold her, not if she doesn't want to press charges against anyone.'

'It's difficult to tell how old she is, according to the doctor, the usual standards don't apply. Not with someone this malnourished.' She took back the photos and tidied them into the envelope. 'Even if we had an address and found her family we'd still need an Emergency Protection Order, given these injuries.'

Pav looked down at the girl with mixed emotions. This could be another dead end, another recruit to the growing army of the sex trade. As Finn said earlier – low-grade police work, nothing to get ROCU excited. On the other hand; East European, violent abuse – and who was the man chasing her earlier? How ironic for this girl to turn up on the day she decided to knock Operation Hexameter on the head.

'You'd think the hospital would find her a bed for the night,' she said to Pauline.

'"Doesn't fit the criteria" – wonderful phrase, isn't it, like a get-out-of-jail-free card.'

'What about your lot in Social Services?'

'Most of our carers for emergency placements are already up to their ears and we can't find anyone who's used to dealing with asylum seekers. We even tried out of county, but everyone's in the same boat.'

The girl looked blankly in their direction from the other

side of the glass, then turned back to her contemplation of the floor.

'We thought we'd found her a roof for a few nights in Abertrothy,' said Pauline. 'Robbie and Dawn, lovely couple. She's already got one of our babies and a four-year-old, and we thought we could talk her into our new little waif, but no joy.'

'So what are you suggesting?' Pav asked. 'Give her a packet of Elastoplasts and send her on her way?'

'Oh no! Nil desperandum, as my granny used to say. Do you know The Swallows, up near Aberhonddu?'

Pav knew it well enough, a secure unit for troublesome children in the middle of nowhere, on the slopes of the Black Mountains. She'd been there a few times; three staff to every inmate, and very expensive. Someone had told her it cost five thousand quid a week per child; the Ritz would be cheaper.

Pauline smiled coyly. 'I spoke to Joe, my boss. I told him The Swallows was our only choice and I'd be very cross if he said no.'

'I bet he's quaking.'

Pauline ignored her. 'I called the supervisor there, Isobel Correa, and she agreed to take the girl for a few days, at least until I can find somewhere cheaper. So what do you think of that, Parvati? A result!'

'Excellent news,' said Pav. 'The sooner she's out of this place the better.'

'Ah, I need to talk to you about that. The Swallows is at least forty minutes away. I have to be in court in an hour and I need to pop home, change into something more suitable. I asked around at the office, really, but no one's free.' She looked at Pav. 'I wondered...'

Through the glass the girl wound a strand of hair

through her fingers, twirling and pulling, looking into unfocused space. Take your chances where you can, thought Pav. If it hadn't been for an accidental meeting in the street she wouldn't be here at all; this was down to the local police and social services. But; the injuries on the girl's back weren't the result of a jealous boyfriend, and the Hexameter files hadn't been packed away and archived, not yet.

'I'll take her to the unit,' said Pav, 'unless, of course, using my car is against Local Authority policy or the Health and Safety Act or the nuclear disarmament treaty.'

'I won't say a word, Parvati, promise. And bless you for helping!'

'Go away and give evidence or whatever you're doing. I know Bella – I'll ask her to call you later and confirm the girl's settled down.'

'I can trust you with this, can't I?' asked Pauline. 'No wafting her off to some secret service interrogation dungeon. She's ours until anyone tells me otherwise.'

'Guide's honour. You know me, Pauline, Little Miss Co-operation.'

THREE

The road narrowed to a single track and the girl beside her was still silent, but at least she had a name now – Eva. A month's salary said it wouldn't be the one her mother gave her, but at least it was contact of a sort. They'd stopped for petrol at a service station a few miles back and the girl came in with her when she went to pay. Amazing how much friendship you could buy with a couple of packets of prawn cocktail crisps.

'They don't exactly go in for street names around here,' Pav said, hoping for a response, but Eva ignored her. 'You'll like The Swallows. You get your own room; there's a TV and music, books, you can go out for walks – with one of the staff. And it's safe – no-one can get at you there.'

She didn't say that it was the next best thing to a prison without the bars. Or that there would always be somebody watching her, and at night the whole place would be alarmed. Bedroom to bathroom and back would be okay, anything else and the place would sound like a slot machine paying out the jackpot, with bells going off all over the shop. '*Unless you have the right keys and the right codes, no one gets in or out*,' Bella had said the last time Pav was there. Perfect.

She realised she'd missed the turning, after driving for miles along the lane as it twisted its way up into the Black Mountains and then reached a cattle grid, where even the stunted hawthorns stopped and the moor began. There wasn't much room to manoeuvre, but a slow seven point turn later and they began the drive back down, paralleling the track of the infant river that glinted twenty feet below. Eva aside, it would be good to see Bella again. How old was she – late 40s or early 50s? – but she'd probably looked much the same at twenty and would at sixty. Eyes like cinders, black hair in a flamenco bun, that irresistible Castilian lisp, and a laugh that would make Satan blush.

Pav glanced at Eva; the girl was staring out of the window across the valley but it was impossible to know what she saw. What pictures does the mind learn to make after so much damage, Pav thought, was there anything which didn't seem tainted and alien? And she remembered the girls that Jess nearly gave her life to save, and shivered with the memory.

She focussed back on the road; it was easier to spot the turning from this direction, an even narrower lane running between steep, grassy banks on either side. Another half a mile, and the banks fell away as the track stopped by security gates set into a high perimeter fence. Pav gave the camera her best smile as she pressed the intercom and said her name; in the rearview mirror, the gates swung shut automatically behind them as they approached the buildings. A wing had been added to what started out as a low, stone farmhouse, and across the gravel courtyard a couple of outhouses sat next to a metal-sided barn that could have hidden a light aircraft. They pulled up near the main door. The hillside rose in earnest beyond the paddocks, just behind the house, but the slopes were still shadowed from the mid-morning sun hiding behind the ridge.

The engine had barely stopped turning before a woman walked out from the main house. The girl didn't move from the front seat as Bella opened the passenger door. 'Eva – did I get that right? Come on in – I'll show you to your room.'

Pav watched as the girl unstrapped herself obediently and followed the older woman; from here they could be mother and daughter. She tracked them at a discreet distance and then waited in the kitchen at the back while the others went upstairs. A coffee machine bubbled away on one of the kitchen units; her last decent drink had been at home that morning, surrounded by the detritus from what passed as her relationship with Ash. She looked around for a spare mug but couldn't see anything, and none of the cupboards or drawers would open. She always forgot, even though Bella had explained; '*Knives, matches, bottles of bleach – the whole place is childproofed with a vengeance.*' With the sort of damaged kids she got, who could blame her?

The house was silent as she sat at the farmhouse table and looked out through the windows at the hills. At this time of day they were little more than silhouettes against a pale sky, featureless masses of deep purple. Beautiful but threatening; somewhere this isolated needed all the light it could get.

She heard a sudden sound from behind and swung around to find Bella in the doorway, smiling.

'It's the stone,' she said, 'it seems to soak up the sound. You'd think there would be echoes, but no. Strange but true.' The way she spoke made Pav think of a dark oloroso by a fireside in winter.

Bella poured two coffees and joined Pav at the table. 'I left Eva upstairs to settle in and get used to her room.' The shadows under her eyes were faint smudges of charcoal.

'What about you?' Pav asked. 'Do you get much time away from this place at the moment?

'Not that easy when it's your own business – you always feel you can do things better than anyone else.'

'I remember when I first met you. I thought you were just the manager, and an unusual one at that.'

'This is my third career, I think – sometimes I lose count. This...,' she encompasses the room with her arms, '... this is a beautiful place, and working with children is a blessing, no? Plus, I like being my own boss, not to mention that this business is a good investment. I don't pretend to be an angel; at least, not all the time.'

'I'll give you this, you're not like most of the social workers I've met.'

Bella smiled. 'This is my life, Pav. One of the lessons I learned – don't lean on anyone. We come into the world alone, we leave it alone. Why buck a trend?' She finished her coffee. 'And how about you? I heard on the grapevine that you were promoted last year; I was surprised to hear that you would be Eva's taxi driver.'

'Just a favour. I was the one that brought her in this morning after she had a slight argument with a van.'

'She is a lucky girl – not everyone would have bothered.'

'Old habits.'

'And how about your chap? You were having trouble with him the last time we met. Some financial whiz kid, you said – or did you end up succumbing to the charms of your colleague, the one who had a passion for you? A little stolid, I thought, unless you wanted a quieter life.'

'Finn? God no – he works for me now, definitely not my style, and he's married. As for Ash, he's gone as of last week. I told him to come back when he's finished evolving – I'm still not sure whether he's stuck at snake or weasel. Actually, more like mollusc.'

'I confess, I was surprised when you said you had a man in tow, not really your style. Who would go back to bread and cheese and warm beer when they have enjoyed the delights of lobsters and truffles and fine wines?' Was that the hint of a wink? 'Do you ever hear from Jess? She sounded challenging, but fun. Or the one before her, Annie, the rich one who moved to New York. You have a habit of letting them slip away.'

'Jess sometimes. She's still based in Venice and making a name with her photography. As for Annie - nothing. She was in a different life, no regrets.'

'No comment. At least I see you kept the car.' When Bella stood, it was like watching a waterfall in reverse. 'We shall do our best by Eva. And it has been too long; you should come up to the house now that you are a free woman. I am only a couple of miles outside Abertrothy – you know Stonefield, near the studios? – and although I say it myself, my taste in wine is exemplary as long as you like it rich and dark and Spanish. This Sunday, I insist.' She scribbled on the back of a business card. 'My address and phone number – eight o'clock if that will suit.'

They both turned at a sound from the hallway; Eva, staring at them with unreadable eyes. Bella took a bottle of Coke from the fridge and handed it to the girl. 'What do you say we go outside – it's too nice to stay in here.' She paused. 'Pav, do you have to go yet?'

Eva had said nothing useful so far, and this might be the chance to make the trip worthwhile. Pav followed Bella through the back door and around the corner of the building to a small concrete terrace furnished with a cheap set of patio furniture, soft metal covered with flaking green paint. The air was fresh and clear this evening, free of the late summer haze. Three rabbits hopped around on a patch of scrubby grass near the perimeter fence, oblivious to the pair of buzzards circling a few hundred feet above, and Pav watched them for a few moments before joining the other two at the table.

'Another hour or so and we shall have supper,' said Bella, 'and then you will meet our other guest – she is with her counsellor at the moment but I am sure that you are going to get on, she is really friendly.'

The girl shrugged and stared at the table. 'I already have friend, is name Mira.'

There was something about the way she said the name, the tone of voice used about someone special who had died or left forever. Holding on to mist.

'How long have you known Mira?' asked Pav.

The girl played with some flaking paint on the table surface as she answered. 'Maybe three month. She still in house I run away from, with bastard man Defrim.'

'Defrim – he kept you in the house? Was he the man who chased you this morning?'

'Of course. Your police, I hope they break his arms. Is not good man.' She spat on the ground.

'This guy, Defrim,' Pav asked, 'where did you meet him? Does he have any friends?'

'Is stupid man, has no friends. He talk to people on phone, I don't know names. You ask him, maybe, and then you break arms.'

Pav tried to hide a smile. 'Your friend Mira, did you know her before you came to this country?'

'She come to house one week after me. We don't know each other before, I think maybe she is Bulgarian girl. I think maybe they don't want her too much, her arm is...' She flapped her left hand around. 'I don't know word. Accident when she was born, hand was... mmm, too small, not strong.'

'Were there other girls in the house with you?' Bella asked.

'They come, they go. No-one last long. This is why I get away, before I go too.'

'Go? Go where?' asked Pav.

Eva looked from one to the other of them, as if searching for something. 'When they get sick, or customers don't want them no more, they go. They take medicine but still everybody get sick, everybody get tired, everybody go. Why not?' She shrugged again and looked away.

The daylight had changed. The corner of the patio was already in shadow and the line between light and dark was moving almost visibly towards the table. The rabbits had disappeared.

It seemed strange, what Eva had just said, about girls getting sick and disappearing. 'Do you know what happens to them, or where they're taken?' asked Pav.

Eva shrugged. 'Defrim – he say when girls no good for business anymore, they get job they came for, au paire, cleaner. I don't think so.' The late rays of the sun shone purple lights through her black hair and she was sitting upright now, defiant. No wonder she was the one to run away; there was a feistiness about her that resonated. Some people are born to be victims, Pav thought, some aren't.

'How about you?' she asked. 'were the customers getting tired of you, were you getting sick?'

Eva gave her a sideways look. 'Maybe I get lucky – was why I leave. You know, these men very unclean. First one they send in to me, I am sick and it go over all his shoes – I remember colour – brown, with broken lace. When he take clothes off, smell of fish market at home. And he look like dead fish, white skin, too wet. Maybe Mira go with him now.' There were tears in her dark eyes. 'I think maybe I take her with me when I go, but she is too young, too slow. And not being at house long; too early to get sick, too early to go. Tonight for her is no good, no good.' She shook her head slowly at the thought of what would be happening to her friend.

Something about this didn't sound right. 'The place you ran away from,' Pav said, 'I don't suppose you know the address? I could tell the police, ask them to fetch Mira and make her safe.' She ignored Bella scowling from the other side of the table. 'The address, Eva, do you know it?' she asked.

The girl smiled for the first time. 'I can show, not tell. The address I do not know – maybe I recognise. Is near where I had accident – you will take me? Then maybe we get Mira.'

AFTER TEN MINUTES, the two of them alone in the kitchen, Bella still wasn't persuaded.

'She's in my care now – if anything happens to her, I'll be responsible.'

'I'm not exactly a stranger, Bella.'

'This is a job for the police, not you secret service types.'

'I work for a government agency with links to the local

police, and we're nothing to do with the bloody secret service. Anyway, you can see the girl's easily spooked – we didn't even have a name until I got her away from the police station. She trusts me, we need to take our chances where we can.'

'I still say it's not our job.'

'Maybe, but it is our duty. It's up to you, come with us or stay behind.'

THEY DROVE in Bella's car, a spotless Audi that still smelled of the showroom. Eva seemed lost in the back seat, wearing borrowed sunglasses and a baseball cap.

'I am still not convinced,' said Bella in a half whisper, trying not to let Eva hear. 'No one ever accused me of being a flake, but searching for brothel keepers and kidnappers is a job for the police, not the middle-aged owner of a residential unit.' She swung onto the A479 heading south. 'And what about the girls getting sick? That does not sound right to me.'

'Sex workers aren't exactly the healthiest people in the world,' said Pav. 'They come into contact with every disgusting disease around. I bet Eva hasn't seen a doctor since she's been in this country. At least, not until we caught up with her. Trust me, that's all she's describing. If a girl gets too sick to work, she gets turned out onto the street and told to piss off. The medicine they're given is probably nothing more than vitamin C, if that.'

But despite her reassurances to Bella, loud bells were ringing, had been ever since Eva talked about girls disappearing. Maybe the bet was paying off; with luck and a fair wind, the girl sitting in the back of the car could be one of the missing victims of the traffickers.

'Perhaps you are right,' said Bella, but there was no conviction in her voice. 'And I guess all we are doing is taking a drive. No heroics, huh?'

'Whatever we find out, we'll pass it on,' Pav said. 'We can't let the police have all the fun now, can we?'

HALF AN HOUR LATER, they started burrowing through the tight streets of Uskmouth. As the fields gave way to buildings, Pav twisted round to smile encouragement; Eva had slipped imperceptibly down into the back seat, trying to hide despite her impromptu disguise.

This could be difficult. The roads all looked the same; the houses were huddled together in repeating patterns of crumbling windowsills, concreted front gardens and satellite dishes with cables that ended in midair. When they reached the street where she'd first seen Eva that morning, Pav told Bella to slow down. They cruised slowly, all the doors locked, waiting for a sign from the girl, but by the time they reached the corner where the van had knocked her down, there was nothing but silence from the back seat. Bella crossed the junction, held up two rows of traffic while she turned in the narrow street and returned the way they came. They were almost at the end of the road again when Eva grabbed Pav's shoulder.

'Do you recognise something?'

The car slowed to a crawl as Eva pointed across the road, hesitantly. 'That house with side door – is where I got away this morning. And red curtains upstairs – they are always closed. I know that room.' Her voice was as small as a child's as she stared at the house. 'I never saw from outside except when I arrive and then it is dark. They say I will be nanny for children.' She took off the sunglasses as if fascinated by the sight, even though there was no obvious difference between that house and any of its neighbours.

'Pull up,' said Pav, although there was no need. They had the address, what more did they want? And yet; only this morning she'd been parked just down the street, never suspecting what was happening a few metres away on the other side of a brick wall. And she'd always seen rules more as guidelines, suggestions to be followed if there were no better options. Which there usually were.

Bella stopped the car but seemed uncomfortable. 'We should go, there's no point in attracting attention to ourselves...' but the front door opened before she finished.

Pav recognised the man instantly, the one who'd jostled her that morning. He stood there for a few seconds, talking to someone in the shadowed hallway, before he pulled the door shut behind him and walked down the path towards the street. At first he looked through them as if they were invisible but then, like the patterns in a kaleidoscope clicking into place, he noticed the car double parked opposite and lumbered towards them.

In the back seat, Eva was making small, animal noises as Bella swore and pulled away. Pav checked her door mirror; the man was standing on the pavement, staring after them.

'Damn, he recognised me,' she said.

'He knows you? How can that be?' Bella sounded almost relieved.

'I bumped into him this morning when he was chasing Eva.' She relaxed as they turned the corner, out of sight of the house. 'He doesn't know who I am, but I guess we must have spooked him. At least now we know where it's all happening – time to call in the cavalry, wouldn't you say?'

• • •

PAV CALLED Finn before she left The Swallows and asked him to organise a raid by the police. He knew half of them from when he was in Uskmouth CID, and as far as she could tell they still saw him as one of theirs, not like her. The upstart tart, they called her behind her back, not always bothering to say it quietly. She'd been called worse, a skinny brown girl growing up near Glasgow, and there weren't many insults she hadn't heard after years working with various crime agencies.

It didn't matter. The raid would have to be police led; they had the foot soldiers, and the protocols needed to be followed. She'd do the same in their shoes, protect their prerogatives against an agency they saw as encroaching on their territory. Turf wars; might as well be dealing with rutting stags, she thought.

THE DAY HAD DISAPPEARED without her noticing. There was no point in going back to the office, so she headed south to Abertrothy and then took the road parallel to the river, until she reached home. Blackbrook might not be the most attractive village in the world, but after living there for the last few years she felt part of the community. Almost. She'd bought the terraced cottage outright with the money she made when she moved in with Annie in Avonport and sold her apartment in London. Her pre-Jess life - everything had looked so different then.

But this wasn't so bad. No mortgage, no worries, and at least she was close to her parents. Pa had worked in a paper factory outside Glasgow until he retired a couple of years ago, and Ma did the books for a small firm of solicitors, until her memory gave up the fight and began to lead her down false and tricksy paths. They'd moved south to be near her; a responsibility that, to her shame, sometimes felt more of a burden.

She parked the car on the verge opposite her cottage; it had been days since she last spoke to Pa, and a couple of weeks since she last went round to visit, even though their house in Lydford was fifteen minutes away at most. More guilt; she knew how much it meant to Pa even though he'd never understand how hard it was for her, trying to talk to the woman who used to be her mother, the woman who'd forgotten who her daughter was and no longer cared. Saturday, she told herself as she locked the car, I'll call round then, give Pa a break.

There was a missed call and a voicemail on her mobile, but she deleted it as soon as she heard Ash's voice. Don't call, she'd said, but that was always wishful thinking. She could block his calls or even get a new number, but was he worth the bother? If she'd thought relationships with women were sometimes challenging, Ash was in a different league.

Bastard; even the thought of having to talk to him put her in a bad mood. At least there was no danger of him coming round, not after what she'd called him the other day. And Blackbrook wasn't his style, thankfully. The recreational drug of choice for most people in the village was warm bitter from The Queen Bess and a bit of weed from time to time. Ash's style was more like rolled up fifties in the loos of a lap-dancing club in the Tottenham Court Road.

A workout, that would get him out of her mind. Too late to book a session with her sensei at the dojo in Uskmouth, so she changed into her running gear, the new Nikes she'd bought as a bugger-off-Ash present to herself, then set her watch and kicked off up the footpath behind the cottage. A steep climb onto the Dyke, through the undulating woods, and then back via Fancy Farm. A good three miles up and down the sides of the valley and then she'd be ready for a couple of glasses of house Shiraz and a plate of cheesy chips. Diets, Pav thought as she hit her stride, were for other people.

FOUR

He should have realised this would be a day for memories, a day for ghosts, this failing day on the cusp between summer and autumn. There was a chill in the air, but it seemed even colder inside the crumbling flat carved from a grey suburban terrace. Wood Green, north London. A good place for refugees, for people running from rather than to.

Sebastian hung his jacket behind the door and picked a fresh wood shaving from the sleeve. He should have a shower, rinse the sawdust from his hair and skin, and leave the day behind, but he didn't have the energy. Food first, shower later; it wasn't as if there was anyone else to please.

He heated the last two fish fingers, charring them as usual under the old gas grill, then buried them under a hummock of cold baked beans. Cooking on this stove, enamelled in grease, was always a mistake. The smell would linger through the night and, in spite of the cool evening air, he would have opened a window if someone hadn't nailed them all shut long since.

This was a day for temptations, for recriminations. He

took the plate back to the curtained-off kitchenette and left it in the sink. He was going to lose that thumbnail, for sure. It was already turning black from where he'd trapped it between two planks of wood on the job earlier, some bespoke kitchen units for a conversion in Hornsey. The husband made films, the wife made children, and they'd offered him glasses of Chardonnay in the afternoon while he measured and sawed and nailed. They had no idea.

There was a time when he would have prayed; Jesus, Mary, take this load from me. There was a time when he might have heard an answer.

He reached up to the unread section on one of the high shelves he'd built in both alcoves, but stopped himself before his fingers touched the cover. The photograph was still there, hidden in the pages of one of his father's old books; Schopenhauer, well thumbed – *On the Fourfold Root of the Principle of Sufficient Reason*. He'd read it once, in his first year at Ushaw seminary. Cause and effect; the change in state of one thing leads to a change in state of another. No need for God. Father Giles had seen the book and smiled: *'Good work, Sebastian – it always helps to know how the enemy thinks.'*

Yet what was the harm in looking at this memory? He turned back to the image; a young woman in a simple summer dress, waving at the camera, smiling at the photographer. Happy to be captured in time. Happy to be remembered.

It would be a long night.

His thumb was throbbing; there was aspirin somewhere in the flat but he couldn't remember where and couldn't be bothered to look. He wished he'd kept the TV.

The sound of raised voices drew him to the window; Urdu, he was becoming good at the languages around here.

Recognising them at least – understanding was for other people. A family passed by on the pavement outside; the patriarch striding a few steps ahead of his wife and daughter, shouting as he walked, unable to see the barely suppressed smiles of the women behind him.

Sebastian watched until they were out of sight. He could do with a drink, but the pubs around here weren't his style and he'd never discovered the habit of drinking alone. A book then, and some music, enough to fill the hours until he could go to sleep.

HE JERKED awake on the small sofa as the doorbell rang for the second time, an unfamiliar sound. A private person, Sebastian, a quiet man. The street lamp outside angled a shaft of amber light across the room, but it was too dark to see his watch. Must be late, though; his neck ached from where he'd slumped awkwardly in the chair as he slept, and he worked his shoulders to loosen the muscles.

Why should anyone be using his bell? No-one knew where he lived, and even the cards he gave his customers had nothing more than his name and mobile number. Rootless, he was, like something pulled up and left to die by the side of the road. He was halfway down the stairs before he thought – *I should have checked from the window first* – but it was too late now. He could already see the shape outside the floor length, rippled panel in the front door, and felt as if he'd stepped into quicksand.

The figure outside was motionless, barely up to Sebastian's chest; a shadow seen through waves. Seb hesitated for a moment with his hand on the lock, safe for a few last seconds behind the corrugated glass, and then slowly turned the handle.

'Father?' The boy tried to smile, showing a gap where his front teeth used to be, and then his eyes rolled upward as he collapsed like a discarded marionette.

'Sweet Jesus!' Sebastian caught him and lowered the body to the ground. Silviu was recognisable despite the emaciated body, the ragged scar on his cheek. As Sebastian leaned closer, the boy's sleeve rode up to reveal a succession of smudges on the inside of his arm, with dry, puckered skin, like cigarette burns.

'He doesn't look too good,' said a voice behind him. 'Friend of yours?'

Sebastian lifted the unconscious boy and turned to face his landlady from the downstairs flat, barely registering the dressing gown and cigarette. 'It's all right, Mrs Mostyn. Nothing to worry about – I'll look after him.' He paused at the foot of the stairs. 'Would you mind closing the front door behind us?'

'No funny business now – I know what goes on,' she called after him. 'A man like you without a woman – it isn't right.'

Sebastian ignored her as he carried the boy upstairs and laid him on the sofa. 'Silviu – can you hear me?' The boy's breathing was shallow and fast, as if he was dreaming of being chased, and his forehead was dry and hot. Sebastian fetched a damp dishcloth from the kitchenette and mopped the boy's skin. He hadn't known, when he saw the shadow at the door, which of them it would be. There had been so many over the years, and he'd always known that one of them would track him down, find him, ask the questions that he didn't know how to answer. Why me?

Why me?

The same question he asked himself every day.

He knew he should call a doctor, or take the boy to a

hospital. Yes, that would work. Drive him to A&E, give a false name, and then walk out. The system would take care of him, doctors and social workers and foster parents if he was lucky. But Silviu had found him once and would find him again, and if Silviu knew where he lived, who else might come knocking on his door late one night? Someone who wasn't helpless, someone who wouldn't even try to smile. Maybe you could never run far enough away.

The boy's breathing was calmer now, as if he'd fallen into the sort of sleep that children were meant to have, but his skin still burned with fever. Sebastian fetched a couple of spare sheets from his bedroom next door, carefully covered Silviu and started the long night's vigil. At least there would be no dreams tonight.

THE MARKS on Silviu's arms had spread in the night and turned black, and new patches had crept up his neck and onto his cheeks. Not cigarette burns, then. A shame; it would have made things easier. He'd regained consciousness once in the night and asked for water, but by the time Sebastian returned with a glass, the boy's eyes had shut again.

There was a new presence in the flat; rotting meat. It hadn't registered until he returned from the corner shop with a carton of milk and a sliced loaf, but when he opened the door to his flat, it hit him like the smell of overflowing waste bins on a hot summer's day. Silviu hadn't moved in the fifteen minutes he'd been gone, but the boy's clothes were soaked with sweat and the marks on his neck were starting to join up. Sebastian checked his arm; the skin on the original patches had cracked and a thick yellow pus was oozing out and drying into a crust.

Sebastian found the number of a local surgery online, but hung up as soon as they answered. Maybe he could still remain anonymous, keep away from the prying fingers of the police and social services and everyone else who would want to know why the boy picked his door.

He forced Silviu awake and gave him some hot, sweet tea. Enough strength for the boy to get downstairs and into the van, that's all he needed. He could carry him again, but the landlady would be watching, as always. The more normal, the better. He found a comb, ran it under a tap, pulled it through the boy's hair and then threw it into the bin. The sheets that had covered the boy were crumpled into a bundle and kicked against the wall; he'd deal with them later, when he got back.

They made their way downstairs slowly, Sebastian balancing the semiconscious body between himself and the wall. It wasn't difficult, Silviu was as light as a child half his age, but Seb was careful not to touch the weeping wounds. He could have bandaged them, somehow, but what was the point? A waste of time and energy, and time was of the essence.

They half walked, half staggered to the white van, and Sebastian strapped the boy into the passenger seat. Not a moment too soon; Silviu quickly slipped back into unconsciousness, as if the exertion had used the last of his energy, and his dark hair left a greasy smear on the side window. Time to go.

The Royal Free, that was the place. They still had an A&E department, so he could take the boy in, register under a false name, and then disappear. He'd be off the hook and Silviu would be safe; a relative term, he knew, but better than any alternative.

· · ·

HALFWAY DOWN JUNCTION ROAD, he realised that something was wrong. He looked sideways at the boy; there had been no sound, no rattle in the throat, no ultimate seizure, but Sebastian knew without conscious thought what had caught his attention; the silent slipping away of a soul. He swore, then said a silent prayer, hoping that it wasn't too tainted. A taxi horn forced him back on his side of the white line and he turned off the main road as soon as he could, pulling up in a side street with no pedestrians in sight.

First things first; grieving could come later. He checked for a pulse at both the wrist and the neck - nothing. This changed everything. It was one thing leaving a sick boy in casualty, another turning up with a corpse. Do that and there would be no slipping away for him, no easy exit.

He had to make sure that there wasn't any way to connect him to the boy. One option would be to find some waste ground and turn the body out, but what if someone saw him? And Silviu deserved so much better than that. Seb considered driving east, towards Epping Forest – the only wild space he could think of so close to London – but it was unfamiliar territory and in the end he found himself heading west instead, down to the North Circular and onto the M4. Stupid in a way, it would take so much longer, but the pull of home was too strong. And maybe he needed the delay; take the time to persuade himself that what he was contemplating was right. He had, after all, connived at far, far worse.

Two hours later, he turned off towards the old bridge. He glanced across at the boy; anyone looking in would think he was asleep and at least the toll booths had gone, one less chance for questions to be asked.

At Gwenstow, on the other side of the estuary, he turned north towards Abertrothy but stayed on the Welsh side of the river. His father had always liked the woods around here, clinging to the narrow side of the gorge. Before the mines closed, further west, they would come here on a Sunday; him, his dad, his mother. Picnics and walks, and the odd rant from his father about blacks and queers and the Tories and how they should all go to hell. Happy days.

But things were different now. He found the place where they used to park, a small lay-by on one of the narrow, winding roads through the trees. You could stay here all day and not see more than a couple of cars. Sebastian turned off the engine, stood outside, and listened. A light breeze rustled the leaves, and a buzzard mewed, high and out of sight, but there were no engines, no voices. If he worked quickly, he should be okay. Of course he would be okay. Especially if he could make the trembling stop.

He walked to the back of the van and looked through the tools and building materials, but nothing seemed right. Why couldn't he have been a builder instead of a carpenter? Improvisation it was then. An off-cut from a piece of beech shelving; that could stand in for a shovel. And would he need anything else? This was a new game, he didn't know the rules. He let his hand touch the various objects, as if contact with the wood and metal would provide an answer. A screwdriver, a chisel, a hand drill; how many ways, he thought, how many ways? There should be a manual for times like this, for neophytes, for the uninitiated.

At last, when he'd made the decision, he opened the passenger door and dragged the boy out. He half expected the movement to bring Silviu around, to pull the soul back; for his eyes to open, for his dry lips to speak, but there was no sound. The time for words had passed.

He scooped the boy into his arms, the body still warm and loose, kicked the car door shut and walked into the shadow of the trees. Not long now and it would be over, if he could find the courage to do what had to be done. And then there would be one less to remember, one less to haunt his dreams.

One less to call him Father.

4:30 a.m. on Tuesday, with the sky beginning to pale. Pav recognised most of the faces assembling in the police station yard as the stab vests were handed round and the final briefings given. The DI in charge, a tight, bullet-headed man, took her to one side.

'I know it's a forlorn hope, Pav, but I'd appreciate you staying out of the action. I don't need to remind you that this is a police operation. We need to keep the responsibilities clear, if you take my meaning. If it were my decision, I wouldn't have you people anywhere near.'

'"You people"? Classy. I know your Chief Constable and my boss would happily knock the shit out of each other, but you know my background, Jim. You wouldn't be here at all if it weren't for me.' She tried to drop her voice low, but a couple of the others had turned round to listen. 'Don't worry, I'm not going to piss on your parade – believe it or not, we're all on the same side.'

They sat in silence on the short drive across town to the house that Eva had picked out the day before, with the DI checking from time to time to make sure that the vans were following in close formation. Pav glanced out of the window as they got closer; the sky had changed colour without her noticing, winning the fight against the sodium street lamps. They waited at traffic lights as a heavy woman, wearing a dull, shapeless skirt and a nylon puffa jacket, waddled across the road in front of them; on the other side of the street, a couple of hundred metres further down, an ancient orange Fiesta puttered into life and moved away in a series of controlled jerks.

The lights changed and they rounded the corner. 'Let the guys go in and do their job, okay?' said the DI. 'Just because we didn't sign up with you glory boys and girls doesn't mean we're all muppets.'

A bulb was still glowing behind the red curtains in the upstairs room, and as they approached the house, a thin man left, adjusting his white cotton cap and then his trouser fly.

'Today's his lucky day,' said the inspector. 'If he'd taken an extra Viagra we'd have picked him up with the rest.' He pulled into the space between a couple of Vauxhalls, let the vans roll past to double park outside the house and then unlocked his door. 'Here we go...'

THE MAIN ACTION was over within minutes. The house emptied like an unblocked drain; first a small clot of male officers, then four teenage girls one after the other, almost identical with their long, dark hair. One was still wearing a miniskirt that needn't have bothered, the others shivering in T-shirts and tracksuit bottoms, each of them supported by a woman officer leading them to the second van.

Something was missing. The girls wouldn't have been

in there alone, and the man who'd left before the police arrived was clearly a customer. But the procession of people ended, the van with the girls drove off, and the other was gradually filling as the street cleared of police. Four hours sleep lost for nothing. And then she saw the man with the flapping belt who'd run after Eva in the street, letting himself out through a side gate about ten houses down. He must have realised what was happening and escaped through the back gardens.

Jim Spears was still by the open front door, talking to someone on his mobile, and hadn't noticed the escapee. Pav looked back to see the man almost at the corner, a messenger bag slung over his shoulder. Another hundred metres and he'd be away, lost in the morning crowds. So Spears had told her to stay out of the action, so what? This was payback time for Eva, and if she couldn't catch him, no-one could.

He must have heard her footsteps when he was only a few houses from safety. He glanced back over his shoulder and then attempted to clamber over a front garden wall, but tripped and fell into an ambiguous shrub with spiked leaves, wriggling like an upended tortoise.

This was almost too easy. Although he weighed more than her, he struggled like someone who didn't get to see much daylight; within seconds she had him restrained amongst the foliage, and as she hauled him to his feet the inspector appeared, breathing noisily through his mouth and looking like someone who'd just lost a bet.

'Nice timing,' she said. 'I'd forgotten how much fun this is.'

. . .

ON THE WAY back to the station, she noticed Spears' left eye twitching in short, regular spasms.

'I know,' she said. 'Glory girls always screwing up the work of the professionals. Don't worry, a simple "thank you" will do.'

The inspector braked sharply as they pulled into the station yard. 'You've got balls, Pav, I'll give you that. Just let me know in advance the next time you decide to play Wonder Woman.'

'I prefer Harley Quinn. And there's no need to beat about the bush – if you want to ask me out, just say so. Won't get you anywhere, but...'

For the first time, the man smiled. 'I'm not your style and anyway, I don't think my heart could stand the strain. Go home, Pav, get some sleep.'

As if.

SHE DIDN'T NOTICE the cuts until she was standing in the shower, enveloped in a steaming cloudburst. She looked down at the tiny geometries of red lines on her legs and forearms, stinging in the flow of water. They must have happened when she jumped over the garden wall, but she hadn't noticed at the time, other things on her mind. She closed her eyes, tipped her head back and let the water run over her face.

THE CAR PARK was almost empty at that time of the morning. She locked the Porsche and looked across to the new bridge, soft focus in the early mist from the estuary. On a clear day, a small hummock of land was visible further down towards the sea, but today its shape was lost in a blanket of white. Island or lump of rock, she'd never been quite sure which; perspectives always seemed different over water. She walked towards her building, wishing it had at least one window. The job description hadn't promised glamour; at least they got something right.

HALFWAY THROUGH WRITING up a report on the morning's work, Finn called into her office.

'How did it go earlier?' he asked.

'I would have preferred a lie-in. All that for four girls and one guy – I guess he was the one running it. I saw him yesterday, chasing Eva.'

'Anything else in the house?'

'The guy had a laptop with him – he made a run for it, but I managed a little interception.'

'Glad to see that normal service hasn't been interrupted. Where's the laptop?'

'The police, for now. As far as they're concerned, this was just another raid on a brothel and they'll check it for anything out of the ordinary. Make sure you stick your nose in; diplomatically, of course. You never know, they might find something useful.'

'You still think Hexameter has legs?'

'Haven't decided. I know I asked you to close the case, but we won't lose anything if we talk to the people they picked up this morning and have another pop at Eva. She may feel safer now her pimp's in custody. Call The Swallows, tell them we'll be there this afternoon.'

Five minutes later, Finn was back. 'All sorted?' she asked. It wasn't like him not to meet her gaze.

'Not exactly. Sorry boss, there's no easy way to say this: it's Eva, she's gone missing.'

The words were like a punch to the stomach. 'What do you mean, missing? What's the point of all that fucking security if the inmates can simply waltz out any time they want? Jesus, Finn, this is a complete balls-up.'

'She wasn't at The Swallows. She'd had a good night, eaten some breakfast, and everything seemed fine, so it seems one of the staff took her – can you believe this? – on an outing to Aberhonddu. They went into a clothes shop, the idiot who was meant to be looking after Eva turned her back for twenty seconds and the girl legged it, probably through a staff entrance. What is it with these people? We try to protect them and look at how they repay us.'

'She probably thought we'd deport her to Rwanda.'

'Not that far off the truth. On the other hand, at least she gave us the house before she decided to disappear, and the clown you brought in should have a few stories to tell.'

AT TWELVE O'CLOCK, Pav settled herself in one of the interview rooms at Uskmouth police station, with Finn sitting beside her. No sofas in the rape suite for the girls who were picked up earlier, as if what had happened to them was somehow their fault. And maybe it was, in some convoluted way. She knew how it worked; they hadn't been kidnapped from the streets of Bucharest or Tirana and brought here as sex slaves. They'd come voluntarily, looking for gold at the end of the rainbow, a job that would let them buy decent clothes and the latest iPhone and maybe hook themselves a decent guy. You'd think word would have got back, you'd think by now they'd know what was waiting for them when they clambered out of their hiding place in the back of one of the lorries that had brought them halfway across Europe. And in a small part of her heart she thought; maybe they did. Maybe they thought it was a price worth paying. Maybe they had just enough hope that they would be the lucky ones. Someone had to be.

The interview room smelled of stale coffee and sweat. The door opened with a clatter and a girl walked in; a sullen teenager still wearing her short plastic skirt. The bruised shadows under her eyes were no charcoal smudges but the dull purple of tired blood, and her legs should have gone out of fashion with rickets. She sat on the edge of her chair without so much as lifting her eyes from the floor.

'Corrina? My name's Pav.' No reaction. 'I want to talk about a girl called Eva – she was in the house with you; is that right?'

The girl looked up, trying to seem uninterested. 'Eva – I don't know this person.'

Pav described her, but Corrina shook her head. 'I am here two days – all girls, two days. When we come, nobody else in house.'

'No-one? Not a girl called Mira? One of her hands was injured.'

'I said, no-one, just the man Defrim.' The girl's skin was the colour of candle wax, and her low-cut top only half hid an open sore next to her bra strap. 'There are other girls, maybe, before we come. On bed sheet, I can smell them.' In spite of the bravado she looked close to tears and rubbed unconsciously at red, swollen wrists with barely healed scars patterning the skin.

'What happened to your hands, Corrina?' Finn asked.

The girl looked away and folded her arms to hide the marks. 'Is nothing.'

'I don't think so. Has the doctor seen those?'

The girl shrugged. 'What can doctor do?' She looked across the table. 'Can he make it not happen? Can he take me home, can he make me forget all this shit?' She almost spat out the last word.

Pav wanted to reach out and take the girl's hand, but who would she be comforting? 'You're right, Corrina, you've had a shitty break. But you're okay now – all we want is to find the other girls and keep them out of danger.'

'I don't think so – end of story, huh?' She pointed at Pav's bag on the floor. 'You got cigarette maybe?'

Pav ignored her. 'You said you'd only been at the house for two days. Where were you before that?'

'Bucuresti – one year. I had shitty room, working streets. Then this man, Defrim, he offer five hundred dollar to work here. Why not?'

'Five hundred dollars? That's a lot of money – do you still have it?' asked Finn.

'You think?' She sniffed, wiped her running nose with a bare arm.

'What about the other girls,' asked Pav.

'Same as me. We come together, in van.'

Her eyes closed in a blink that lasted a moment too long. Exhausted, damaged, stoned. All three, probably.

'WHAT DO YOU THINK?' asked Finn when the girl had gone. 'Doesn't sound right to me. Why pull them off the streets in Bucharest and bring them a couple of hundred miles to Uskmouth, then throw them out after a few weeks.'

'Who knows? Perhaps we'll find out more when we've seen the man.'

He was brought in a few moments later, a small,

angular creature with a pitted face of flat planes that might have inspired Picasso. The top two buttons on his shirt were missing, the Aertex vest underneath hadn't seen an optical brightener for a while and the dark patches under his arms were spreading by the second; even from the other side of the table, he smelled sour.

Pav let Finn take the lead and watched for the tells, the giveaways in Defrim's body language and speech. He was frightened, she could see that, but not of them. After twenty minutes of evasion, she took over.

'We can help,' she said. 'So you had a few girls working for you – that's not so bad. No one's interested in you – just who you work with. How do you find the girls? How do you get them here? Vans, lorries, boats? It's your choice Defrim, you know how this works. Give us what we need - the people who organise all this - and we'll go easy on you.'

It took another ten minutes, but in the end he asked for a pen and paper and wrote down a web address. 'Like online service,' he said. 'When customer want something special, I put in order. How they come to this country is nothing to do with me.'

'You're saying you order people the way you would a curry? Like a take-away?' said Finn.

'Perhaps. Girls are delivered and taken away.'

'I don't understand,' said Pav. 'You mean a girl is brought in for one customer and then taken away again?'

'No! New girl arrive, she stay. But girl who don't work out, girl who get sick – she go back.'

'Very efficient,' said Finn, drily. 'How do you pay?'

'Give money to delivery driver. If no girls he come anyway, once a week.'

'Describe him,' said Pav. 'Is it always the same man?'

Now the fear was back. Defrim looked from one to the

other of them, but said nothing. He'd told them all that he was going to, at least for the time being.

———

BACK IN THEIR office on the edge of the estuary, Pav watched while Finn tapped in the web address.

'Nothing,' he said, 'not that I had much hope. Even if the site was real, someone's taken it down - probably as soon as they knew about the raid. We can possibly find a cached version, but if we've stumbled on Hexameter, the operation's likely to be pretty well oiled, not the usual bunch of boyos from Albania. So where do we go next?'

'The girls we picked up are too new – they know nothing. Defrim's another matter. Let him stew overnight and then we'll have another session. As for Eva – make sure her description's circulated.'

'A teenage girl on the run? You'll be lucky.'

'I know. If someone like her wants to disappear, then no one's going to stop her.'

———

PAV HEADED towards the dual carriageway. It was on days like this that she missed Jess. If nothing else, she would have been around to hear her sounding off, an excuse to talk to someone who cared. She couldn't do that to an empty house, not too often.

Perhaps, she thought, it was time to get a cat.

CHAPTER
SIX

There were more sirens tonight. He was sure of it, rising and fading, edging closer and then disappearing. Teasing him. The first night had been bad enough – he hadn't even gone to bed – and then he spent yesterday inside with his mobile off, watching the street like an old lady. Now, fifteen hours later and counting, Sebastian lay stiffly on his back in the room half lit by the amber street lamp outside. The cheap cotton curtains didn't quite meet, leaving a bar of sodium light angling across the room to the shelf of books in the corner.

The latest two-tones faded into the distance, but Sebastian couldn't relax. He was conscious of his hands hidden under the thin sheet, still stained with red mud. The dirt had burrowed under his fingernails and nothing could shift it, even though he'd scrubbed until blood welled out from a hundred hairline cuts.

It wasn't just the mud. Burying a body always seemed so easy in books and on television, but they never gave you the details. What was he supposed to do but improvise? Perhaps if he'd known what to expect, if he'd been ready for the residual warmth of the corpse as he laid it in a shallow grave, if he'd been prepared for the way the limbs cooperated as if they still had a life. You read about these things: muscles reacting after the brain was dead and the soul departed. That's all it was. That's all it could possibly be.

Perhaps because he hadn't slept, his mind began to float; there had been a girl in his street, when he was thirteen – older than him by four years, unattainable and exotic. She wore long Indian skirts of turquoise and white, and one day she dyed her hair and nails with henna. Her father threatened to cut off her hands when he realised that the colour couldn't be removed and would have to grow out. At least, that was the rumour. His daughter, the tart, and him a chapel man like most of them. A righteous man. A thug.

Just like me, thought Sebastian, even if he'd swapped his family's austere Welsh religion for the bells and smells of Rome.

It wasn't just his hands. Even from the narrow bed, hard and damp with sweat, he sensed the van parked outside as if it were alive, as if he could hear it breathing. No-one had seen what happened in the woods, but the van was there. It knew. The passenger window still had a smear of grease where Silviu's head had lolled against it; there must be flecks of his skin, fallen hair, molecules of the air he'd breathed. And even after the one hundred and sixty miles of motorway and the most expensive car wash he could find, traces of that damned, rusty red mud remained in the grooves of the tyres and under the wheel arches.

There was nothing for it, the van had to go. Yes, that would do it; he could feel the load getting lighter. He dressed quickly and stuffed a bin bag with the clothes he'd been wearing, as well as the sheet which covered the shivering body of Silviu on the night that he'd kept vigil, listening for the passing bell. He strapped on his watch and checked the time; 5 a.m. It would be light soon; no more time to waste. He was almost out of the door before he realised... of course, it wasn't just the van.

He sighed, sat back on the bed, and looked around the room. He had few enough possessions, but it was still hard to let them go. Perhaps it was just as well, another leaving. He'd always known that one day it would be time to move on, time to attend to the unfinished business that he couldn't ignore forever. He reached under the bed and pulled out a well-used backpack in dark green, one of the pockets roughly mended with duct tape. The hole had appeared when a mouse bit through to reach some forgotten food, a chocolate bar he'd forgotten to take out after a day hiking on the Pembrokeshire coast. A lifetime ago.

Someone else's life.

He wouldn't need much, not that there was a choice. A change of clothes, a few things from the bathroom – and, at the last minute, the book with its hidden photograph. Why not, he thought, we all need an anchor.

He moved about quietly, not wanting to wake Mrs Mostyn in the flat below. Her face behind a twitching curtain was the last thing he needed; a lady suffering a strangulation of the spirit, as one of his tutors might have said. With the backpack on his shoulder and the bin bag in front of him like a shield, he trod carefully down the stairs, using his Yale key to close the front door behind him.

The van seemed spotlit under the street lamp. Sebastian threw the two bags across onto the passenger seat and pulled away as smoothly as he could, waiting until he reached the corner before shutting his door properly. He'd already decided where to go; a patch of waste ground between the railway and the old gasworks. At first he thought of the original plan for Silviu's body, Epping Forest, but every second he was on the street he felt naked. More than that, flayed, even his skin stripped away to leave nothing behind.

After driving for less than ten minutes, he turned down the road running behind the ladder of Victorian streets, and reached a high fence guarding an area of urban scrub. The rusty metal gates were swinging open and he drove through onto a patch of dusty grass. This wasn't a place for security cameras, not that he could see, but he kept the hood up on his sweatshirt all the same.

He should have brought a can of petrol, but it was too late now. That's what comes of being a newcomer to the game, he thought, and then remembered the sheet he kept in the back of the van, the one he used to cover the floors of his customers' homes when he was working. He ripped off a strip, twisted it into a long roll and fed it into the petrol tank through the filler tube. When it couldn't go any further, he pulled it back out; lucky he filled up yesterday on the way back; the strip of material was sodden with fuel and its heavy perfume surrounded him.

Sebastian pushed the dry end back down into the tank, and then hesitated again. Life had been easy once; a vocation, a mapped-out future. Certainty. And only himself to blame for what changed everything. One moment, one choice. He could have walked away, but no. Not him. Weak, needy, fallen. And now he was about to cross yet another line.

The sky was definitely lighter now, a pale blue-grey. In the early morning quiet, cutting through the distant sound of the first cars, a single bird had started to sing. As if grateful for the diversion, Sebastian looked around but the song could be coming from anywhere; there were no trees, no bushes, just the outline on the ground of buildings that had been removed to their foundations, and the huge skeletons of gasometers a few hundred metres away, preserved from another age.

Enough delay. He swung the backpack over one shoulder, settling the weight, then struck a match, touched it to the fuel-soaked rag and began to run.

CHAPTER
SEVEN

Perhaps Defrim would have remembered a little more after a night in the cells. Strange that he hadn't asked for a solicitor, not that it would have made much difference. Even stranger were the mail order girls being delivered and returned. Follow the money, though, always good advice. The driver who left the girls and took the cash; where did he go, who did he answer to?

The web address Defrim gave them yesterday had led nowhere so far; the site had been taken down and tracing the servers to a physical location wouldn't be easy or useful in the short term. So it was back to the man himself. Time to squeeze a little harder and hope that they found some worthwhile juice inside. Maybe it would be best to see him on her own. Maybe he'd feel less threatened by a woman; one could only hope. Men showing how superior they believed themselves to be, always such fun.

The line of traffic ahead had already bunched up as she reached the roadworks on the way into town, and she turned right to wriggle her way round the back streets to

Uskmouth police station. The clouds were heavier today, low shades of grey covering the distant hilltops, and her windscreen was misted with fine rain. She was still ten minutes from the police station when Finn called on her mobile.

'Where are you, boss?'

'Outskirts of Uskmouth, on my way to interview Defrim – why?'

'A call just came in to the local police. Some workmen were about to start preparing a disused building for demolition and it seems they found a girl. They're not sure if she's alive or dead, which is weird. Not the sort of thing we'd normally bother with, but with Eva missing...'

'...then we might get one of our witnesses back. Where is she?'

'The old primary school on the Gwenstow Road, near the library. Do you want me to go?'

'I'm two minutes away; trust me, Finn, I'm flying.'

She found the site easily enough, a semi-derelict Victorian building surrounded by suburban terraces. There were shadows of her own junior school on what would have been the asphalt playgrounds; even here, standing outside the gates, she could smell the damp cloakrooms and the musty gym, hear the echo of voices and feet down the long corridors.

Disquieting; those weren't the best of days.

All long gone, though. It must be decades since children were learning here; the board by the main gate called it the Uskmouth Centre for Adult Education, from what she could make out through the fluorescent graffiti, but the pilates classes and craft workshops had long since deserted the place for the hospitality of a new college, half a mile away. Not that anyone could blame them; this old building had the air of a mausoleum as it squatted heavily behind its high walls.

The main gates were half open, with a small group of men in hi-vis and hard hats clustered just inside, muttering like a secret cabal. No police yet, no ambulance. One of the men walked over to her. 'You don't look like a copper, love.'

'I'll take that as a compliment.' She flashed her ID. 'They said there was an injured girl – where is she?'

'The boiler room, down in the basement.' He seemed uncomfortable. 'Seriously love, you don't want to go in there, no offence. You'll need a strong stomach.'

'With great respect, I'm not your love. Detective Inspector will do just fine. And whatever's down there, I've probably seen worse. Did you talk to her, see if there was anything you could do to help?'

The man looked away and said nothing. How bad can it be, she thought, even if the girl is dead? 'Are you going to show me,' she said, 'or do I have to waste even more time and find my own way?'

The air inside the gloomy building was cold and dry, and small black mouse droppings peppered the layer of dust on the window sills of the corridor. As Pav followed the man through a door and down some stairs, it felt as though she were entering a tomb.

'It's in there,' he said, as they reached a door in the basement. 'You sure you don't want to wait?'

It, not she.

Pav pushed past him and went inside. The smell hit her first, a mixture of barbecue and butcher's shop. And then the heat, dry and oppressive as a city street on an airless heatwave day. The door hung open on an old boiler in the corner, but the dull, red glow of the dying fire inside barely penetrated the gloom.

Someone had been burning something, and that didn't seem right for a derelict building. Pav stood in the doorway, playing the torch beam from her mobile across the room. It took her eyes a few moments to adjust and then she saw the girl, huddled by a wall against a pile of broken pallets.

She picked her way carefully across the detritus on the floor towards the crumpled body, shrunken and jaundiced in the torchlight.

The workman called from the door. 'We didn't like to move her, see? Health and safety.' He filled the door frame, a shadow against the light.

The girl on the floor sighed softly as her wizened left hand fluttered, trying to grasp something just out of reach, but her eyes remained shut even when Pav felt her forehead and said the girl's name.

'Mira – Mira!' It had to be her; younger than her friend, the withered arm and hand just as Eva described. Now that her eyes were more accustomed to the gloom, Pav noticed the thick red weal around the girl's neck, angry and raw; it reminded her of the marks on Corrina's wrists. The girl's face and lips were swollen and bruised, with one arm bent at a strange angle as if the elbow joint had reversed itself.

There was something else, a mark on her face that seemed different from the bruising. Pav looked more closely; not a mark but an open sore weeping a thin, yellow pus. There was another on her unbroken arm, larger and more ragged, as if something unwholesome was trying to break out.

Near the floor, the smell was even stronger. The torch beam picked out the boiler, a Victorian contraption of dark iron spattered with pale green paint on one side, the same colour as the walls in the corridor upstairs. The cinders of a recent fire were still glowing inside.

Dark stains mottled the cement floor; someone had stashed a heap of broken wood against the wall on one side of the boiler, with a pile of white plastic sacking a few feet away, and a fine layer of pale ash covered every surface. It had to be everywhere, Pav thought, conscious of the barely visible motes picked out by the torchlight, and she tried not to breathe too deeply.

She noticed another mound of rubbish near the sacking, a small hillock almost three feet high. Pav left the girl's side to investigate and the man by the door called out. 'Don't go there, love! You don't want...'

But it was too late. As she moved closer, the mound of soft geometry resolved itself into a slag heap of ash and fragments of bone – the eye socket from a skull, the fossilised snake of a spine – and next to it was a smaller pile; joints of meat, slabs and cylinders of flesh piled together and bound with a glue of brown, dried blood. And there, attached to some anonymous gobbet, was a piece of stained blue cloth with a small white button. A shirt, a blouse. Clothing covering flesh.

She was staring at a pile of human remains, of butchered bodies. She was standing in a charnel house. She could be outside an oven for people at Auschwitz.

The room lightened for a moment as the man in the doorway moved away. Pav heard voices through the buzz in her head, and then Jim Spears was in the room with a couple of paramedics who went straight across to the girl.

'Again?' said the inspector. 'You're like a bloody stalker. And sweet Jesus, what is that stench?'

She pointed at the mound of flesh and concentrated on keeping her breakfast down. 'Looks like we're all a bit late. The girl over there, I think her name's Mira. She used to work at the house we raided. At least she's still alive. And now, if you don't mind, I think I need some air.'

POLICE HAD ALREADY CLOSED the street outside the school with barricades of blue and white tape, all except the pavement on the opposite side of the road. The beginnings of a crowd had gathered near an ambulance parked by the gates, not enough yet to push at the tape, but idly curious for the sight of someone else's misery.

The menagerie of voyeurs annoyed her. She craved somewhere private to empty the images of what she'd just seen; all the training in the world couldn't have prepared her for that sort of carnage. But as she turned to go back into the schoolyard, a man caught her eye, standing at the back of the other onlookers. A bantam with a blonde crew cut and a well-trimmed moustache – even from this distance, his sharp blue eyes stood out like splinters of sky against the tanned skin of his face. It took her a moment and then she remembered where she'd seen men like him before, in old newsreels of the Blitz. Men who wore camel hair coats and smoked thin cigarettes, men who looked like ferrets.

She sensed a movement behind her as the paramedics wheeled a stretcher from the school gates to the waiting ambulance. Mira was strapped down, unmoving and unconscious, her face blanched and soft like something that had never seen the light. As the paramedics loaded her into the vehicle, Pav looked up and caught the eye of the blond man: he stared at her, blinked once like a camera lens and then, as if not trusting his memory, pulled a mobile from the maroon leather bag dangling from his wrist and took a snapshot. Whether of her or Mira, it would be hard to say.

As the ambulance pulled away and the crowd began to disperse, she called Finn and told him to follow up on the girl. The sight of her lying in that slaughterhouse wouldn't be an easy memory to erase, and as for what would have happened if the builders had started work a week later – it didn't bear thinking about. But now it was time to pick up the threads of the day and see Defrim; after this morning's revelations, she had a little more to talk about now.

At Uskmouth police station, she had him brought into the same sour room. A night's reflection hadn't improved him, and a fine, white crust framed the sweat stains under his arms.

She decided to start gently. No need to rush into this with accusations of murder and scare him into a permanent silence. 'The website you gave us doesn't exist,' she said. 'What was the point of lying?'

'They change address some days, for security maybe. Driver gives details.'

'The man who drives the take-away girls? That's fine, we have a watch on the house. We'll pick him up next time he comes round, but you could do yourself a favour and save us all some trouble if you describe him to me.'

Defrim laughed. 'He will not come, not now.'

'Why not?'

'He will know. These people, they know everything. Me, I am already a dead man.'

His eyes were blank. She knew that look, someone who'd put up barriers. A shame; sometimes the people in that chair couldn't wait to tell their stories, and more than once she'd felt like a confessor, except that she never offered any absolution. Perhaps Defrim already knew that; why confess the truth if there was no reward?

'You mentioned dead people, Defrim. What about the bodies?'

'Bodies? There are no bodies.' He shuffled in the chair like a small child with a full bladder.

'The bodies in the school basement. Arms and legs, torsos, some of them incinerated. The girl was there too; Mira.'

That got a reaction; his top lip sprouted a moustache of sweat, but he still said nothing.

'Remember Mira, the girl with the withered hand?,' said Pav. 'Eva told us about her and helped us to find you.' No need to tell him that Eva was missing. 'We have a link, Defrim. You to Eva, to Mira, to a room full of murdered children. We have enough to put you away forever and then some. Do you know what happens in prison to people like you? You won't need a name anymore, you'll just be someone's bitch.'

His mouth was working, but his lips stayed pressed together. She should have known, she told herself later, but who would have suspected?

Still staring at her, he reached inside his mouth with a couple of fingers, as if to clear a food scrap caught between his teeth. He winced slightly and then pulled out what looked like the crown of a tooth. They both stared at it, so unexpected, and then the man ground his jaws together.

'Oh shit!' Pav turned to the officer standing by the door. 'Medic – now!'

But it was always going to be too late. The man had already slipped off his chair and onto the ground, his face a rictus of pain, and the faint scent of almonds hung above the table.

THE PHOTOS from the basement were waiting for her back at the office, and Pav had them printed and pinned to a board in the open plan area outside her tiny room. She felt a kind of catharsis, seeing the limbs and torsos reduced to two dimensions, like earthing a memory. They'd become objects now, not parts of people; abstract shapes, mottled and patterned with cuts and tears.

There was something else, though, a common thread. She studied the images more closely, looking at the suppurations that disfigured so much of the remaining skin. Lesions; such an unemotional word, wounds that never managed to weep themselves dry. She traced the shapes with her finger, comparing one with another. These weren't caused by a knife, but by something more insidious. Something they shared with the living girl she'd found a few feet away from that pile of death.

She remembered what Eva had said; when the girls fell sick they disappeared, taken away by Defrim's delivery man. Some sickness. Was that what killed them, she wondered, or something else?

She called the hospital, and it came as no surprise to find that Mira had been admitted to the intensive care unit. 'There's no point in coming now,' a nurse said, 'tomorrow will be time enough.'

Time enough for what? She needed samples of the lesions to be analysed; whatever caused those wounds might not be the whole answer, but it was sure as hell pointing the way.

· · ·

SHE WOKE the next morning to the sound of hymns on the radio, a gospel choir clapping and swaying; even with her eyes closed, she could see their ecstatic smiles and she wondered – do they have the slightest idea about the shit their god allows to happen in his name? It was all too much for a Sunday morning, especially when she'd promised herself a lie-in. The memory of Defrim's death seeped back slowly into her mind, then the basement and Mira with the bodies. All that and no nightmares, what a blessing, although the half bottle of scotch probably helped. A little more than half, if she was honest.

She hit the button on the bedside radio and then sank back into the pillow, hoping there was paracetamol somewhere in the kitchen drawer. At least home was a place of safety; she didn't know how she'd survive without the cottage. Sure, she could afford something more in keeping with her job, maybe one of the new apartments overlooking Uskmouth Bay, but she liked the isolation here and the way this building fitted around her in a village where no one cared about what she drove, what she did, or who she was. It might not be a Batcave or a Fortress of Solitude, but a hero complex had never been her thing.

THE LIE in was a short one. No resting on the seventh day for her, not with a case that seemed to be rising like a phoenix from its own bed of ashes. Even on a Sunday the hospital was a thirty-minute drive from home, but the NCP gods were smiling; the car park looked full but someone backed out of a space as she arrived, and handed her an unexpired ticket.

The intensive care unit was on the second floor, but the concourse by the lifts and stairs was more crowded than

usual with weekend visitors doing their duty. She jumped
out of the way as a porter barely missed her in his rush to
reach some internal appointment in the bowels of that
soul-stifling place, and the elderly woman on the trolley
gurned an apologetic smile.

There were too many people for her mood and she took
another route, through the radiography department and up
another set of rarely used stairs. She walked quickly
through the holding area near the scanners and X-ray
machines; the people waiting looked plaintively at her as
though she had the power to release them. She pushed
through the double doors to leave the department and
another trolley clipped her elbow, forcing her against the
wall. She knew why this one was in a hurry; the static
figure on the bed had sheets drawn up over its head, but
from the contours it was - had been - a person. Pav watched
as other people moved out of the way; if she were wheeling
a dead body around, please God she'd have the sense to
keep it out of public view as much as possible. Hospitals
were bad enough without being reminded of the possible
outcome.

She ran up the stairs to the second floor, checked in at
the nurses' station, and asked for Mira. One of the women
ran a finger down her list. 'Looks like she's been moved to a
ward – Aspen.'

'She was only admitted to ICU yesterday. Can you check
again - she was in a pretty bad way when she came in.'

The nurse ignored her as if she were an irritating child,
rifled through the wad of papers again, and then called one
of her colleagues and showed her the list. 'Aspen ward –
that's geriatric,' she said. 'There must be a mistake on the
paperwork.'

The Sister checked for herself. 'Mira – she shouldn't

have been moved until she was stable.' She noticed Pav for the first time. 'And you are?'

She showed her ID, already knowing that something was wrong; she could see it from the way the nurses exchanged glances. While the Sister paged a registrar, Pav ignored the pointed looks and called Finn.

'I'm at the hospital,' she said. 'It's Mira, she's disappeared.'

'What do you mean?'

'Gone. Taken away. May just be a screw-up by the hospital, but after what happened to Defrim... push some buttons, Finn, I want that girl found.'

'I'll call hospital security,' he said, 'get the place locked down. I'll be there as soon as I can.'

A young doctor arrived within a couple of minutes, breathing as though she'd just finished a marathon. 'I've checked Aspen Ward,' she said, 'but she's not there, and she's way too sick to take herself off anywhere. When did you notice she was gone?'

'How should I know?' said the Sister, 'I just got on duty.' She turned to her colleague. 'Did you see who moved the girl?'

The younger nurse looked frightened. 'I was down in pharmacy – ask one of the others.'

Something surfaced from Pav's memory. 'I saw a porter,' she said. 'He came out of the lifts at the radiography department, wheeling a dead body on a trolley. I assumed it was dead – the sheets were pulled up over the face.'

The doctor and the Sister looked at each other. 'That lift comes down from here,' said the doctor. 'But we'd never take a body down that way.' She suppressed a shudder at the thought.

Pav didn't need to hear any more. It wasn't more than

ten minutes since she'd seen them; the girl could still be somewhere in the building. She took the stairs three at a time, stopped by the lift outside the radiography department and tried to remember which way they'd been going. This was a crossroads of corridors and she checked the overhead signs. Through the waiting room? Unlikely with so many people watching, so that left a choice of three directions.

The man with the trolley must have wanted to kidnap Mira rather than kill her here, otherwise all bets were off. But if she was right, he'd want to get outside as soon as possible and into a car or van. She closed her eyes and tried to picture the layout of the building; there was another entrance at the back for the A&E department, separated off from the main body of the hospital. When Ma was first ill, she'd been brought in there more than once when she'd fallen badly or burned herself. People came and went all the time; no one would notice another trolley, or a sick girl being taken to a car.

The only public access to A&E was from the outside of the building – only staff were supposed to walk through from the main entrance or the wards. Time for a change of career. She ran down the corridor, but the double doors at the end were locked and she didn't have the code for the keypad. The wards upstairs all had bells and intercom systems, but usually the door was opened with no inquisition if someone pressed the intercom; no harm in trying that here.

Within a few seconds, the lock clicked as it released and she pushed through into another identikit corridor lined with what looked like offices. A few people gave her startled looks as she sprinted the fifty metres or so to the far end, slammed the door release and came out at the end of the waiting room for A&E.

Whatever Finn meant by lockdown, the message hadn't got this far. The sliding glass doors to the real world were unpatrolled, and a man was helping a boy on crutches to limp outside, heading for the car park. Two ambulances were waiting in the bays by the entrance, but their back doors were open and when Pav checked, there was no-one inside. The small car park was a hundred metres away, behind some low bushes, and she ran across to look, but there was no visible activity. There were still empty spaces on this side of the hospital, and the parked cars were silent and motionless.

She'd made the wrong call. Perhaps the body on the trolley wasn't Mira after all, perhaps she was still somewhere in the hospital, perhaps she was already being taken out by the other entrance. Pav scanned the car park once more but still nothing, and it wasn't until she was halfway back to the main building that she saw them coming out from the entrance used by the paramedics; a man with sunglasses and a hooded jacket supporting a thin girl who seemed barely able to move her legs. Despite the woollen hat jammed over her hair, the second figure was obviously Mira, a weeping sore on her cheek and her eyelids fluttering with distress. At least she was still alive.

There was no time for thought or making decisions. Pav ran towards them, already wondering if this was such a good idea; the man was a six-six megalith with a shaved head showing under the front of his hood, and jaws that were gritty with dark stubble. In an ideal world, he would have abandoned the girl and run, not tucked her under one arm like a load of washing. As Pav got closer, she saw him bunch his other hand into a fist. Speed versus strength –

never an easy call. She stopped just out of arm's length, blocking his way.

'Let her go,' she said, 'the roads have been closed, you won't get far.'

The world hadn't become any more ideal. For a reply, he ran straight at her like a testosterone fuelled bull; she dodged to one side, span around behind him and jumped to get him in a head lock. With firepower like his, she needed to be a tad tricky. With his free hand he tried to pull her off but she bit into his left ear - needs must - feeling her teeth ripping through the cartilage and tasting the hot salt of his blood. Enough to turn anyone vegan.

The man bellowed, dropped Mira and, with both hands free, pulled Pav's arms from his neck. He had her on the ground now. Her face was on kissing terms with the asphalt, and her attacker had forced one arm behind her back and was attempting to push it higher. Another moment and something would break, surely. Struggling would never get her free, but at least it diverted him from her arm, and then she heard voices shouting and footsteps getting closer.

The man was as heavy as a fallen girder, still kneeling on her back with his knee threatening to rupture her kidneys. He leant down with his mouth next to her ear and she waited for the pain, but instead she felt only his hot breath on her cheek.

'I know you now, bitch,' he said. 'You are so fucking dead!'

And then, with a final twist which sent pincers of agony through her shoulder, he pushed her free and ran off through the car park towards the main road.

Pav rolled over to see Mira crumpled a couple of feet away. The girl was semiconscious; the woollen hat had fallen to the tarmac, and a blood was already welling through cuts on her face where she'd hit the ground. As Pav clambered to her feet, a couple of paramedics reached them.

'Are you okay? There's blood all over your face. Bastard ran off before we could get him.'

'I'm fine – look after the girl. She should be in ICU, he tried to kidnap her.' She flexed her arm and winced; bruised and torn, but nothing serious.

'It's okay, we'll take it from here, see she gets back safely – you get yourself seen to.'

'I can wait; where she goes, I go.'

The Sister arrived from ICU, harassed and nervous, all the earlier arrogance gone. She bent over Mira, checked her pulse and eyes, and nodded at the paramedics. 'Take her up, quick as you like.' She studied Pav for a second. 'You'd better come up too - the police are on their way. When we get upstairs, I'll have a look at that cut for you.'

Pav spat on her hand and wiped her mouth. 'Not my blood, it's from the bastard who took her. If a man turns up needing an ear transplant, he's the one.'

They arrived at the entrance to the ICU at the same time as Spears and a couple of uniformed officers.

'That was a bloody close shave,' said the inspector.

'It didn't occur to you to have someone guarding her? She may be part of my case, but it's your responsibility to keep her safe.'

'We're stretched.' To his credit, he looked embarrassed. 'A girl like her, I didn't think she was that important – I got it wrong, mea culpa.'

'Too bloody right. I need her, do you hear me?'

Spears looked around the unit. 'This place has as much

security as Brighton beach; even if I had someone here full time, I can't guarantee that she'd be safe.'

'If they tried once, they'll try again. I'd put her in one of our safe houses if she weren't so sick.' She thought for a moment. 'I'll speak to the medics,' she said. 'If this fuck-up hasn't done her too much additional harm we could try moving her to another hospital, somewhere they won't think to look for her, and book her in with a false name. It's not perfect, but if we're careful it might keep the bastards away from her for long enough.'

As Spears moved away to question the nurses, Finn arrived, breathing hard. He stared at her mouth.

'What happened, boss? There's blood...'

'Not mine, don't worry. I just hope he didn't have anything catching. We should take a sample though, see if there's a DNA match somewhere.'

'What about Mira?'

'The doctor's with her now – she was in a bad enough state already and this won't have helped, she was pretty shaken about. I blame Spears for this, security was down to him.'

They were interrupted by one of the paramedics who'd helped her earlier, a twig of a man with a soft, fey voice.

'Sorry to butt in,' he said. 'Just wanted to see how you are.' He turned to Finn. 'She's a feisty one, your missus. Hanging onto this bloke she was, like a monkey. And when she bit him! The size of that bastard, I'd have thought twice, I tell you.'

Finn waited until the man was out of earshot. 'Like a monkey? Bit him? You're meant to be setting me an example. He could have you for GBH with some lawyer arguing about his human rights.'

'We have to catch him first and anyway, it was appropriate force. Didn't work, he would have broken my arm if that ambulance hadn't pulled up. At least he let go of the girl.' She worked her shoulder to loosen the muscles.

'You want me to massage it for you?' Finn said. 'I've got some magic embrocation at home; it should still be okay. Excellent when you get a bad tackle on the pitch, not that I've played for a year or two. Three, if I'm honest. I could come round, rub it in.'

'In your dreams.'

'No need to be like that, I'm just trying to help. So what was this man like?'

'Six inches taller than you, and when he knelt on my kidneys he felt like a bloody elephant. Bald or shaven head; I couldn't see properly because his hood was up, but a boxer's nose. Oh, and he told me I'll be dead when he catches up with me.'

'Let's hope that wasn't a prediction. And what about his accent?'

'London,' Pav said, 'but don't ask me which part; Albert Square wouldn't be a million miles out.'

'It cuts out some people,' said Finn. 'Short fat women, monopods, Scottish psychopaths – come on boss, don't beat yourself up; if wasn't for you, we'd be finding Mira's dead body in a ditch somewhere in the next week or two.'

WHILE SHE WAITED in the family room for the consultant to arrive, Pav rifled through the papers and magazines on the low table; a Daily Telegraph from last week, a couple of Country Livings, the till receipt for a bunch of flowers from a petrol station. Although the room was empty, the air seemed damp with other people's tears. She tried to open a window, but it was sealed shut. This was where people were sent to be told bad news, somewhere private and out of sight. No need to embarrass the dying.

The room was at the back of the hospital, looking out towards the hills, mostly green. Nothing dramatic; a cracked landscape, when you got there, papered over with tough grass and low fences of wood and wire. Sheep, sometimes. A place to drive through.

As the minutes ticked along, she wondered what it was like to be Eva, on the run. She wondered what it was like to be Mira, halfway to hell. At their age, she was still living with her parents. Homework every night for her GCSEs, a sort-of a boyfriend who turned up one night with a bright yellow pustule by the corner of his lips and she had to pretend to be ill, couldn't bear to see him. Arguments with her parents that always ended with a hug. Pain was not being allowed to go to a party that started after 8 p.m.

As for sex, she'd still been a virgin at nearly eighteen, even after those fumbling few minutes in the back of his brother's car with a guy she met in a club one night. At that age, she still thought she had to do what people expected of her. No, men had never really stepped up to the mark for her, which made the Ash interlude even more ridiculous. There were rebounds, and there were huge mistakes.

At least Ash wouldn't have been one of the customers abusing Eva or Mira. Not his style. Over the past few months he'd developed a taste for whores drinking overpriced champagne and doing coke at his expense in lap-dancing clubs filled with damp estate agents, used-car salesmen and wannabe management consultants. Get the girls far enough gone and he wouldn't have to perform; a watcher, Ash, not a doer. Not these days. Not that he'd ever admitted it, but she knew. Men had so little shame and word got around.

And if he couldn't arrange a live show, then some internet porn and a strong right wrist, that was his idea of a good time. Be thankful for small mercies.

The door opened behind her, and someone called her name. The man was wearing a suit that looked as if it had just come from Savile Row, and when he shook her hand, his fingers could have belonged to a violinist. In a joint compact of informality, they perched on the edge of red foam armchairs, with cigarette burns on the pale wooden arms; the doctor rested a clipboard on his lap.

'I'll come straight to the point, Miss McNeil. Mira is a very sick girl and right now whatever's causing this illness is foxing us – I don't think that this morning's adventures were much help.' The light South African accent was unexpected, and he studied his manicured fingertips before looking back at her. 'The injuries from the attempted strangulation are the least of our problems; her infection led to a dangerously high fever last night and we're having trouble getting her temperature down. She also has a couple of very unpleasant lesions in her skin; they've opened and spread more quickly than we would have expected. I understand she was involved as a sex worker? We've run standard tests, including HIV – all of them were negative. But the symptoms are very like those you get with compromised immune systems, particularly some kinds of fungal infections. And we're not talking thrush here – these can be fatal if they're not treated soon enough.'

'So why not give her whatever medicines she needs?'

'If I knew what was causing it, I would. As I said, the tests were negative – we sent samples off for analysis, but there are never any guarantees. Her liver's already dangerously enlarged, and if the fever doesn't come down... To be honest, I don't know how much time she has. We're seeing the first signs of multiple organ failure and her body's collapsing under the stress of the disease.' He studied the clipboard without focusing on the words, and then looked up. 'There's something else, a build-up of fluid around the brain. She may already have sustained irreversible damage and unless we operate soon – and I mean today – there's a fair chance that she'll be dead by tomorrow.'

'So why are you waiting?'

'Your visit today is serendipitous. Even if Mira were old enough, she's not in a fit state to give permission for the procedure.' He picked up the clipboard, studied the sheet of paper for a moment, and then handed it across. 'There was a time when we would just have gone ahead, but with all the litigation these days...' He took a thick fountain pen from an inside pocket, unscrewed the iridescent blue cap and handed it to her, expectantly.

This wasn't fair. For a start, he had no right to ask her that, and all the options of moving Mira to a safer place were now out of the window, at least for the time being. 'What about the hospital social worker?' Pav said. 'While Mira's in here it's her case, surely.' She saw the confusion on his face. 'Mira's a potential witness in one of my investigations – I can't make decisions on her behalf. You talk about litigation? I get half crucified if someone I'm interviewing points to a bruise and said I did it. If I give you permission to cut into her brain, I could be done for aiding and abetting a crime.'

The consultant sighed. 'What about her next of kin?'

'If she has any, I'd guess they're a couple of thousand miles away, somewhere in Eastern Europe.'

The doctor put the pen back on his clipboard and rubbed his eyes. 'Miss McNeil, I live with enough bureaucracy as it is. You want me to call a hospital social worker?

Fine – I'll bleep her now, and then I'll tell you what will happen. Nothing. How do I know that? Because I tried earlier today. One is away on annual leave, one has a two-day training course in some godforsaken conference centre near Birmingham, and the other two have decided that it's all too much and decided to stay at their respective homes with what they are pleased to call "stress-related illnesses". Meanwhile, I have a girl in there who'll be dead by the time they all reappear from their shenanigans.' For the second time he handed her the clipboard and the pen.

What the hell. It was only a signature on a piece of paper, after all. Possible imprisonment and loss of career versus a young girl's death - no contest. She passed the signed consent form back to the doctor.

'We'll get her into theatre straight away,' he said. 'And my apologies for that little outburst about the social workers. When you get to consultant, you think you'll catch up on all the sleep you missed as a house officer and registrar – it doesn't seem to be that way anymore.' He shook her hand.

'That's it?' she asked.

'There's nothing else you can do now, really. Say a prayer, if it helps.' He didn't sound convinced.

PAV SAT in the hospital coffee bar for half an hour. The sandwich tasted of plastic, and the coffee of burnt cardboard, but she hoarded her table in the corner and watched the world go by. Hiding, she knew that. Passing time, waiting; not her greatest skill. The doctor had said they'd operate immediately, but she wanted to make sure before she left the hospital.

On reflection, she should have called Pauline Treadaway and dumped the decision in her lap. Passed the buck, let the monkey leap onto someone else's back. And maybe cause a girl to die in the process; approval for an operation was way beyond Pauline's pay grade and she wasn't one to bend the rules, let alone snap them in two and stamp on the remains. Go down that route and who could tell when a decision might get made? What would they put on Mira's death certificate, death by bureaucracy? No, in the end it was no contest, whatever the consequences.

When she couldn't wait any longer, she made her way back upstairs to ICU and asked for news.

'Still in theatre,' the nurse told her. 'There's no need to stay here, we'll let you know when it's over.'

Pav waited until she was in the car park before calling the social worker and having the barbed wire conversation she'd expected. She hung up while Pauline was in full flow, threatening legal action, excommunication and permanent exile. Empty threats, and even if they weren't, she was past caring.

The day felt dry, suddenly, as if something had withered. She could go back to the office and shuffle some paper in weekend loneliness, but it would feel like pissing in the wind. All the same, everyone needed some downtime. Perhaps she should go home and relax, watch an afternoon film on Netflix, sort out the underwear drawer – anything to put her mind in freefall for a while. And then she checked her watch and swore as she remembered; she couldn't fight duty, not when she was due at her parents' for Sunday lunch. How could she have forgotten? Denial, of course. Or maybe she was just getting older, unable to keep more than one thought in her mind at a time. Early onset dementia would be the cherry on the cake.

She thought of phoning Pa and making an excuse; after

the last few hours, she'd save up enough to last a lifetime. But any excuse would only buy a temporary reprieve, and she'd pay in spades later with guilt. No, far better to get it over with today and give herself a breathing space for the week ahead; somehow she knew she was going to need it.

CHAPTER
EIGHT

T he front door opened while she was still only halfway down the garden path. This wasn't one of Pa's good days; he seemed to be shrinking in all directions, like a fresh mushroom shrinking in on itself in a frying pan. His neck smelled of soap as she kissed him; green Palmolive, the same brand they'd used since she was a child. Pav followed him through to the kitchen, wondering which leitmotifs would define her life.

'She's good today, Parvati, so far. Go on, say hello – she's probably having a nap in front of the television. She got quite excited when I told her you were coming.' He fussed with the saucepans of vegetables that had probably been on the boil for at least an hour. 'Dinner won't be ready for another fifteen minutes. Off you go, tell her what you've been doing.'

'Will she know who I am? Last time I came, she thought I was her mother.'

Pa hung the oven gloves carefully over the rail on the cooker and turned to face her; she could see the effort it took to stop his fragile smile from crumbling. 'Give her a hug, she likes that,' he said. 'I've left a hairbrush next to her chair; she was crying yesterday, said she needed plaits for school. I said – Barbs, your hair isn't long enough, not for years, but that only made it worse.' He turned back to the oven, hiding his face. 'She forgets if you brush it for long enough.'

My mother's like a spider, Pav thought, sucking out his juices and leaving little more than a husk. It had been bad enough before her illness, but now there were no controls. And when Pa was empty and gone, what then? Who would she feed on next?

Pav left her father to his smoking roast and saturated greens, and found Ma asleep in the living room. She would look like this forever, it seemed; a bristled face of bloodhound skin capped with grey, unwashed hair, and a scrap of green ribbon tied around a tendril that curled across one cheek. Pav sat in the armchair opposite and watched her, this strange, alien creature, this ageing cuckoo in the nest. How could this have happened to her, to them? It had always been difficult having such a distant mother, but this – this was so unfair.

She wasn't ready.

The television was tuned to a shopping channel. '*She thinks they're talking to her,*' Pa had said once. And perhaps they were, thought Pav. We all have our own illusions – if that's what it takes to keep Ma's shadows back for a while longer, who am I to break the spell?

She was about to go back into the kitchen when Ma's eyes flicked open, grey soft-boiled eggs, and she smiled. Another tooth had gone by the looks of it, crumbled away unnoticed.

'Parvati, love. Is the coal in?'

Pav knelt down and took her hand. 'We don't have coal

anymore, Ma. Remember, that was when you were a girl back in Scotland.'

Ma leant forward and whispered in Pav's ear, her breath smelling stale and yellow. 'Is your father still sneaking around? He has other women – I've heard them, upstairs. They live in the spare room.'

'I don't think so, Ma. I had a look last time – there was no one there.'

'He hits me, you know, he beats me. And he keeps me a prisoner in this – this *place*. If I had a car I could escape.' Her eyes narrowed with suspicion. 'How did you get here? It's such a long way, I expect you flew. That's the way, these days.' She reached up to touch Pav's cheek. 'If only you could get me out of here, take me home.' She whined, like a fractious child.

'This is your home – you've lived here for years. See, this is all your furniture, your pictures. You've always liked this house, that's what you said.'

Her mother struggled to sit upright and looked around the room, blinking, as if she was seeing its contents for the first time. 'How did they bring it all here, to this...' She struggled for the word. '...this hotel?'

There was no point in fighting it. Pav tucked the tendril of hair behind her mother's ear. 'Probably a van.' She stood up. 'Set the table, shall I? I think dinner's nearly ready.'

'You can't go on like this, Pa.' Pav finished washing up the last saucepan and put the roasting dish in to soak. 'When did you last do something you wanted to? I bet you haven't been to a football match for months.'

'How can I? If she's not sleeping she follows me everywhere I go, and the things she says to me...' He sounded hunted. 'I leave her notes when I go to the shops, to remind her, but she still panics. Last week, I came back from Tesco and found her walking down the street, looking for me. It was a miracle she got herself dressed, even if she thought her dressing gown was a coat. You'd think someone would have noticed and taken her in.'

'People don't like to interfere.' They were back in the well-travelled groove. 'You need professional help, Pa; just because her life has gone doesn't mean yours has to as well – she needs 24-hour care. What if she really hurts herself, or you? You can't watch her all the time – what if she gets out again and goes missing? It's for her sake as much as yours.'

'How can I, Parvati? She paid for this house just as much as me. She has a right to live here.'

And then he started to cry, the way he cried almost every time they spoke these days. It all felt so wrong, and yet there was nothing she could do to make it better. Would it have been different if Saj were still alive, she wondered?

Fifteen years between them; he'd been the success story, the firstborn, the wanted one. Manager of a local supermarket until the day he drank a bottle of scotch, attached a hose to his exhaust and sat in the car with the engine running. Two days after her fourteenth birthday. It was hard enough knowing yourself, she'd realised; what chance did you have with other people?

Pav hugged her father the way he used to hug her; a promise of protection that she knew she couldn't keep. 'We'll work it out. I'll come round more often when I can, to give you a break.'

'You got your own life, Parvati. Your mother's my job. I've always done what's right, best I can, and I'll not stop now. She stuck with me through all the nonsense when we first got together. It wasn't easy back then for a Scottish lass to be seen with brown lad from Punjab. The things people said... Oh well, better or worse, eh?' He dried his eyes on the tea towel. 'What say I make us all a nice cup of tea? You don't have to go yet, do you?'

The kettle had barely begun to sigh when her mobile rang. She took the call in the hallway; from the sound of other voices in the background and the crackle of the wind, Finn was somewhere outside.

'Sorry not to have called you earlier, boss – bit of a show on here at the moment. I'm in the woods a few miles shy of Tryleg, above the river.' He raised his voice over the sound of the breeze. 'There's a body here, youngish lad by the looks of him. Jimmy Spears gave me the nod and I think he was right, we might have an interest.'

She felt her shoulders drop. This was how it had started for Jess, all those years ago, with the body of a boy in the woods. 'Any idea how he died?' she asked.

'We haven't moved him yet, still waiting for the pathologist to arrive. Strange, though, the way he was buried. Assuming he didn't dig a hole, get in and cover himself up again, someone else brought him here. But he wasn't dumped or hidden quickly; this was a proper grave. Shallow, I'll give you that, but he'd been laid out with respect, and someone left an ivory crucifix in his hand. Expensive, not your usual high street jeweller's tat and not the hallmark of a casual murderer, in my experience.' He paused and Pav heard a voice in the background, calling his name. 'Look, I can't talk now,' he said. 'Do you want to meet up later? I'll fill you in.'

'Catch me at the hospital, I want to check on Mira. Until they tell me she's dead, there's still hope.'

Back in the kitchen, her father had already put away one of the cups.

'Sorry Pa, I have to go,' she said, taking the opportunity. If she stayed any longer she'd start shouting at him to put Ma in a home, and neither of them deserved to go through that again, not today.

'On a Sunday?' he said. 'At least in my day we got the weekends off.' But there was no anger in his voice, just the defeated tones of someone who'd grown too used to losing.

'It's difficult,' Pav said. 'I'll explain next time. Give Ma a kiss for me, I'll call, promise,' and as she drove away, she could still feel him watching from the front door.

SHE FOUND the last remaining parking space in the shadow of the hospital incinerator's towering, stainless steel chimney. She could have phoned for news, but somehow it felt more respectful, coming here in person. The South African surgeon from earlier had already left, but a registrar took her to the bed in ICU where the girl was lying with her eyes closed, tubed up with drips and oxygen.

'Was the operation a success?' she asked.

'That depends on your definition of the word. We relieved the pressure on the brain, at least for now, but the underlying infection is worrying and she was in a pretty weak state to start with. We found evidence of GHB in her bloodstream, one of the date rape drugs. Given what was done to her, it was probably a blessing in disguise.'

'What about her injuries?'

'When she was admitted there were signs of abundant recent sexual activity, and not the sort that most people would consent to. Apart from the internal injuries, one of her arms had several fractures and from the bruising to her neck, I'm guessing that someone attempted to strangle her. It's just possible that's what saved her; a combination of asphyxiation and the drugs may have fooled them into thinking she was dead.'

Pav took a couple of deep breaths. 'Will she be okay?' A stupid question, she knew. How could Mira ever be okay after this? 'You know about the other bodies that were found,' she said. 'She's a potential witness and I really need to talk to her.'

The doctor shook his head. 'Count on at least three or four days, minimum, before she regains consciousness and we can assess the extent of any brain damage – that's assuming a miracle happens and we get the infection under control.'

'Have our forensic people been in touch with you yet about the infection? They have good links with the National Institute for Medical Research in London, and if those guys can't work out what's causing the infection, no one can.'

'We sent samples off first thing this morning, but I wouldn't get your hopes up. The drugs she was given have the side effect of amnesia, which can be permanent in some cases. She might never be able to tell you what happened and if you want my opinion, that would be a blessing.'

PAV PUSHED the door release to leave the unit, desperate to get out of the building with its smells of over-boiled vegetables. The glass walls of the corridor looked out onto miniature courtyards, two floors below, planted with sprawling scrubs and empty benches; from what she could see, the only way down there would be to abseil. Someone had pushed an abandoned trolley against the wall a few metres further down, and Finn rounded the corner towards her as she reached it.

'Sorry boss, I thought I'd be here earlier,' he said. 'I tried your phone, but there was no answer.'

'The signal's always rubbish here. I think they do it deliberately to stop the inmates from plotting their escapes.'

She gave him the details about Mira as they waited for the lift. When it arrived, they rode it to the ground floor in silence, standing either side of an orderly in charge of an empty stretcher piled with crumpled blankets. The small space was filled with the smell of bandages and misery. Pav tried not to stare; she'd sat up half of last night, flicking between channels on the TV, trying to block out the images of body parts and ash and trying not to think of the soft, heavy dust that invaded her lungs in the cellar.

They let the stretcher out first, made their way outside and perched next to each other on a low wall by a block of shrubs, away from most of the patients with their portable drips and serial cigarettes.

'They probably did this to her because Eva ran away,' said Finn. 'But I don't understand; the girls must be more valuable to them alive. As for the other bodies; they couldn't all have been working in that house.' He offered her a stick of chewing gum and they waited as a grey-haired woman shambled by; small brown stains like islands stretched in a dirty archipelago towards the hem of her faded primrose dressing gown.

'It's no good, I need to get away from here,' said Pav. 'How about that Brazilian place in Abertrothy? You owe me a drink or two.'

SHE STOPPED for petrol on the way, and the clock above the bar showed 5:30 p.m. when she walked into the overdesigned bistro. Finn was waiting at a table in the window with two Sols, the necks stuffed with wizened chunks of lime.

'Standards haven't slipped then,' Pav said, flicking the fruit out with a fingernail. 'Sorry your Sunday got screwed up. How's Mrs W. taking it?'

'Off in Avonport for a day's shopping with one of her best buddies. If it hadn't been for all this fun and games, I'd have been at home on the sofa – Sky sports, don't care what's on – and a few too many beers.'

'I saved you from yourself, so that's two good deeds in a weekend, not bad. How about the locals; are they talking to us again?'

'Jimmy Spears? He's a softy when you get to know him. Believe it or not, he thinks you're the dog's bollocks, Not that he'd ever tell you to your face. It was him tipped me off about the boy in the woods, thought we might be interested.'

'Like I keep saying, we don't get involved in run-of-the-mill murders.'

'Well, how about this for a Sunday treat? Teenage boy, white, badly malnourished, probably East European. And he has lesions on his arms and neck, just like the ones on Mira and the other bodies.'

'You saw this? Yourself? With your own eyes?'

'Scouts honour. I've registered our interest, persuaded them that the post-mortem needs to be done this afternoon. A lot of whining, but it'll get done.'

'You need to get back in touch with Spears; we need samples from the boy sent to NIMR in London so that they can cross match with Mira and the other bodies.'

A small brindle whippet wandered in and sat by the bar, followed by a twenty stone Michelin man wearing a grey tracksuit. Pav half turned her back and looked out of the window. 'Friend of yours?' asked Finn. 'He looks familiar.'

'Schedule 1 offender – he's working his way through every single mother in Uskmouth, though God knows what they see in him. I came across the bastard soon after I joined ROCU, and ended up giving evidence against him a couple of years ago. I'm not exactly top of his Christmas card list.'

'You want to go?' asked Finn.

'He's the mouth breather around here. I'm not going anywhere.'

Finn looked round at the bar. 'I can't say he's a good match for the ambience in here.'

'Ambience, eh? That's a big word for a poor little Welsh boyo.'

'I've spent too much time hanging around with you, boss. It's all that culture, see, rubbing off on me.' He pointed at her empty bottle. 'Time for another?'

He came back from the bar with two more Sols. 'I told them to hold the lime and send it to a fruit museum instead.' He pushed the bottle across the table. 'Is there any more news on the bodies that were found with Mira?'

'You sure you want to know?' She took a long swig of the cold beer. 'Going by the bone fragments and the quantity of ash, they'd been burning bodies for some time. Forensics can't be certain, but they're guessing at between twenty and thirty.'

A classroom of children turned to dust. There were times, she thought, when thumbscrews and the rack didn't seem like such bad ideas.

'The door to the fire chamber's quite small,' she said, 'that's why they cut the bodies up, to make them fit. Something must have disturbed them before they could finish the last batch – Mira's lucky to be alive.'

'Batch? That doesn't sound like you boss. They weren't chickens being slaughtered.'

'Sorry - maybe callousness is catching. You think I had sweet dreams last night? I've arranged DNA matching on the bodies, but if that doesn't throw up anything we're a bit stuck for identification.'

'How about facial reconstruction from the skulls?'

'There wasn't a single one intact. But we know one thing – some of those kids were pretty ill before they died. You've seen the photos; an infection caused those lesions.'

She had a sudden thought. 'At hospitals, when they do operations and remove something from a body, like an appendix, or if they amputate a limb... what happens to the bits they don't want? They don't exactly put them out with the bins.'

'Incinerate them, I guess.' He looked sideways at her. 'You're not suggesting...'

'Why not? Parts of bodies, evidence of disease; what's the common denominator?'

'So where does Mira fit in?' asked Finn. 'And if they brought those bodies from the hospital, why not burn them on site in the first place?'

'Botched operations, deliberate overdoses of drugs, someone trying to hide the evidence. I don't know. I'm flailing around in the dark here, Finn, give me a break.'

'What about the basement itself; is there any significance in that?' he asked. 'The place used to be a school – maybe there's a connection with an ex-pupil.'

Pav ignored him and tried to think if there was anything else she'd missed. 'The basement, no, but after the police arrived, I went outside to get some air. The street was half blocked off and there was a crowd of people, you know the sort. But one guy stood out, he didn't seem to fit. I'd put money on him not being local – he had a leather wrist bag, took a picture with his mobile.'

'No law against that,' said Finn. 'There are some weird people out there. You know the sort, uploading crap to their social media to get more likes.'

'But that's the point. He didn't look like the sort of guy who cares about his Insta or Facebook. And the picture he took – it was when Mira was brought out to the ambulance, but I could swear he was pointing the camera at me.'

'You'd just had a pretty big shock,' said Finn. 'Doesn't do a lot for clear thinking or powers of observation.'

'That's what I told myself. Just being jumpy. And now I'd better let you get back to being a Sunday afternoon couch potato; something tells me we won't be socialising much for a while.'

PAV GUNNED the Porsche across the bridge and turned onto the valley road. Another ten minutes and she'd be home for another evening of her own company. She glanced over at the river, tracking the course of the road through the valley. The early evening sun had turned the calm surface into a mirror, reflecting the willows that lined the opposite bank; if only life could be that perfect.

Her mobile rang a few hundred metres before she reached the edge of the village. She glanced at the screen and threw the phone back onto the passenger seat without answering. What was it with Ash? Pride, probably – couldn't stand the thought of a woman rejecting him. She pumped the brakes to slow down in time and turned up the track to the terrace of cottages. The phone buzzed again as she parked, a WhatsApp this time. She waited until she was inside before reading it; a gif of an animated, crying teddy bear and the words – *Missing You!*

THE BOTTLE of Pinot Noir in the fridge only managed half a glass. Not that it mattered; there was another bottle begging to be opened and the alcohol would to do more for the ache in her shoulder than any amount of massage or paracetamol. Then it was lock the doors, turn off the mobile and settle down for a bath, a book and then whatever rubbish she could find on the TV.

But first she took the glass back into the living room, sat at the small dining table, opened the laptop and checked her messages. There was the usual dross; an invitation from someone she met once at a conference and hadn't thought of since, asking her to become a Facebook friend, and another message from Ash. The man was beginning to feel like a particularly irritating rash, but she couldn't delete the message without reading it.

'Hi babe. Sorry about the other day – it all got out of hand. No hard feelings. How about we go to New York for the weekend – I already booked flights and our hotel, the one you liked so much last time ;) Remember? I'll pick you up Friday night, okay? Kiss and make up, like always.'

The arrogant bastard. Typical Ash; throw money at the problem. He'd turn up with some present that would have cost her at least two months' salary, and within five minutes he'd be expecting her to apologise for his infantile behaviour. Before she deleted the message, Pav sent a reply. *'Not around next weekend, not around this lifetime, go by your-self. Don't call again.'* And then she couldn't resist another. *'The room was crap, by the way, and so were you.'*

Pa had never quite mastered the art of cooking, and he'd

passed on that gene to her. She was famished. Toast, that was the answer. The only decision was cheese, beans, eggs, or all three. The bread was already in the toaster when her mobile beeped with a diary reminder. She swore, sagged and turned off the sound, not needing to look. Forgetting two appointments in one day; the senior moments had come early.

Sunday, Bella had said, come round for a meal. It had seemed like a good idea at the time but now, after a day like this? She could phone, of course, and rearrange for another day; tomorrow, next week, sometime never. That would be the clever thing to do, give herself a break. Or she could get off her lazy, antisocial butt and act like a normal person for one evening, the sort of person who had friends.

The toast popped up, golden and inviting, and she threw it in the bin.

AT SEVEN THIRTY THAT EVENING, Pav pulled up outside the house near Stonefield studios, not far from the golf club. At first she thought it had to be the wrong address, but there was no mistake. The black and white timbered mansion sat well back from the road in manicured grounds that fell away gently, with views over the rolling Vale of Prescoed; live here and you'd never want to leave.

Bella waited by the open front door as Pav parked on the drive next to the silver Audi, and then led her through the front door to a stage set; the square entrance hall had the sort of curving staircase that made her think of American films from the 1940s, and if the signatures on the framed paintings were real, any one of them was worth more than her cottage.

They made their way through to a room at the back;

dark, wood furniture on the marble floor, with large folding doors opening out onto a patio with a stone balustrade and views across the Vale to soft focus mountains in the distance. Bella had already set the mosaic table with a bottle of fino, two glasses, and some small bowls of food.

'I thought we would eat tapas tonight, if that is agreeable. Gambas al Ajillo, Patatas Bravas, Croquetas de Jamòn, Tapenade, and some beautiful scented green olives. At home, I revert to my Castilian ways.'

'When I'm at home I eat beans on toast; I think I need to raise my game. Don't tell me you do all this on your salary.'

Bella laughed, a cliché of sparkling black eyes and small, perfect teeth. 'There's no mystery. I graduated in economics in Madrid, then I got my doctorate, then I taught for a few years, then I got bored with living in poverty.'

She picked up an olive between her forefinger and thumb - perfect fingernails, the palest pearlescent pink - studied it for a second, and then bit it in half, closing her eyes as if to savour the flavour better.

'I can't imagine you ever lived in poverty.'

'Relative poverty for sure, but my contemporaries were driving BMWs and I was driving a Seat, and I thought – I can do better than this. I found a job in the UK, working for a small management consultancy; within two years I was on the Board, I had share options, and then came the Dotcom crash.' She speared a prawn swimming in a dish of oil and garlic. 'I was lucky. I had seen it coming and already cashed in some of my share options, those that I could, and then I thought – now is the time to do something different. So I changed the business suits for jeans, took a degree in social work, moved out here and then set up The Swallows.' She sipped her chilled sherry, looking at Pav over the top of the glass. 'I hope that was concise enough for you.'

This woman was in a different class, a Spanish version of Annie but ten years older. This could get complicated - best keep the conversation away from anything personal. After the Sols and now the sherry, her guard wouldn't just be down, she'd be putting out the welcome mat and asking when they could adopt their first cat together. 'So you didn't fancy working for Gwenstow social services?' she said, trying to keep it casual.

'Look at me, what do you think? I confess, I have never been very good at kowtowing to other people. And while I was training, I realised that there was a real need for somewhere like The Swallows, a place for the kids who cannot cope without help. And it makes money. £5,000 per week, per child. We only take four at a time, but it adds up.' She poured herself another glass. 'Enough about me - any more news from Ash?' she asked. 'Is he still being a nuisance?'

'I can cope.'

'Of course! But men are always like animals once you get below the surface. And not just the men, although I only say that to you as a friend. The girls are almost as bad. I know it is in the biology, but still you hope that civilisation tames the beast.'

'And does it?'

'You tell me – you have seen them in the streets at night. Be honest, my friend. Maybe it is the fault of the parents, maybe it is the fault of the system, I don't know, but half of them are little more than teenage sluts, leading on the boys.' Her wine glass hit the table with such force that the stem snapped, and pale wine dripped over the edge of the table and onto the tiled patio floor. 'My apologies,' she said, finding a tissue to mop up the mess. 'All the 'wokeness' at work, sometimes we need to be honest with people that we can trust.' Bella brought another glass and a bottle from a concealed fridge by the drinks cabinet.

'I was so ashamed when Eva ran away that I thought maybe you would not come tonight. She was not a prisoner, but I feel responsible. I have to make a confession - I was the one with her when she disappeared, me! I know, you are right to look at me like that.'

'Jesus, Bella. She'd only been here a day; why the hell did you allow her out? As for taking her yourself - don't you have staff for that?'

'Mea culpa. I felt sorry for the girl, something about her touched me. I made a mistake to take her out, I recognise that now. But at least she is no longer being abused, and we may be thankful for that. I just hope she is safe wherever she is.'

'Amen to that. But the trouble is, I needed her - she's a potential witness in a case I'm working on.'

'I thought you came across her by accident? Working with these child abuse cases is a past life for you, no?'

'Not quite. I spread my net wider these days, that's all. At least she gave us a lead on the house.'

'Her friend with the damaged hand, did you find her? Eva was so worried, I remember.'

'Do you listen to local radio?' Pav asked. 'There was a report about some bodies found in a school basement and Mira was with them; badly injured and very sick, but alive. She's in hospital now but it's touch and go.'

'Oh, my dear Lord!' Bella walked over to the balcony and stared out over the Vale; slivers of cloud had turned pink and grey in the pale evening sky and a soft breeze brought the scent of newly mown hay. 'This is terrible, terrible; I shall say a novena.'

Pav joined her, leaning on the balustrade. 'She had an

emergency operation today on her brain. We won't know for a while if it's been successful.'

'And what about the house? Did you find anything that might help?'

'A computer with a wiped disk, and the man who was running the place. Unfortunately, we had a problem with him too – and this is for your ears only. He killed himself with a cyanide pill while I was interviewing him, so Mira's our only link between the brothel and the bodies.'

'Cyanide pill? Is that not a little old school, not to mention very painful? said Bella. 'He must have worked for someone; perhaps they could not allow him to tell his secrets, and death was preferable to whatever they would do to him.' She picked up the last prawn in her fingers, studied it for a moment, bit it in two and then swallowed the halves without chewing. 'There was a time, many years ago now, when I was consulting to a software company near Newbury. Their technology was pretty damn expensive, took them years to develop. We heard rumours that another company was starting up with a very similar product. To cut a long story short, one of my client's employees had been selling their secrets to a competitor.'

'Industrial espionage,' Pav said. 'That's fairly common, especially in tech.'

'Common, perhaps, but not acceptable, not for our clients. Believe me, I was not involved, directly or indirectly, but the guy who thought he could shit on his *colegas* finds it is time to start a collection of walking sticks. No, I am not saying that I agree – of course it should never have happened – but when people forget their obligations, perhaps it is time to teach them a lesson.'

H e'd have to travel light; a change of clothes, the small radio, a sandwich of stale bread and the last of the cheese, a bottle of water. And the book, and the photo. He looked around the small flat for the last time; moving there had once felt like a penance, now it seemed a sanctuary. How small his life had become, he thought, each step down was another diminishment. Giving up possessions was supposed to be a stage on the way to enlightenment, but he felt only failure and loss.

He spent that day wandering almost aimlessly, heading vaguely south and downhill towards the city that rose in the distance, and the light from street lamps had replaced the fading sun by the time he passed a cash machine outside a bank. He checked his wallet – £26 and a few pence. Best to empty his account now; anyone looking for him could trace his movements by the places he used his credit card. Once things settled down, yet another new identity would be in order.

There was less than he thought; a little over £200, the sum total of his world. Seb wandered on until he found himself outside the bright window of a burger bar; he'd reached King's Cross, unfamiliar territory. A man brushed past him, a palimpsest of newspaper, string, cloth and hidden flesh; a walking midden of rank odours. As Seb stepped backwards into the gutter, he collided with a young woman who pushed him away, stronger than she looked, swearing and laughing with her companions as they clattered into the café.

The smell of frying onions enveloped him, riding on the gust of damp air from the open door. How long had it been since he ate? His mouth was watering, and he suddenly craved the taste of salt and hot fat. Inside the café, he took a table away from the window, behind the women he'd followed in; three of them, a pack. The one who'd sworn at him a few minutes ago turned to look over her shoulder; under the fluorescent lights, her skin seemed almost yellow and one eye was skewed down as if the skin at the corner had melted.

He swallowed two bites of the burger, then pushed it away. Maybe this had been a mistake after all; the inside of his mouth felt as though it had been painted with a layer of grease, and the lukewarm tea tasted no different from the food. He stared through the window; cameras sneaked on the streets outside, tracking the crowds, but how many millions of faces did they see every hour, every day? He'd be safe enough for a while. Yet now that his hunger had given up, he realised that he'd need to sleep somewhere that night.

He found a hotel on one of the side streets; cash in advance, how many hours? The bedroom walls were stained in unlikely places, the washbasin was clogged with dark pubic hairs and the whole room smelled like a urinal. Seb turned the pillow over, folded himself onto the bed fully clothed, and gradually fell asleep to a muted lullaby of traffic outside his window, and rusty orgasms from the adjoining rooms.

TWO DAYS LATER. The hotel had been a haven, but money was running out. Reluctantly, he left his room for the last time. He hadn't shaved since he abandoned his flat and he scratched through to the skin, wondering if tiny insects were already planning to nest there.

Today felt different. He detected a scent of change in the air, and instead of heading towards the river and the crowded alleyways of the City proper, he crossed the Euston Road and then took side streets at random until he found himself by an Italianate church set in large grounds, overlooked by a hospital. Seb let himself into the empty churchyard and found a seat, uncharacteristically tired. He'd forgotten to eat again this morning. No, not so much forgotten as decided against, but now his stomach had a familiar, hollow feeling. He scrabbled in his bag and found the sandwich that he'd made only two days ago, but in another life. The bread was a mouldy rock but the cheese was salvageable, just, and he chewed at it like a beggar.

He should have packed more clothes. Even though he'd washed as best he could in the cracked basin at the hotel, his skin felt sticky. The thought of a hot shower took him over for a moment, and he fantasised about the dirt sluicing off his body. *Fastidious little bastard*, his father had called him when he was young – *might as well be a girl, put your hair in bunches.*

The ancient cheese made him feel bilious. He should have eaten more slowly, and he sat back on the seat to straighten his body. Everything has a cause; that's what his father used to say. Nothing stands in isolation. Seb couldn't help himself and took the picture of the girl from his bag; Anca, posing by the church, smiling under a hot, Romanian sun. If he were to trace events back far enough, was Anca the reason for him being here? The inciting incident, the proximate cause?

If he were to go back even further, though, there were other causes. Why had he gone to Romania in the first place? To do good, that's what he'd told himself at the time. To go into the orphanages, raise funds for the children, help them to a better life. And for at least a year, it had worked; the state-run orphanage in Bucharest where he'd met Silviu, a beanstalk with a shaven head, dressed in pyjamas despite the freezing temperatures – punishment for trying to run away again, the Director had said.

And then he'd moved to the project in Sintana, a village in the mountains a hundred miles from the capital. Helping to build a school – the first time that he'd used a saw or a chisel – the place where he'd met Anca. Fourteen years old, she was, and shy as an unbroken pony. How many months had it taken before she'd said her first words to him? But once she started, the flow never stopped. His own, personal serpent pretending to be Eve; he'd never thought temptation could hit so hard. It took over two years for the disguise to be sloughed off like an outgrown skin, to see her as a woman, not a girl. He should have known that the devil stalked slowly.

For a moment, he was back in the remote Romanian village; he could almost smell the chickens and pigs, the sour reek of poverty. But Anca in her pale blue dress was a teenage Madonna, and madonnas were meant to be worshipped. So simple, so pure; what priest could resist the temptation to touch his goddess? It was nothing at first; a chaste kiss on her forehead, his trembling hands pressed lightly to her waist, both of them hidden from sight in one of the dust-soaked alleys between the school and the house where he had his room. But as she'd pulled away, a faint blush of pleasure on her cheeks, he'd pulled her face up to his and kissed her lips – bit them – slipped his hand inside the thin cotton of her dress and onto her breast; even now, the memory made him burn and harden.

They'd rutted like animals, pressed against the mottled concrete wall. He could still smell her, sweet and salt; he heard her small sounds; he saw her eyes closed – with joy and fulfilment, he'd told himself, not with pain and disgust.

It had seemed so innocent; two virgins consummating their love and surely pleasing to God. But that night, sitting on his bed before dinner, he'd realised that his life was over. He'd been tested, and failed. An hour later, with a glass of cheap wine inside him, he told the Project Leader, Lorenzo Bonetti, that he would be leaving and not coming back. *Personal reasons*, he'd said, *I should go tomorrow.*

And instead of the argument that he'd expected, Bonetti handed him a photograph; a girl pressed against a wall. There was no innocent joy on her face, only pain as she tried not to cry out, while the man...

He'd pushed the photo away, not having the words to explain, but Bonetti slid it back across the table.

'*A memento,*' he'd said, '*don't worry, we have other copies.*' And then he put his dry hand over Sebastian's.

'*Men are weak, my friend, there is no blame. Not in my eyes. But the eyes of the world, they will see something different; a teenage child and a concupiscent priest. Unless, of course...*'

The memories, and the sun in the quiet churchyard, had made him weary. Seb closed his eyes and leant back, emptying his mind as he felt the warmth on his face.

. . .

HE DIDN'T HEAR them arrive. The first he knew was the photo of Anca – not Bonetti's blackmail betrayal but his own innocent image, the way he wanted to remember her – being wrenched from the hand that had fallen onto his lap as he slept. There were three of them, standing a few feet in front of him, laughing at the image. One of them licked it slowly, swivelling his hips at the same time. Fourteen years old, maybe fifteen. Kids.

The one on the left, the smallest, spat on the ground. 'Fucking nonce!' He was dancing from foot to foot, not sure what expression to wear. 'You sick, man.'

The oldest boy, the one with the picture, swaggered forward a couple of steps. 'He right, you know, my brother. Sick fuck like you, want to mess with young girls. Am I right?' He squatted down, his face level with Seb's. 'Tell you what. You pay us, maybe we let you go. Like a fine, yeah? Come on bro, give us the money. We all got places to go.'

Seb pushed himself upright on the bench. He could smell the boys from here, cheap aftershave barely masking the sweat. Or was that his own fear leaking out? He tried to get to his feet, but the boy in front of him jerked upright at the same time and pushed him back, hard.

'You not listening, bro. You pay or we gonna have to fine you. Your choice.'

'I don't have any money,' said Seb. 'Leave me alone, please.'

'Leave me alone, pleeease!' The third boy tried to mimic his accent, and then snatched Seb's bag and emptied it on the ground. 'Fuck all here.' He picked up the book, flicked through the pages and then threw it to one side. He kicked through the few pieces of clothing and then pulled a knife

from somewhere inside his shapeless jacket. 'Give us your wallet, man. No messing about; like my colleague say, we all got places to go.'

Seb couldn't take his eyes off the blade. He pulled out his wallet, slowly, and threw it on the ground at the boy's feet. 'It's all I have – take it.'

The oldest boy picked it up and checked the contents. 'Okay, this is a good start, my brother, but we can do better. Two hundred pound don't go nowhere these days. You and me and your credit card, we going for a walk, get some more cash. Then maybe we let you get back to the girls.' He laughed, waved the photograph in Seb's face, and let it flutter to the ground.

'I've told you before – get out of here! I'll call the police, now leave him alone!' A large man in his sixties lumbered down the path from the church, waving a walking stick with a thick, round end. The smallest boy was already halfway to the churchyard gate and Seb tried to grab his wallet while the others were distracted.

The oldest boy turned back to him. 'Your lucky day, my friend, you only lose your money.' With the skill of long practice, he scooped the cash and credit cards from the wallet and lobbed it back. 'Live happy,' he said, and then they were gone.

'I'm so sorry.' The man sank on to the bench beside Seb, panting. 'They know no reason. I've tried to talk to them but they infest the place. The church, you see, it draws the lonely. And the lonely so often are vulnerable. They took your wallet, I think. Will you be okay?' He picked up the creased photo of Anca and handed it to Seb. 'A pretty girl; is she your daughter?'

Seb shook his head. 'A friend. I haven't seen her for a long time.'

'But a good friendship never dies. If it's God's will, you'll see her again.' He wiped the sweat from his forehead, took a deep breath and levered himself to his feet. 'To stay and talk would be a pleasure, but I regret that I have a sermon to finish. May God keep you safe.'

Seb felt himself trembling as the vicar disappeared into the church. God's will, the man had said, but where was God now? Not that it mattered; while he'd slept, something had clicked into place, and now he knew what to do next. Only one thing was important, only one person. '*I'll keep her safe,*' Lorenzo had said, his arm around Anca's shoulders on the day that Sebastian left Sintana. '*Just remember our bargain and no one will come to any harm.*'

The contents of his bag were still scattered on the ground in front of the seat, and Seb gathered them up slowly. He had to go back to The Mission; Bonetti wouldn't have been fooled by his disappearance, even though he'd planned it so well and tried to tie up every loose end so Anca would remain safe. He must have been deluded.

Bonetti had always been vindictive; what if he'd taken his revenge on Anca, and put her in one of his whorehouses? Seb tried, and failed, to ignore the image of her flattened and helpless under a series of sweating strangers.

There was no choice; he had to go back to the Mission in Uskmouth and confront the man. Kill him if need be; it couldn't be that hard. With no God, who was there to judge? And then he'd find Anca and they could disappear again, together.

Forever.

CHAPTER
TEN

The corner shop Chianti after she got back from Bella's had been a mistake in both quality and quantity. She'd woken in front of the television at 2:30 a.m., cold and bent around a cushion; the last half-drunk glass had tipped onto the carpet and left a dark stain. When she left for work that morning it was still there, covered in a mound of damp, pink salt.

Pav took another sip of machine coffee to wash down the couple of painkillers that she'd cadged from Finn. The hangover might be self-inflicted and therefore blameless, but the bruising to her shoulder and kidneys had spread during the night, leaving her with slow, tentative movements.

She checked her messages, starting with the analysis of Defrim's laptop. She'd hoped for some clue to lead them to another link in the chain, but the machine's hard drive had been wiped clean by industrial grade software – he'd prob-ably set it off as soon as he realised the raid was happening. Another door slammed.

A light knock on the office door interrupted her. 'I hope

you feel better than you look,' said Rachel. 'Gus wants to see you upstairs asap. Wasn't looking too happy; I think he heard about yesterday. Fuckin' well done, by the way.'

'Somehow, I don't think Gus will take the same attitude.'

This was a summons she could do without. On the other hand, Gus had to fight the battles in London for resources and budgets, and what had she given him to work with? Two missing witnesses, one of them on the run, one of them dead. Another who might or might not regain consciousness, and who might not remember anything even if she did. Add to that a butcher's shop of diseased limbs and torsos, and a few sackfuls of incinerated bone and fine grey ash. And, perhaps, the anonymous body in a shallow grave. They still hadn't traced a single trafficker or found any living victims, except for Mira.

She pushed her notes aside, finished the lukewarm coffee, and walked up the back stairs to Gus's office. This wasn't one of his good days, she could tell from the way he pulled his earlobe every time he looked at her.

'Thank you, Pav, for continuing to make my life interesting. It isn't as if we don't have enough problems about exceeding authority.'

'Just trying to help, Gus.'

'Come on Pav. You know as well as I do that these bastards can't wait for us to fail so they can grab our resources for themselves; local police, Home Office, even the bloody security services. I'm trying to calm the waters and build relationships while you're crashing around like an out-of-control RoboCop. Please tell me you had a good reason for authorising brain surgery on a teenage girl. Please tell me it was for sound operational reasons and not some misguided feminine empathy. Well?'

'You want reasons? I'll give you reasons. First, any delay and Mira would be dead. End of life, end of our only witness. Second...' She paused and then gave up the attempt. 'I think the first reason is more than enough.'

Gus checked the name on an incoming call to his mobile, cut it off, and slumped back in his chair. 'As it happens, I agree with you, but the Director of Social Services wants me to deliver your trussed body for ritual slaughter. Strange woman. I've told her you will receive a severe reprimand and a note will go in your personnel file, although the latter action may just slip my mind. Matter closed.' He took a tissue from the box on his desk and polished the lenses of his spectacles. 'As for your karate demonstration in the hospital car park, I trust there's no permanent damage. You seem to be moving a little stiffly.'

'A word of advice, Gus, don't go all koala bear on brick shithouses, and definitely don't bite their ears. You never know where they've been and they taste foul.'

'I shall exclude the practice from my repertoire with immediate effect.' He took a slim cigar from a tin in the drawer of his desk, passed it under his nose as though it were a delicate flower, and replaced it. 'So tell me, am I girding my loins for a battle on your behalf at Vauxhall this Wednesday or not? Something to work with, Pav, that's all I ask. Despite all your frenetic activity, I have a sneaking sense that you're flying blind.'

Working for Gus had its upsides. Loyal, clever, and usually not around - always a desirable attribute in a boss. On the downside, he had an annoying habit of mind reading. 'We both know Hexameter's passed its sell-by date,' she said. 'I was the one who recommended that we pull the plug. But everything's changed; a pimp with a cyanide pill? Please!'

'What about the incinerated bodies? I assume they were part of the traffickers' stock, depreciated to death.'

'Not the phrase I would have used, but yes. And there's Mira. If - when - she regains consciousness, we may have a decent witness; it's a long shot, but we've worked on less.'

Gus was still looking lazily at her; not a man to play at poker.

'The clincher's the infection,' Pav said. 'Some of the kids who died had it, so does Mira. So did the boy they found buried up by Tryleg.'

'Has the post-mortem report come through yet?'

'I should have it this morning.'

'Then tell me more about this sickness,' said Gus. 'What do we have from forensics?'

'Nothing. They've passed it on to NIMR in Mill Hill.'

'You've been a busy girl. Sorry. Busy *woman,* and don't look at me like that. It's all a bit early for me, haven't turned the 'woke' filter on yet. Write everything up and let me have it by tomorrow lunchtime.'

'Any chance of extra help on this?' Pav asked, ignoring the dismissal. 'Finn and I will be pretty stretched.'

'Use Rachel and Amir as and when. I can't reassign them full-time, but they can take some of the strain. As for you, be careful; I don't want parts of your gangling body turning up in another basement somewhere.'

'My sentiments exactly.'

FINN WAS WAITING for her downstairs in her office. 'The PM came through on the boy. First, they found traces of sawdust on his clothes, but on the surface, not worked in. It's likely he picked them up from whatever vehicle brought him there. Seasoned oak and mahogany, so we're probably talking carpenter rather than woodcutter. And second – you're going to love this – according to the pathologist he was already suffering multiple organ failure, just like Mira. Whatever caused that would have killed him within days, if not hours.'

'What about the lesions?'

'Identical to the other bodies. And Mira.'

She could almost feel the cogs meshing. 'So if the infection didn't kill him, how did he die?' she asked, not sure that she wanted to know the answer.

'This is the unpleasant part.' He paused. 'You have to understand, even though the grave was shallow, the earth around Tryleg is pretty solid. It's mostly clay, and someone had tamped it down around the body. Movements of arms or legs were out of the question.'

'What movements? He was dead, right?'

'By the time we found him, yes. But the post-mortem found small traces of soil in his nasal passage and his lungs. He was still breathing, just, after he was buried.'

Two weaknesses that she'd never admitted to anyone, and barely even to herself. Being constrained in a small, dark space, and not being able to breathe. That poor soul in the woods had lived and died in her worst nightmare. 'He would have struggled, surely, not just lain there,' she said.

'It's possible he'd fallen into a coma. If I were feeling charitable, I'd say that whoever buried him might have thought the boy was dead, especially if he was panicking about having a body on his hands. Which points to the burial being done by someone who isn't used to this sort of thing. Not a professional.'

How long did it take to suffocate? A minute, five? Twenty? How long did a minute last when you were dying? Time was relative, after all. She'd heard that people in comas might still be conscious, might still be able to hear and feel even though they couldn't make any response. What about this boy? Had he felt the earth being shovelled onto his limbs, pressing on his chest, covering his face, grains of soil invading his lungs with each infinitesimal breath?

Sometimes she wished her imagination wasn't quite so vivid.

'When did all this happen?' she asked. 'Are we talking days, weeks?'

'The forensic entomologist is playing with larvae as we speak, but the burial probably took place less than a week ago. One thing's sure, though, he'd been abused not long before he died. We don't know whether he was willing or not, although "willing" doesn't mean much in someone his age - seventeen or eighteen, but underdeveloped for his age. Malnourishment, probably. I'm still waiting for toxicology reports for evidence of drugs.'

'What about the samples from the others? Do we have anything yet from Mill Hill?'

'Still waiting. And there's something else. We're not exactly blessed with CCTV up in the woods where they discovered the boy, but there's a patch of mud just off the road with some recent tyre impressions.'

Perhaps there was a God after all. 'Mud?' she said. 'Apart from today, it hasn't rained for weeks.'

'There are springs all over the slope up there. In some places, the ground never really dries out. The tyres were typical of a small van, and unless the driver took the back doubles, it's odds-on he came through either Gwenstow or Abertrothy. I've corralled the CCTV footage for the last four days and told the chaps to look for vans heading towards Tryleg.'

'Rather them than me – that could take weeks. And why four days?'

'They found a few things in the boy's pockets,' Finn said. 'A few coppers and a receipt, dated four days ago, from a corner shop in North London. He'd bought a Mars bar and a packet of crisps, and that's all they found in his stomach. Looks like the last meal he ever ate.'

'Some meal, poor bastard.'

'So he's in London less than a week ago, then his mutilated body ends up on the Welsh Borders. He was probably buried about the same time that Mira was dumped in that basement.' Finn shook his head. 'But this is what I don't understand if you're looking for connections. The bodies you found with Mira were butchered and dumped, like meat. But whatever happened to the body in the woods, I'm laying money that someone said a prayer as they shovelled the earth over his face. God knows what the killer would have said if he'd known the boy wasn't dead.'

'Assuming the person who buried him also killed him. You don't think he knew the lad was still alive?'

"Possible, if this was a punishment or revenge killing. But the way he was laid in the grave doesn't fit the profile.'

'You're saying two different people did these murders, always assuming the boy's death wasn't accidental.'

'Or one person with two different motives. It's still possible they're completely unconnected, but I know where I'm placing my bet. My gut tells me that if we find the source of the disease, we'll find our killer.'

Finn's intuition wasn't bad for a man. Not that she believed in gut instinct - no better than woo woo as far as she was concerned. But the evidence did seem to point that way. 'Maybe the boy really is a coincidence and we're wasting time on him, but I agree he looks interesting. What about the shop where he bought the crisps? Any security cameras?'

'No point, they said. The kids who nick things always wear hoods.'

Finn broke away to take a call, scribbled some notes on the corner of a grease-stained paper napkin, and then turned back to her, grinning. 'Oh yes! God pats me on the head and says, "Good boy Finn."'

Pav looked at the semi-legible notes; the only recognisable part was a postcode. 'Are you going to let me in on the secret?'

'You remember I told you about the tyre tracks in the woods near the grave? The police already have a visual on a van that fits the bill – it was picked up on CCTV in Gwenstow last Friday. Nothing special in that, but I asked for a correlation with ANPR, and now we have the same van crossing the bridge at 11.32, in Gwenstow heading towards the Tryleg Road at 11.40, and back on the bridge, heading east, at just after 2 p.m.' He picked up the napkin. 'The van's registered at this address; Wood Green in North London, a hop, skip and a jump from Tottenham where our body bought the Mars bar the day before!'

'I bet when you were a kid you used a hammer to make jigsaw pieces fit; there must be five hundred white vans driving through Gwenstow every day.'

Finn was still grinning. 'Don't need a hammer. There's a patch of wasteland near Harringay station; a white van with the same plates was torched there on Saturday. Someone complained about the smoke, and one of our bright sparks picked up the report by doing a routine database sweep on the van we caught on camera in Gwenstow. Damn, I love technology.'

Pav grabbed her bag. 'Looks like we have our day

mapped out. We'll call in at Mill Hill on the way back and see where they are with analysis of the infection. See you in the car park in ten – you can drive. I'm probably still over the limit from last night.'

'I shan't ask.'

'Good call.'

THE RAIN HAD STARTED, a thin, miserable drizzle. Through the car's windscreen everything looked distant and blurred, matching her mood. Pav fell asleep on the almost-empty M4, just after the Avonport turnoff, and came to only when Finn shook her awake as they passed Bounds Green tube station. The satnav took them to an address on one of the ladders of streets tucked behind Wood Green Shopping Centre.

This was bedsit land, and the house where they'd stopped looked dilapidated and unloved, with dark green paint flaking from the window frames. Pav pushed the top bell again, but there was still no answer, and she tried the lower flat. She looked down the street of Victorian villas while she waited; half the front gardens had been turned into parking bays, and the rest were overgrown with scrubby hydrangeas or badly pruned privet.

The street was early afternoon empty. Pav banged on the front door and noticed one of the grey net curtains twitch aside for a second. She banged again; Finn tapped her shoulder and smiled at the downstairs window, where an old lady was peering out at them.

'Don't do that,' Pav said. 'She'll never come out.'

The curtain fell back, and a few moments later the front door opened. The woman seemed well enough, apart from hair that looked as if it hadn't been washed for a year, and clothes that had been stranded on the shores of fashion circa 1955.

Pav flashed her ID. 'Sorry to bother you, but we're looking for a chap called Sebastian Evans from the upstairs flat. I don't suppose you have any idea...'

'Gone! Buggered off. Left me a month's rent and just disappeared. Left all his stuff, too. Books, clothes – what good's that to me? Never trusted him. Creepy, he was, wore a crucifix. Only poofs wear jewellery. And he was too quiet. A man should make some noise sometimes, or what's the point? Eh?' She ignored Pav and studied Finn's left ear as if it had a message for her. 'Who did you say you were?'

Pav held out her hand and backed the woman slowly into the hallway. 'Delighted to meet you Mrs...?'

Finn closed the door behind them; the narrow corridor smelled of incontinent cats. 'You told us he'd "buggered off",' she said, savouring the words. 'In that case, I wonder if you'd mind letting us see his rooms.'

'Done something wrong, has he? I run a decent place here, always have, always will. People see the police nosing about gets me a bad name, that's why I keep meself to meself. Ask me no questions and I'll tell you no lies – that was my Harold's motto and I still swear by it.' If the Queen still sent telegrams to centenarians, this woman would be near the top of the list.

'We'll be very discreet, I promise,' said Finn. 'Ten minutes upstairs and then we'll be out of your way.'

The woman squinted at him. 'You look just like the gasman – he was here the other day. Said there was a leak. And you sound like him.'

'Who – the gasman?'

'Mr Evans, your friend Sebastian, if that's what his name is! Never trust a Welshman, that was my Harold's motto, specially as a lodger. For all I know you could be after me life savings, much good may they do you.'

Finn took out his ID card and showed it to her, gently this time, as if scared that she'd attack him if he moved too quickly. 'Regional Organised Crime Unit, that's what it says here. We do things discreetly, not like the regular police, but if we don't get to see those rooms pretty damn quick, I'll have to call my colleagues. They'll turn up in a squad car with sirens and flashing blue lights and what will the neighbours think then?'

The old woman backed slowly towards her open door. 'You come here waving yourself around like you own the place. Bloody police state, I blame the socialists. Some of us keep ourselves respectable, not that you'd know anything about that.' She took another step back as Finn advanced towards her. 'All right, all right, keep your wig on. Just give me a minute and I'll get the key.'

THE TINY FLAT WAS AN ANTICLIMAX, as they usually were. What had she expected? A monster's lair, perhaps, with blood on the walls and a couple of stained axes? But this was so ordinary. Two rooms, cheap furniture, a fridge empty except for a half carton of rancid milk and an open tin of baked beans. A wardrobe with four wire hangers, but no clothes.

Finn sniffed loudly as he wandered back into the living room from the tiny, curtained-off kitchen. 'Bedsits always smell the same, don't know what it is. Socks and sausages, at a guess, and I'll bet the windows don't open, they never do.' He lifted one of the brown cushions on the plastic sofa, then let it fall back. 'Interesting that he sounded Welsh, at least it fits with the name.' He looked up at the framed print hanging opposite the chair. 'Now that's weird. No, not just weird – whoever painted that was on a trip and a half.'

Pav joined him. 'It's a Dali, you peasant. Anyone would know that. "The Madonna of Port Lligat" – it's famous.'

'Not to us Valley boys.' He studied it from another angle. 'Didn't know you were an art historian on top of everything else.'

'My brother liked the Surrealists. Had loads of books on them – I used to sneak into his room and look through the pictures when he wasn't there.' She studied the image which she knew so well. Everything seemed to be floating; the seated woman with her transparent torso showing the horizon far behind, and the infant Christ hovering above the cushion on her lap as if there were no such thing as gravity. Waiting to escape.

She focused back into the room; Finn had already turned away from the picture to study the bookshelves. 'Eclectic tastes but not exactly my style – philosophy, religion. Get a real nutter and you can bet he's an intellectual.'

Pav joined him, pulled out one of the books, and started to flick through it. 'St Thomas Aquinas, the *Summa contra Gentiles*. You can't get much more Catholic than that.' She checked out another. 'Jean-Paul Sartre, and it's in French. Now that's a different matter; Ash would love it. Come to think of it, he's got the same edition.'

'I thought you said he was an ignorant prick?'

'Ignorant, no. But as for being a prick – I'll give you that.' She slotted the books back into place. 'We need to have this place looked at properly, see if we can pull out any leads, but I bet anything worth knowing about went up when he torched the van.'

She stopped by the door. 'The landlady said he wore a crucifix, and that's what your body was holding. Then there's the book by Aquinas and that painting of the Madonna. If he's into religion, maybe he went to a church nearby. Perhaps Mrs whatever-her-name-was knows something –worth an ask.'

The woman was waiting for them downstairs, lurking by the front door. 'Seen enough, have you? I'd burn the lot.'

'We'll send some people round,' said Pav, 'save you the trouble. As for Mr Evans; you said he wore a crucifix. Can you describe it? Was it silver, gold, wood?'

'Plastic! That's the Welsh for you, won't spend a penny if a farthing will do.'

'Are you sure?'

'Creamy colour, it was, with bits of brown. He couldn't even be bothered to keep it clean.'

'Perhaps it was ivory?'

'What would I know about that?' She squinted at Finn's ear again. 'And why are you so interested?'

'We were wondering if he was especially religious,' said Finn, 'if he went to Church.'

The landlady gave him a sideways look. 'I said he was Welsh, didn't I? I told him when he moved in – there's a nice Methodist Chapel just down the road, me and Harold used to go there every Sunday, regular as clockwork – but blow me down if he doesn't turn out to be a left footer. Nasty business. Too much thinking about virgins can't do you any good, that's what I told him, but he still used to take himself off to Muswell Hill on a Sunday to worship his painted idols. All that incense – he'd come back smelling like a tart's boudoir. What my Harold would have said doesn't bear thinking about.'

. . .

THE PRIEST INVITED them to sit on folding chairs in a side chapel. 'Sick, you say, this man you're looking for? He would be in the majority then, of the people I see. What was his name again?'

He sank slowly onto the chair as if every joint in his body was filled with sand. Pav couldn't help staring at his trembling hands and his eyes like undercooked eggs; was this a man that a killer would have confided in? And if he had, surely the priest would claim the sanctity of the confessional to keep any secrets.

'Sebastian, Sebastian Evans,' said Finn.

The priest's polite smile faded, and he stared up at the high ceiling. 'Ah yes, I knew a Sebastian, a strange, tortured man. Never knew his surname.' He paused, his fingers twisting as if telling an invisible rosary. 'Knowledgeable, he was, knew his bible and his doctrine.' He shifted uneasily in the chair and looked straight at Pav. 'I speak to many people. They unburden their souls, and what they tell me is known only to them, to me and to God. And that is how it should stay.'

'This man may be sick, Father,' Finn said, sticking to the story they'd agreed to beforehand. 'If we don't find him, he could die.'

'Could, but perhaps not. Whatever happens is God's will, you must see that.'

Before he could say anything else, Pav interrupted. 'Perhaps God sent us to you because he wants this tortured man to be found. Perhaps God's given you the chance to perform a service and save a life.

The old man smiled. 'Perhaps you put too much value on this existence.'

'It's the only one I know,' said Pav.

The priest was silent again as he studied them both.

'You mean no harm,' he said, eventually. 'And this young man; our disputes were informal, you understand. He refused to take confession. He felt himself to be unworthy, he had no faith in the power of forgiveness. My counter was that he displayed the sin of pride in such feelings, but it had no effect. And he argued with me like a Jesuit, albeit one that had lost his faith. It is always hard, I think, to find what you've lost, but much harder to find what you've thrown away.'

'You mentioned forgiveness, Father,' said Pav. 'For what?'

'I'm afraid such secrets were between Sebastian and God; I was never privileged with that revelation.'

'Do you know where he came from, Father, before he moved to London?' Finn asked. 'Perhaps he mentioned his home or his family?'

'The memory of his own father was a burden, I think, but not an unbearable one. And which of us hasn't railed against our parents? As for the whereabouts of his home; the Welsh valleys, I would say, from his accent, but you'd know that if you had spoken to him. And his father worked in the mines as a young man until they were closed. The devil takes strange forms.'

His eyes shut while he was talking, as if he'd fallen asleep. Finn looked across at Pav, but she shook her head and stood up. 'Thank you for your help, Father,' she said quietly, and it wasn't until they reached the door that she heard the priest's voice.

'You will find him, if it is God's will. If not, put your faith in his mercy.'

. . .

FROM MUSWELL HILL to the research lab in Mill Hill took less than fifteen minutes. The road hadn't changed since she'd taken part in an animal rights demonstration outside the gates, when she was studying for her degree; she hadn't thought about that for years. Funny how some memories hid themselves away.

The laboratories hadn't changed either; protected in their 1930s complex behind high walls and razor wire, set back from the road. As they drove up to the gates, she wondered how many people realised what went on in there. At least you knew where you were with criminals. People who poisoned and tortured and eviscerated live animals in the name of science were something else.

The man that met them at reception looked disconcertingly like Justin Bieber, but in a grey, polyester suit and an ill-judged turquoise tie. Who on earth would voluntarily dress that way and work in a place like this? As they followed their guide through the labyrinth of corridors, even though she knew it was her imagination, Pav could almost hear the cries of invisible animals and smell the singed fur.

When they eventually reached a small anteroom, the grey man gave them white coats, plastic hats, thin latex gloves, goggles and masks, before punching a code into a security lock and leading the way through into a brightly lit room. It smelled like an operating theatre, with its faint chemical miasma, and Pav wondered what all the precautions were for when there was so little to see.

'We usually like a little more time – this has all been rather rushed.' The man sounded apologetic.

'You said you'd found something interesting,' Pav said. 'For a three hundred mile round trip, I hope it was worth it.'

For the first time, the man smiled. 'Oh, I think so. We

wouldn't normally get involved in something like this, you understand, rather outside our remit. But with the same idiopathic pattern from three sources in almost as many days, how could we say no? The hospital was unable to identify the agent causing her disease, although it resembled a particular strain of thermally dimorphic fungus, a penicillium to be precise.'

Finn glanced over and raised his eyebrows, but Pav ignored him.

'And that's what was so strange,' the man continued. 'You'll be familiar, of course, with *P. Marneffei*, the little chap that causes penicillosis – no?' He barely suppressed a sigh. 'It's not that common in this country, except for patients with compromised immune systems, especially those who've recently travelled in Southeast Asia. Think HIV, AIDS, that sort of thing.' He was beginning to sound quite excited again.

'And now we come to the main show,' he said. 'We've managed to grow both forms of the culture from skin samples, as well as blood from the girl. There's no doubt; the strain that infected them all was identical and we haven't seen it before, not in this mutation.' He spoke into an intercom on the wall. 'You may bring the first one in now.'

A young woman joined them, holding a clear plastic cage, and placed it on the operating table. Now Pav knew what a miserable rat looked like; this one had a strange, squashed nose and tiny black eyes, and it sat huddled in the corner of its prison, shivering.

'We infected this one with a culture taken from one of the basement bodies,' said the man, 'identical to the agent that infected the girl. In Asia, these bamboo rats act as reservoirs for *P. Marneffei*.' He noticed Finn trying to back away unobtrusively. 'Don't worry – as far as we know, humans can only catch it by breathing in aerosols from infected rat faeces. But there's the rub; as I said, this isn't *P. Marneffei*. Similar, but not the same. And the differences are enough to make our current treatments for penicillosis useless.'

Which meant, if Pav understood him correctly, that Mira was in real trouble.

'Let me be clear on this,' said Finn. 'The boy we found up in the woods, and the sick girl, both show evidence of the same disease. So was that what killed the anonymous bodies in the boiler room?'

The man shook his head. 'I investigate the agents that cause infection, I'm not a pathologist. But penicillosis kills more often than not if it isn't treated quickly, and a drug-resistant mutation out there... For most people, it's unlikely to be a problem if the immune system's up to scratch. But for people who are already compromised – let's just say you wouldn't need to worry about Christmas presents for them this year.'

The rat shuffled from one corner to another, like an old man trying to find somewhere to keep warm. 'How long will it be before the poor creature dies?' Pav asked.

'Die? No, I don't think so. He's suffering the equivalent of a bad case of flu – he'll shake it off in a few days. Rats and humans, one or two differences in physiology. Mind you, a healthy human might react the same way; fever, maybe a weeping sore or two, but within a week he'd be back to normal, especially if he were treated with some antibiotics. He could end up as a carrier, though, a Typhoid Mary. We need to do more research on transmission, but if our assumption about aerosols is wrong, then an otherwise healthy but infected person might pass on the infectious agent to someone who couldn't shake it off, and we'd have ourselves a very sick person, just like your girl. As for young ratty here, I bet you a tenner that when we open up this little chap, we'll find that he's harbouring our bug. Liver, spleen, the usual suspects.'

Pav tried not to picture what he was talking about. Rats were bad enough when they were moving, but dead, eviscerated rats...

'I'm still not sure what you're telling us,' said Finn. 'Is the only way to catch this disease from contact with one of these poor buggers?'

'"Probably" is the best I can give you for now. Which, from your point of view, is a good thing, because these little fellows don't live around here. China, Vietnam, Nepal, Indonesia – that's their stamping ground.'

'How about Eastern Europe?' Pav asked. 'We think that's where the girl in the hospital came from.'

'I doubt it, wrong habitat. Not a great traveller, your bamboo rat. A nice warm burrow on a Chinese mountainside and he's happy. Perhaps he knows something we don't.' The cage was taken out again and the air suddenly felt cleaner. 'Give us a little more time,' said the man, 'and we'll find the right treatment for your girl, I promise. We nearly always do.'

THEY ORDERED a late lunch at the Cain and Abel pub a couple of hundred metres down from the complex. The smell from the room was still in her hair, an appetite killer, but she attempted to force down a cheese baguette and salad; Finn seemed happy enough to hack away at his rare steak and chips. A pale sun broke through and they sat in the otherwise empty garden at the back of the pub, barely able to hear the rumble of buses on The Ridgeway. Pav picked at the baguette for a few minutes and then pushed the plate aside.

'I don't know how you can eat that steak, not after what we've just seen. I should have let you come by yourself – that whole place is a torture chamber.'

Finn mopped up the last of the meat juices with a chip. 'Which butcher would you prefer – the one in that building or the one chopping up a few spare Bulgarians and Romanians and God knows who else? Needs must, and we've got villains to find. Can't afford too many principles, not in the sort of job we do.' He wiped his mouth with a paper napkin. 'Bloody good steak that, all the same. Wife's a veggie; if I want meat, I usually have to cook it for myself. Whatever happened to love, honour and obey?'

CHAPTER
ELEVEN

Sebastian sipped a cup of coffee at Reading services on the M4, paid for from the few coins loose in his pocket. At least the boys in the churchyard hadn't found the Oyster card he kept in a separate compartment of the wallet; enough credit for him to take the tube from Kings Cross to Hounslow West and then start walking. He'd headed west until a van stopped for him as he stuck his thumb out, more in hope than expectation, on the main road running along the side of the airport.

At least it was a start. Another hundred plus miles to go before he'd be back in Uskmouth to face Bonetti, always assuming he was back in the country. Seb drained the cup – God alone knew when he'd get another drink. Now he needed to find another ride. He walked round to the lorry park, but none of the drivers were interested as he approached them on the way back from their meals. The way they looked at him, as if he were some sort of insect. Most turned away without speaking.

He wandered back to the services. A van would do, and there were a few dotted about the car park, standing out above the hatchbacks of the road warriors and the tourists. Seb felt like a private investigator, waiting by the glass doors and noting the path of everyone that left, watching for anyone making his way to one of his target vehicles.

He was coming down with a cold, or flu. He'd felt semi-detached all day, even before the churchyard, and the sudden recognition of the thick, unbalanced feeling in his head was almost cheering. A cold, nothing he couldn't cope with. He scratched unconsciously at a small, unhealed cut on his hand and winced when an edge of his nail caught the wound. He should put a plaster on it; they'd sell them somewhere inside. He was halfway through the door when he remembered that, yes, they'd sell them. To people with money.

He shambled back to his waiting post and realised that one of the vans he'd been watching, a large white Luton, was edging backwards; he'd missed the driver coming out. Seb grabbed his bag and, trying not to look too desperate, ran towards it. The man at the wheel, a twenty-something with pierced eyebrows, shrugged and then opened the passenger door.

'I stop at Gwenstow,' he said. 'That any good?'

Good? Nearly perfect.

THE MUSIC WAS SO loud that there was no chance of a conversation, and Seb realised he'd been asleep only when the driver braked sharply. This wasn't the motorway.

The driver turned down Snow Patrol. 'Forgot to tell you, slight diversion. Had to pick something up in Malmesbury, then this little lady sticks her thumb in the air. What with you being out for the count I thought a bit more company wouldn't hurt.'

For the first time, Seb noticed the young woman by the side of the road. Denim shorts, T-shirt and a baggy patchwork cardigan. An uncertain smile.

'Move over,' said the man. 'Give the lady a seat, why don't you?' As Seb shuffled closer, the man pushed him away. 'She goes in the middle, fuckwit.'

The girl seemed unembarrassed as she squeezed past and sat between them. 'You saved my life,' she said. 'My last lift dumped me a couple of miles back – don't even know where I am.' Seb felt the warmth of her bare thigh pressed against his, and a flick of her bleached hair rested on his shoulder. She sounded faintly antipodean.

The driver winked. 'No problem, my darling. Avonport, Gwenstow and all points west if that's what takes your fancy. Or anything else, for that matter.'

The van picked up speed along a tree-lined country road, and the man rested his hand on the girl's thigh. She didn't complain and Seb tried to move away, embarrassed by the so much female flesh, so close. He felt like an intruder. The girl was much the same age as Anca would be now, he reckoned. He closed his eyes and tried to sleep again, but his mind was too full of images; Silviu sweating to death in his room, Anca smiling in the sun, Bonetti's smug face with its all-knowing smile.

They slowed down again, pulling into a small lay-by near a farm gate. 'Sorry mate,' said the driver, 'but this is where you get out.'

'What, both of us?'

'No, fuckwit. You smell like shit and you're offending the lady.'

He didn't even think of arguing, what would be the point? 'You sure?' he asked the girl, but she simply smiled and shrugged, and he suddenly felt very old.

He jumped to the ground, but the cab was higher than he'd thought, and he stumbled on the rutted grass verge. As he righted himself, the van was already moving away. He watched it disappear around a bend in the road and realised that he was glad to be out of the moving vehicle. He felt lightheaded and a little nauseous, and the privacy of a small copse, a couple of fields away, was a welcome relief.

It had been a dry summer, and the patches of parched grass were like straw as he propped himself against the trunk of an old oak. He checked his watch, but it was hard to focus; catarrh in his sinuses, probably. From the look of the sun, it was early evening, and the air was warm and still. He could do worse than sleep here; tomorrow would be a better day.

THE SMELL of the earth reminded him of Sintana, back in Romania; the thick woodland above the village where he used to walk in the early mornings. Bonetti had come to him there, the day after the incident with Anca and the photograph of their love. The morning after his fall.

His mother would have called Lorenzo "well-groomed", with his carefully cut blonde hair and unfashionably military moustache, those sharp blue eyes and his skin and nails buffed and polished. In the early morning light, on a Romanian hillside, he looked as out of place as a racehorse drawing a plough.

'You haven't told me what you want from me,' Sebastian had said, already knowing that he'd lost.

The Italian dropped his cigarette butt and ground it into the earth with the toe of his shoe. 'Like you, we simply want to help; unlike you, perhaps, we have money to spend.'

They stood together on the hillside, looking down as

the light from the morning sun hit the valley floor, and they made the deal. More a capitulation, if he was honest. Bonetti's charity would provide the funding and Sebastian would set up a religious mission in Uskmouth, a conduit for Bonetti and his partners to take young people from Romania and God knows where else, and sell them into jobs in the UK.

'A recruitment agency,' Bonetti had said, 'we all win. And with you as our public face, the young Catholic priest, we shall be respectable, why not? Sure, the kids will have to work hard – cleaners, au paires, builders – but would you have them stay in the squalor of places like this?'

Sintana was below them with other villages further down the valley, shimmering like mirages in the distant haze. A mediaeval landscape with its own beauty. A simple life, but who wanted that these days? Who would choose to stay if there were a way out?

'And if we make a little money along the way,' said Bonetti, 'so be it. Remember the parable of the talents? God, my friend, he works in mysterious ways.'

Such a small step, it had seemed. For over a year, he'd pretended to himself that this was God's will. A busy year setting up a new charity; finding the large house in Uskmouth with its rooms and cellars and wild, overgrown garden with plum trees and thickets of shrubs, teaching himself to repair and decorate. Preparing for the young people they would help. He'd loved that place.

Once it was up and running, a group of refugees would arrive almost every week, see the doctor for a health check, and move within a few days. 'We arrange boarding houses,' Bonetti had said. 'Very cheap, very clean, close to where they work. No need for you to be involved in that side of the project.'

No need to find out the truth, not that he ever tried.

HE HADN'T NOTICED the sound last night, but in the daylight it was unmistakable – a bass note to the birdsong like distant thunder, even though the sky was clear. The sleep seemed to have worked and he could read his watch now – 6.30 in the morning, a good time to start moving again. He made his way through the trees to the edge of the copse, standing on its slight rise. The ribbon of a motorway snaked across the landscape a couple of miles away, glittering with the reflection of the rising sun from a thousand car windscreens. As good a direction as any.

Only after he'd been walking for ten minutes did he realise that he no longer had his backpack; he must have left it in the van yesterday. But what did that matter? A few scraps of clothing, but other than those, what was there to regret? We all come in to the world naked, he thought, and at least the photograph was safe in his pocket. His talisman, his own sacred icon.

He carried on, slowly moving downhill across the fields and lanes, making his way towards the motorway in its own valley. At last he reached a fence at the top of an embankment that dropped onto the hard shoulder. He sat with his back to the wooden rails, watching the cars. The walk had cleared his head and even his hand felt better. A rusty scab had formed, and it barely itched anymore. Yes, today would be better; only one thing was wrong – the cars on this side were heading east, back toward London.

Watching the flow of traffic was hypnotic. As Seb waited on the stained grass, the vehicles seemed to be moving more and more slowly as they approached his position, accelerating again as they raced away, as if time were running at a different pace in the patch of air before him. Doppler vision, if there were such a thing. No problem. He could easily pick his way between the cars and the lorries that were moving like slow-motion dinosaurs, cross to the other side and then hitch a ride home. He slithered down the bank and stood on the hard shoulder.

Fast or slow, fast or slow. The speed was hard to judge now that he was here, and exhaust fumes had replaced the fresh air from his early morning walk. Still, it shouldn't be too difficult. Find the first gap, run through, wait for the next, do the same again. Step by step he'd get there, and now was the time to start.

The klaxon from the trailer was as loud as the hooter of an ocean liner, and it shocked Seb into immobility, leaving him like a statue on the edge of the slow lane, Moses waiting to part the traffic. Time had sped up again; each lorry that passed sucked the air from his lungs, leaving him fighting for breath until at last there was a long enough gap and he ran the few metres to the central reservation. He clambered across the crash barrier and then sank to the ground, feeling as if he'd been sleepwalking for the past hour and had just woken up. The sound was deafening, and the fumes threatened to choke him.

Seb closed his eyes but the noise refused to diminish, and when he looked again – tentatively, through half-open eyes – the traffic stretched both ways in unbroken lines, trapping him. He'd have to wait, keep a low profile. At some point there would be a lull in the traffic, even if only at night.

Patience, that's all it would take. He could walk, of course. There was nothing to stop him moving west, safe in his little central strip. Every step would be a step closer to his destination, even if he wasn't sure what he'd find there.

He got to his feet, aware that every joint ached, turned his back to the sun and began.

HE COULD HAVE BEEN WALKING for ten minutes or an hour, but at least he was feeling a little stronger, and his head was no longer so tightly packed with cotton wool. The sound of the traffic had become almost comforting, like the regular in and out of waves on a beach, until there was a break in the rhythm and a sound that didn't grow and die but stayed with him. As he turned to look at the police car, stopped in the fast lane a few yards back, the driver vaulted the barrier and caught up with him, taking his arm as though to prevent him running off.

'Not the best choice for an afternoon ramble, is it mate?' Pause. 'Are you ok?' A voice for children, the old or the stupid.

Seb was suddenly conscious that he hadn't cleaned himself properly for days. 'Sorry – didn't mean to be here – got stuck. Stupid mistake.' He spoke to the ground, barely able to hear his own words. And then he felt himself falling and spinning as he collapsed into darkness.

HE WAS LYING in his bedroom at home, although the curtains looked different, closer to the bed. Seb closed his eyes and let the mattress take his weight, wondering what had happened to the duvet. His mother would come in soon, pretending to be angry that he still wasn't up and telling him that breakfast was ready. This was the best time, these stolen minutes of solitude before the day started. He tried to recall what lessons he had at school that day and whether he'd finished his homework, but the memory stayed just out of reach.

He sensed movement in the room and opened his eyes again, but it wasn't his mother. Right build, wrong colour. And the man behind her, too young to be his father. The woman bent over to study him; funny, there was no smell about her at all. She stepped back and the man came forward, a stethoscope around his neck.

'That's a nasty wound on your hand, bit of infection. We've put a dressing on and given you some antibiotics – you'll be right as rain in no time. We'll keep you here for a couple more hours, check your blood pressure and so on, make sure you're steady enough on your pins. Okay?' He went without waiting for an answer, along with the nurse.

Not flu then; no wonder he'd been feeling so groggy. He pushed himself upright on the bed and studied the dressing on his hand. He should have kept a plaster on it before, but it felt better now. Contained, controlled. And he could almost feel the antibiotics knocking out the infection and clearing his mind, unless that was in his imagination too.

But what if the police came back? Not that he'd done anything wrong, not really, not that they would know about. Nothing that counted. But there was no sense in staying around to find out. He swung his legs carefully over the side of the bed and sat quietly for a few moments. No dizziness, no problem. He found his trainers by the side of the bed, put them on and then carefully pulled back one of the curtains; the nurse and doctor from earlier were nowhere to be seen.

A set of double doors beckoned, no more than twenty yards away; wherever they led, it had to be away from here. One more check, both ways, to make sure that no one was watching, and he made his bid for freedom.

CHAPTER
TWELVE

It was nearly eight o'clock before Pav dropped Finn off in the car park outside the office. Had the day moved them forward? She wasn't sure. All they'd discovered so far was a religious man who seemed to care about the boy he'd buried alive - which was weird - and then disappeared. Pav consoled herself with the thought that at least there were no signs of a struggle, no scrabbling as the boy tried to escape into the air as clods of heavy clay covered his body.

Then there was the crucifix, possibly plastic, possibly ivory. Tantalising but circumstantial. Neither common nor rare, depending on your lifestyle; in her world like hen's teeth, but in Sebastian's?

Last but not least was the infection. They had confirmation now of a link between the bodies in the boiler room, Mira, and the boy. No sign of it in the girls that were picked up on the raid, but as for Defrim...

She left a voicemail for Gill Rossiter, the pathologist, and told her what to look for and where. Liver, spleen, the usual suspects. Typhoid Mary.

She finished the report for Gus and emailed him a copy; there had to be enough evidence to buy them another couple of weeks at least. And now, at last, it was time to go home and shower the acrid smell of the laboratory off her skin and out of her hair. She thought of fitting in a run, but no, probably not, even though her muscles were clenched and aching from sitting and waiting. Tomorrow evening, she promised herself, the big circuit through the woods, along the ridge a couple of hundred yards above the old farmhouse, down to Smallweir bridge, then back along the old railway track next to the river.

But tonight it was time to leave the day behind and relax with a few glasses of something, anything, with whoever bowled up at The Queen Bess. No need to think, barely any need to talk. Perfect. She wound along the valley road on autopilot until she reached home; by now she could almost feel the hot water running over her body, dissolving away the day. And then she saw the new, black-pack Range Rover parked outside the cottage. Her space, of course, and there was only one person it could be. The car was empty, but her neighbour's front door opened as she walked up to the gate, and Ash swung himself over the low fence into her front garden.

'Hiya babe. Mrs Jenkins offered me a cuppa. Couldn't say no, knew you wouldn't wanna miss me.' He reached up for a kiss, and as Pav swerved her face away, she caught the aroma of the afternoon entertainment. Scotch, at a guess. And coke, from the way he was twitching. All she needed.

'What are you doing here, Ash?'

'I thought I'd surprise you, babe. New motor – like it? Picked it up at lunchtime.'

'There's a dent,' she said, 'front bumper.'

His smile barely slipped. 'Fuckwit on the M32, poxy Lexus. I'll get it sorted.'

'I thought you got a three-month ban?'

'Only a couple of weeks to go – who's to know? Hey – you wanna ride? I thought we could fuck off out of here and go somewhere civilised.'

'Coming up again in the world, are we? Last time I heard they'd made you clear your desk and escorted you out of the building.'

'Loada pricks. Don't need them anyway – on my own now. Couple of ex-clients put up the cash, I use my connections to set up my own desk. I told you before, cream always floats to the top.'

'So does scum.'

'C'mon babe – what do you say?' He must have had a heavy afternoon; his receding hairline was dotted with beads of sweat.

He cranked up the smile and reached out to stroke her hair, but she swayed out of his reach again.

'It's been a hard day, Ash, and I told you to get out of my life. So tell me, just why am I wasting my time talking to you again?'

A bead of sweat broke away and rolled slowly past the corner of Ash's left eye as he put on his contrite face. 'I screwed up, I can see that. It was that old job, the pressure; you don't know what it was like.'

'I have a pretty good idea.'

'I promise, babe, I'm clean now. Haven't touched anything for a week. How about it? A new start, me and you. We could even move in together; you know those new apartments by the bay? I looked at them a couple of days ago, you'd love it there.'

'I love it here. And what I love best about it is being alone. For the avoidance of doubt, that means without you.'

He wiped the sweat away and tried to laugh. 'C'mon kid, you don't mean that. This new job – it'll be different, you'll see.' He stroked the car like a favourite pet. 'Let's have a run, I'll show you how she moves – what do you say? You get changed into something decent – how about that leather skirt I got for your birthday?' He tried to wink and sniff at the same time, but neither worked.

While he was talking, Pav edged between him and her front gate. 'Ash – in case you don't remember the last time we met, I told you to go and play with yourself, or failing that, the traffic. We don't see each other anymore, I'm not driving anywhere with an uninsured dwarf who's totally amped, and for your information the skirt you're so keen on went to Oxfam the day after your secretary posted it to me with that appalling card she signed for you. FYI, she never got your signature right. And now I'm going inside, and you and your pimpmobile can go to hell. Capisce?'

The Range Rover stayed outside for twenty minutes, with Ash inside. Not smiling now, although Pav didn't flatter herself that she'd caused that reaction. Ash always had a fallback somewhere, paid or otherwise.

She took her time getting showered and changed. When she heard Ash's car disappearing down the lane, she waited a couple of minutes before leaving the cottage, just to make sure. The evening air was cool and moist, promising rain, and although the sky was clear, a roll of thunder rumbled somewhere over the horizon.

It wasn't until she was halfway across the village green that she noticed the man sitting at one of the wooden tables used by tourists for their picnics during the day. She slowed down and start, bu it was hard to tell. So many people looked the same, and he was facing the river with his back to her. A big man, though, the sort who could lift a girl with one arm and punch with the other.

She turned onto the curving perimeter path that ran past his table, but after a few steps her foot slipped and she demolished a small mound of dog shit. She swore and wiped her foot on the grass, but by the time she glanced back at the table, the man had disappeared.

This was a hard day in a hard week. She was feeling jumpy; Ash always did that to her these days, and the visit to the lab hadn't helped. She thought about the number of tourists that came through the village to stay in one of the B&Bs for the walking or kayaking – and how many of them wore hooded tops or took a bit of exercise to build up the muscles? Hundreds, probably. She remembered a conversation with Pa, years ago, when she was a little girl afraid of the dark. Fear, he'd said, is what you do to yourself. It's your own mind that makes you afraid, nothing else. Remember that and stay in control.

It was a good lesson. She reached the door to the pub, checked her shoe again, forced a smile and went inside.

SHE'D ONLY MEANT to go down for a quick drink, but after the last few days, who cared? And in the end, it was a good night, a forgetting night. Ash, Eva, Mira – all of them shrunken and lost for a while, submerged in music and words, beer and wine. The band in the corner played Coldplay covers with a drum machine, a keyboard and a guitar held together by gaffer tape, and the bottles and glasses keep refilling themselves as if in some Celtic myth; someone else was paying, so go with the flow, much easier that way.

Eventually a glass of wine seemed reluctant to go down, and she knew it was time to leave when Detta abandoned the deep-fat fryer and began to get pissed with the rest of them.

Pav made her way unsteadily back across the moonlit village green. God alone knew what time it was – she tried her watch, slanting it to catch the moonlight. Nearly midnight; best get the key out now if she didn't want Mrs Jenkins complaining about her dancing around the garden in the early hours like a tart.

The terrace was quiet and dark as Pav turned the corner from the main road. Mrs J would have been in bed since 9.30, and as for Detta on the other side – the last Pav had seen of her she was playing darts, her eyes blindfolded with a dishevelled tea towel, and a pint of lager balanced on her head.

She thought about moving the Porsche, still parked on the verge where she'd left it because Ash had taken her space earlier. On second thoughts, that was definitely a bad idea. No need to annoy Mrs J any more than necessary. She carried on to the front gate, stopped and turned back to look at the car again. Something definitely wasn't right; the boot, not quite shut.

Weird, she couldn't remember the last time she put anything in there as she always threw stuff on the rear seat. She turned back, lifted the boot lid and peered inside. As expected, there was nothing except for a rather grubby rag, a set of jump leads she'd forgotten she owned, plus a half-empty box of thin, latex gloves. Maybe the catch had gone and she hadn't noticed, but it was too late to do anything about it now - tomorrow would be time enough. With luck it would be easily fixed, even if that meant duct taping it shut for now - she sure as hell wouldn't be able to get it to a dealer any time soon.

She skirted round and tried the driver's door, but it was open; she must have forgotten to hit the remote when she came home earlier and saw Ash. Not like her. And she definitely remembered putting the car keys down on the small table inside the front door; a habit she'd picked up from Jess, always leaving them in the same place.

She slid onto the driver's seat. Nothing seemed out of place; yesterday's crisp packets and an empty can of Red Bull were still on the floor by the front passenger seat, and other than them the car was in its usual, minimal state. The places she drove to, she'd learnt not to leave anything lying around.

A shiver ran down her back; perhaps Alzheimer's was catching and these were the first signs. She clambered out of the car and checked her bag – no car keys; they had to be inside for sure.

This time, she noticed the pane of glass as soon as she opened the front gate. The lack of it. That part of the front door which wasn't reflecting the moonlight, a small, square black hole of emptiness. She walked in slow motion along the path, like those dreams where the air turns to treacle, where every movement takes forever. *I should call for backup*, she thought, but instead she unlocked the door and stood on the threshold, half in, half out. She left the light off, as if the darkness were safer than what she might see.

Someone had been there. Ash, perhaps, pissing her around? He'd never given back his front door key and swore he'd lost it. But he also knew about the back door key hidden in the shed; he wouldn't need to break in. Pav called his name, but her voice sounded distant and strangled and she tried again, louder. Funny how different fear felt in your own home.

There was no answer, no sound anywhere.

She turned on the light. The TV was still in the corner of the single downstairs room, not that it was worth taking. Someone had moved the small sofa, though, and as she turned to look at the other side of the room, she realised what the intruder must have been looking for. She always left her laptop on the small pine dining table, but it wasn't there now. Shit and double shit.

She remembered the car keys and checked by the front door, but they'd gone too. Her bag? No, she'd already looked in there. So it was back out to the car, not worried now about Mrs J, and then she found them a couple of feet away, glinting in the moonlight where they'd been tossed onto the grass verge. But if the thief had the keys, why not take her car as well?

She put on a pair of thin gloves from the box in the boot and went back into the house. No need to complicate things for the locals when she got around to calling them.

She looked around the main room and then checked upstairs, feeling almost disappointed. Apart from the broken glass in the front door – and the missing laptop – she wouldn't have known anything was wrong. Kids, maybe, messing around? The ones in the village weren't that bad, but they had their moments.

They would have left more of a mess, though. Kids.

She went downstairs into the small kitchen and checked the fridge. When she'd gone out, there were three cans of lager, and they hadn't moved. She checked the bottle of Pinot on the corner of the kitchen worktop – still almost full. Not like teenagers, to leave alcohol untouched. Who else then? Someone from the old days, someone with a grudge? It was always possible. This was a small world and if someone really wanted to find her, it wouldn't be too difficult. She remembered the man from the wine bar the other day, the one she'd given evidence against; there were plenty like him around.

And, of course, there was the hooded guy she'd seen earlier on the green. Even if he wasn't the same person who tried to take Mira, he could have been a common or garden scrote on the make. Maybe he'd scoped out the area and knew that the Mill Terrace was hidden from view, knew that with her out of the way he'd have a clear shot. The Porsche might have misled him into thinking there were rich pickings inside. But why take only the laptop, unless he knew what she did for a living and thought there would be confidential information that he could sell? He'd be out of luck then; getting into the ROCU VPN would be a real stretch for someone without the right access codes.

At least the house was empty. She'd know if someone else was there – the place was so small that she'd be able to hear him breathing. Pav sat heavily on the corner of the sofa and looked over at the two framed photos on the sideboard; her parents on their golden wedding anniversary last year when Ma could still play the part, just. And the other – her favourite – of her brother, a month before he sat in his car with the engine on and the garage door shut.

She looked again and went across the room, feeling cold. Saj was there, as he should be, but the photo of her parents had been replaced by another. She recognised the scene; the street outside the school, a stretcher being carried from the gates to the ambulance. But history had been changed; instead of Mira's wan face above the blanket it was her own eyes looking up, wide and surprised. Someone had crudely substituted her head for the girl's,

Photoshop 101. Not subtle, but effective. The blond man at the back of the crowd; this must be the photo he'd taken on his mobile; no need for guesses now.

Enough; time to knock up Mrs J even though it was so late, and find out if she'd noticed anything earlier. A one-woman neighbourhood watch scheme, her neighbour; '*I'll bet she even has my periods marked on her calendar,*' she'd joked once to Jess in one of their intermittent post-breakup email exchanges. 78 years old, Mrs J, and sassy as hell, but the best sort of witness.

Pav climbed the low wall separating the two front gardens and then saw what she should have noticed before, that the front door wasn't completely shut. The last vestiges of alcohol drained away, sluiced out by adrenaline. She pressed the bell but heard no sound of movement from inside, so she pushed the door open gently.

'Mrs Jenkins!' She tried again, but her voice sank into the walls.

There could be an innocent explanation. Mrs J often left the door on the latch when she went to nose about; she'd locked herself out once, a few months ago, when she'd complained to Pav about an argument she was having with Ash. But it was gone midnight now, too late for an old lady to be having adventures. Pav switched on the light. The room was a mirror image of hers, but furnished in orange Dralon with thick, blue velvet curtains. The cream, wall-to-wall carpet was pristine as ever, mostly; hoovered three times a day, Mrs J told her once, as if that were something to be proud of.

She wouldn't be hoovering it again.

It seemed impossible that a human body could hold so much blood, especially a sparrow like her neighbour. Pav ran across to the heap of clothes on the floor by the television, felt for a pulse, and then stood up slowly. The body was still lukewarm; whoever killed her had been here within the last few hours.

Mrs Jenkins – Katherine, not that anyone dared call her that – would have heard the noise of breaking glass next door and come out to investigate. She still thought she was a headmistress, that people would do what she told them.

Pav crouched down again for a better look, careful not to touch the body. She couldn't be sure without moving anything, but it appeared her attacker had knifed Mrs J in the side. She couldn't see any sign of a struggle so at least it had happened quickly. A small mercy, but sometimes you have to take what you can get. Pav pictured the choreography of murder in her mind; Mrs J had disturbed the killer wile he was stealing the laptop and changing the photo. She'd run back to her own cottage in an effort to escape but he'd come towards her across her tiny living room, backing her into the corner before slashing out. She wouldn't have stood a chance with no-one nearby to hear her screams.

Pav straightened up and listened; her own house had been empty of intruders, but was this one? She checked the kitchen first, then the rooms upstairs, but the house contained no-one except her and the cooling body.

There was nothing more she could do. She called Finn first, her go-to man, and the hoarse whisper of his answer told her she'd woken him.

'Boss? Jesus wept, don't you ever sleep?' But when he heard what had happened, the tiredness evaporated from his voice. 'Have you called the locals yet?'

'You do it, get hold of Jimmy – might as well have someone we know.'

'I'm on my way. And boss, stay outside until the cavalry

arrives – you'll only piss Spears off if he thinks you've cont-
aminated the crime scene.'

'Thanks for the reminder, Mr Williams. I was just about
to go back in and give the place a spring clean.'

She sat in the car, dimly lit by the single amber street
light, and let her mind roam. The Queen Bess was probably
still open; sometimes it was still going strong at 3am on a
Friday night. Detta hadn't come home yet, but then her
social life was famously vibrant.

Pav looked in the glove compartment, just in case one of
Ash's fag packets was still in there, but no luck. Just as well;
it would only have made her feel worse. She climbed out of
the car again, suddenly feeling trapped, and rested against
the bonnet. A car drove by on the main road thirty feet
below, hidden by the high bank and line of trees that gave
the terrace its privacy. Whoever the killer was, he hadn't
needed to worry about being seen. Only Mrs J, and she
hadn't held him up.

The chill night air was invading her skin; even so, she
didn't want to go back inside the house. No need to annoy
Spears and the locals any more than necessary; at least, not
this time. Another five minutes passed before a single police
car arrived; no siren, a driver, no-one else. Pav recognised
him vaguely, a large, shambling lad with pale eyebrows and
a permanent blush; this wouldn't be his idea of fun on a
Friday night.

'I was told to wait with you until the DI arrives,' he said,
'and you're not to touch anything. Ma'am.' His accent was
pure Forest. 'Are you all right? Is there anything I can do?'

What would he do if she said yes? 'I'm fine – whoever
did this was gone by the time I got back.'

They waited in silence. This wasn't the time for small
talk, and the few words she'd said had caused the boy's

blush to deepen every time. There couldn't be any more than ten years between them, but it felt like decades. At last she heard another car on the main road, slowing down, and then the sweep of headlights brightened the lane.

'You want to show me what happened?' Spears was already looking inside her car, checking the boot. When he was satisfied, Pav led him to Mrs J's front room and showed him the body.

'Made a bit of a mess,' she said, 'but it was probably quick.'

'Bleeding out like a pig? I'll take a rain check. Did you find anything else in here?'

'Nothing obvious – don't worry, I kept my hands to myself.'

'What about your place?' he asked.

Next-door she showed him the swapped-out photo, slightly out of focus but clear enough.

'Who the hell took this?' he asked.

'When the bodies turned up the other day there was a guy in the crowd outside the school. He took a photo with his mobile, but I wasn't sure whether it was of Mira or me. Now I know.'

'You think he murdered your neighbour?'

Pav took the photo and angled it to catch the light. There had been no attempt at realism; this was quick and dirty, her shocked face looking up from the stretcher, too small for the body.

'If it wasn't him, it was someone he knows. I noticed someone on the green tonight. He had his back to me, but it could have been the guy who tried to lift Mira from the hospital.'

'Could have been? Did you challenge him? Knowing you, he's chained up in a cellar somewhere by now.'

'I worry about you, Jim. And no, I didn't challenge him because I wasn't sure. We get hordes of tourists in the summer and before I could get to him, he was gone. I thought I was being jumpy after the last few days; if I'd run after him maybe none of this would have happened.'

'And maybe you'd have a knife between your ribs, too.'

A car outside skidded to a halt and a few seconds later Finn erupted into the room, un-brushed and enveloped in the chill night air.

'Boss, are you okay? I came as quickly as I could.'

'I'm a grown woman, Finn, and I've seen dead bodies before. More than you, probably.'

'Not your neighbour, not next-door to where you live.'

'I don't want to break up this lover's tiff,' said the DI, 'but I need to take a statement. After that, I suggest you find somewhere else to stay tonight.'

Finn touched her arm, unexpectedly gentle. 'I'll phone the wife, tell her to make up the spare bed. No arguments. You'll only get in the way if you stay here, and Gus will be after breaking your balls if he finds out you're muddying the waters again.'

She started to argue, but he was right. Far better to get what sleep she could and then check in the morning to see what they'd found.

'I need to get some clothes, the car keys.'

'Fraid we can't let you take the car, not yet,' said Spears, 'and even if we did, I would be aiding and abetting a drunk driver. Maybe Indiana Williams here can drive you. And you shouldn't disturb anything else in your house, not until forensics have done their bit. Burglary's one thing, but a murder changes the shape.'

THIRTEEN

Sleeping was going to be a problem. Finn's wife showed her to the spare room; pastel pink and blue, hedging a bet. 'For our daughter,' she said, 'or son, assuming we ever get that far.' She smiled uncertainly as she plumped the pillows and smoothed the duvet, a pretty beetle of a woman for whom the word 'scurry' might have been invented.

The night was sultry and stuttering, punctuated by visions of rats hanging from hooks, with blood dripping from their fur and tails. When Pav surfaced at last from the dreams, it was gone eight o'clock in the morning. The duvet lay crumpled on the floor and her body was shivering and damp. Someone had left a towel on the chair in the corner; she showered quickly, then wished she hadn't bothered as she dressed in yesterday's clothes.

She found Finn downstairs in the kitchen, drinking coffee; Pav turned down the offer of eggs, accepted the toast and tried not to slump at the table, conscious of the state of her hair and the shadows under her eyes, conscious of the way Finn looked; scrubbed and polished. He asked how her night had been.

'Draining – you?'

'Not bad apart from Sarah's snoring, so no change there.' He poured her a second coffee. 'With luck, you'll be able to go back home today to collect some clothes, but I doubt if they'll be finished in there until tomorrow. Your neighbour – Mrs Jenkins – they'll take a little longer over that. Bit of a mess.'

A slight understatement.

'Where's your wife?' Pav asked. 'I wanted to thank her for putting me up last night.'

'The OFSTED inspectors have decided to pay her college a visit, so the entire staff are on a three-line whip to get everything in order. She's not the best company at the moment – mind you, she probably says the same about me.' He spread Marmite thickly on a slice of toast. 'Have you spoken to Gus since last night?'

'No, I've decided to live in a state of complete denial and pretend none of this has happened.'

If she'd expected sympathy, she'd been disappointed; Gus had always been selective with political correctness. '*She wasn't related, this neighbour?*' he'd asked. '*No? Good – no nonsense about compassionate leave then.*'

'There's something I forgot to mention,' she said to Finn. 'I didn't remember until I was in the shower this morning.' Not so much remember, as realise that denial was a sub-optimal strategy at the moment.

She told him about Ash waiting for her at the cottage when she'd arrived home last night, and wondered again why she'd said nothing to Spears. Did she have a subconscious desire to protect her ex, or was the idea of his involvement so preposterous that she'd dismissed it automatically? She pictured him swinging over the low wall from Mrs J's and then sitting in his pimpmobile, on the phone.

'Jesus, boss, you like to spring surprises,' said Finn. 'Why didn't you mention this before?'

'I forgot. I've had a lot of practice recently, forgetting Ash.'

'You wouldn't let a witness get away with that.'

'Come on – I'm hardly carrying a candle for the bastard. He was a mistake. A huge, horrible mistake.'

'I thought he was history.'

'He is. I didn't know he'd be there.' She could hear herself sounding defensive.

'Where was he, in the house?'

'His car was outside, a new Range Rover with a knock on the front. I hadn't seen it before, but I knew it had to be his.'

'And he was in the car?'

'Not exactly. To tell the truth, he was in with Mrs J, having a cuppa while he waited for me.' So everyday, so normal. That's what people do, pop into the neighbour, have a cup of tea while they're waiting.

She glanced at Finn, but he was wearing the face that he kept for interviews. 'You know Ash,' she said. 'He could charm the fleas off a dog. Mrs J thought I was a tramp, but she always had a soft spot for him. To tell the truth, I don't think she liked women much.'

'What time was this?'

'Six thirty, maybe. I'm not sure. Yesterday was a bad day.' Her mouth felt dry.

'So why did Ash come round?' Finn asked. 'Come on boss, you know how this works.'

'You'll be reading me my rights in a moment.'

'Better me here, than Spears in an interview room.'

He was right, of course. Was this how suspects felt when they'd done nothing wrong but could see the disbelief in the eyes of their interrogators? 'He was showing off the new motor, as if I cared. I told him what to do with it and he left – he didn't even come inside.'

'How did he seem?'

'The usual pompous bastard. Nothing out of the ordinary.'

'And your neighbour – she seemed okay when you saw her?'

This was the hard part. 'I didn't actually see her. Ash came out of her house and shut the front door behind him. He must have seen me drive up.' She waited for Finn to say something, but he stayed silent. 'She had bad legs, Mrs J, didn't move too quickly. And to be honest, there's no way Ash would've had anything to do with this. By the time I went to the pub, he'd long since gone. And when did Mrs J die? Must have been later in the evening.' She heard herself making excuses for someone she didn't even like.

Finn shrugged. 'Time of death isn't an exact science even now, and her house was like a sauna. We know she was murdered yesterday evening, but nobody's taking bets on exactly when.'

'I should get in touch with Ash,' Pav said. 'Find out when he arrived and how long he was with her.'

'Not a good idea. He might have been the last person to see her alive – for all we know, he's the one that killed her. Look at it from where I'm sitting - he has to be a person of interest. But you're right, we need to talk to him asap, if only to cross him off the list.'

'You're forgetting the photo that was taken outside the school; that was nothing to do with Ash.'

Finn sighed his trademark "more in sadness" sigh. 'You can't talk to him, boss, you're too close. This murder investigation is down to Spears; you have to tell him about Ash.'

'And then what, spend half a day or more being treated like a toerag? You know the man, he'd jump at the chance to score points off me – us.'

'There's another way,' said Finn, slowly. 'You need to tell Spears, that's non-negotiable, but it doesn't mean he has to have first shot. We can't go after Ash directly, but what about one of Gus's other teams? How about the guys on the Minnow op, tracing that cocaine supply line? I could give them Ash's details – you could even call him a legitimate suspect.'

She could almost see him clambering into the gorilla suit and getting his climbing boots on. 'Nice try, but no. I don't want you getting your hands dirty on my account. I'll call Spears and ask him to co-opt you onto whatever they do with Ash. I'm sure the prick's innocent – wrong place, wrong time – but you're right, we need to put a line through his name. As soon as you speak to him, call me, let me know what happened. If he contacts me first, I shan't say anything.'

'Sounds like a plan.'

'It's the best we have so far.'

PAV SLUMPED in the passenger seat listening to the radio as Finn drove her home; perhaps it was a bad night in an unfamiliar bed, but her whole body felt battered. She noticed a small crowd outside the shop as they drove through the village; the news must be out. Finn swung the car off the main road and they were ushered through the cordon blocking her lane; the front door of number one was still open, with a couple of white-suited figures moving around in the black hole of the living room. It seemed ridiculous, how quickly everything had changed. Yesterday she'd been an investigator, now she was part of a crime, and that was an unfamiliar and unwelcome feeling. Just another entry in the accounts, something else to add in when debt collection time was due.

Inside her house, everything seemed wrong. Someone had made an attempt to put things back in their places, but every piece of furniture had shifted a few centimetres away from where it should be, and the cut'n'paste photo had been removed, leaving an empty frame. What had happened to the original, she thought, the one of Ma and Pa? It had been old school, their images caught on film emulsion as if some part of them existed in the photo. Jess would have understood. And now it was probably a crumpled scrap, thrown away like unwanted rubbish.

Traces of fingerprint powder lingered on some of the surfaces; if she were more domestic, she'd get a duster, but she didn't have the energy. There were other calls on her time, work she should be doing now. First, run a check to see if anyone resembling Eva had been picked up in the last day or so. Then trawl the hospitals for people with the same recalcitrant disease as Mira and the others; the Catholic carpenter from North London might have been infected and was now wandering around, a carrier on the loose. Finn had circulated the description they got from the landlady, but as far as she knew there had been no sightings so far.

And she should arrange for warnings to be put out to girls working the streets; take care, take precautions. God knows how often she and the others had questioned every sex worker between Avonport and Uskmouth, evidence gathering for Operation Hexameter. Perhaps one last push with the threat of a killer disease might get one of them talking.

BEFORE SHE LEFT for the office, Pav cleaned up the inside of her car as best she could and decided to take it through a car wash, anything to get rid of the touch of whoever had rifled through it last night, but her mobile rang as she pulled into the petrol station just outside Abertrothy.

'Parvati, pet...' Pa's voice was tremulous, and he was swallowing hard, trying not to cry. 'It's your Ma, she's gone missing again. I've been in every room, I've tried the neighbours, I've been up and down the street. I don't know what to do, Parvati. You know what she's like, she's always somewhere close by when she does this.'

She cut a twenty-minute journey down to fifteen and parked outside the house while Pa waited in the open doorway. After the last time she'd told him – keep the doors locked, keep the keys out of sight – but she knew he hadn't. *'I can't make her a prisoner, pet,'* he'd said, even though that's what her parents had become in the last couple of years. Both of them trapped.

She led him back inside as if this were her house and he was the visitor. 'How long has she been gone?' she asked.

'An hour, maybe more. I was out the back, in the greenhouse. I thought she was asleep in her chair. She always sleeps after breakfast.'

'And what about the police?' Pav asked. 'What did they say?'

He looked so frightened, swamped in his armchair. 'I haven't told them, not yet. I thought – you and me, we could go out together and take your car. I don't want a fuss.'

It was hard not to cry at his helplessness. She took her mobile from her bag, but he reached out to stop her.

'Please, no. They'll want to put her in a home.'

'No, they won't. And even if they did, maybe it's for the best. You can't go on like this, Pa.' She stroked his hand, trying to soften the words.

He pulled away. 'You don't understand, pet. I need her.'

THEY STARTED with the roads on the small estate. 'Where did you find her the last time she did this?' asked Pav

'She was waiting for a bus outside the paper shop. I don't think she knew who I was – said she was late getting home. I remember she cried and said her mum would be angry.'

They cut off towards the small high street, a few minutes away. There were only two people waiting by the bus stop, a pair of giggling teenage girls with bare thighs.

'Twenty minutes, Pa, and then we report her missing – this isn't a good day.'

It should have been easy in a small town like Lydford, a hangover from the days when the Forest was alive with the mines. Today the streets were almost empty apart from two men with Racing Posts under their arms, a straggle of shoppers and a couple of middle-aged hikers studying a map by the clock tower. But no old lady, struggling to find her way to the past.

Pav stopped after they'd searched the car park behind the Co-op. 'Is there anywhere else she might be? She can't have gone far with no money.'

Pa looked away. 'I always make sure there's something in her purse. A couple of £10 notes, some change. She likes to go through her handbag and make sure everything's there; lipstick, hairbrush, mirror, compact. Purse. She takes the money out, sometimes, and counts it.'

She could cry for him. 'Pa – she can no more count than a cat could knit a cardigan.'

'Old habits, you don't understand. It gives her comfort – God knows she gets little enough.'

It had been half an hour since they started looking, nearly two hours since Pa had realised that Ma wasn't in her chair. Pav called the local police station, but there were no reports of an old lady being handed in. She took Pa back home and tried the neighbours again, but there was still no sign of her mother.

'Are you sure you checked everywhere?' she asked. A stupid question, but she needed to satisfy herself. She started in her parents' bedroom, with its brown and orange wallpaper, single beds and tower of Ma's clothes on the chair. In the spare room, someone had found Little Ted and propped him against the pillow on top of the worn candlewick bedspread. A dark button had replaced the threadbare animal's missing eye; Ma, then, while she could still be trusted with something as sharp as a needle.

Pav picked up the soft toy and held it to her face; it smelled strangely familiar, of dust and discarded childhood, as if she were intruding on her own memories. What was in Ma's mind when she found this childhood comforter in some dark cupboard and brought him out into the daylight? Searching for a past because, for her, there could be no future?

Pav put the faded toy back on the bed and closed the bedroom door behind her, quietly. Time travel; not appropriate, not now.

Pa had been right; there was no sign of her mother.

She made them both a pot of tea. 'Have another think, Pa. Did she take anything with her?'

'Her bag, of course.' He looked around the room, as if for clues. 'The quilted jacket you got for her birthday. She loves how it feels; sometimes she strokes the fur around the hood.' He smiled for the first time that day. 'I heard her talking to it once, she thought it was our old cat, Gizmo. I didn't like to remind her that we buried the little fella in the garden at our old house, these ten years since.' The smile faded, his voice cracked and he started to cry.

Pav hugged him close. It still felt like forbidden territory, seeing tears on her father's face. When he was quiet again, she sat him at the round dining table, conscious of putting a barrier between them.

'The police will find her, Pa, promise.' But there was an image in her mind that wouldn't go away, something connected with the night before. She barely allowed herself the thought, but what if - unbelievably - Ash *had* been involved in Mrs Jenkins's death? Perhaps the breakup of their relationship had tipped him over the edge; he knew her parents, knew where they lived... But no, it was too ridiculous. He might be an arrogant bastard and a fool, but not a criminal.

She couldn't wait any longer and called Finn. 'It was nothing, right? You spoke to Ash and sorted it out. Just coincidence, like I said.'

Finn paused before replying. 'Maybe it's coincidence that he's not around, either. His car was left at the motorway services near Gwenstow. We've got CCTV of him driving in last night, around eleven pm. Nothing of him leaving, though, and I don't think he would have walked home from there. And yes, we checked his apartment in London.' Another pause, longer. 'There's no easy way to say this, boss, and I don't want to pry into your private life, but did Ash ever use porn when you were together?' His voice was tight.

Porn... of course he used porn. What man didn't? Unpleasant, but not illegal. Usually.

'Pav – you there?' Finn's voice wasn't unkind, just apologetic. 'It's not like I'm telling you anything you don't know. We found enough charlie to send him inside for dealing, as well as a couple of memory sticks and some DVDs. The trouble is, the files on them are a damn sight more hardcore than I would have expected. At least, if the first few minutes are anything to go by.'

Finn was right. None of this was a surprise. 'That all sounds a bit old school for Ash,' she said. 'Why get the stuff on USBs or discs when he could get almost whatever he wanted online? Though I admit, him falling off the radar like this doesn't look good.'

'You were right to give him the push,' said Finn. 'Whatever he's involved with, you need to keep clear. The people who dealt him drugs in that quantity don't belong to the local Chamber of Commerce, and the porn we found would be a stretch even for the dark web.'

It had always surprised her how otherwise intelligent people could be so stupid. But that was Ash all over; if he wasn't coked out of his skull, he was thinking with his prick instead of his brain. Where did it all go wrong for people like him? When did they get to a fork in the road and make the wrong choice?

'You don't think he had something to do with your mother's disappearance?' Finn said, eventually.

'Why does Ash do anything? He's probably out of it on some slag's sofa – wouldn't have made it as far as the bed. And it wouldn't be the first time he went AWOL for a few days – it was why they kicked him out of his last company. Ash always lands on his feet.'

The shrill of the doorbell made her start; a welcome escape. 'Gotta go, Finn – I'll catch up with you later.' She beat her father to the front door by a couple of lengths; Ma was standing under the porch, holding the arm of a young policewoman. A fragment of torn cloth hung from the sleeve of her jacket, one of her blue slippers was missing and the pop sock was snagged and laddered – tights hadn't lasted more than a few days after Pa became her unofficial dresser.

They helped Ma to her chair in the living room. As her jacket flapped open, the smell of old lady was almost overpowering. Pa still hadn't spoken and Pav watched him looking at the woman in the chair, enveloped by her clothes, as if she was some strange intruder. There was a part of him, she realised, that wished his wife hadn't been found.

'Such a nice young man,' Ma said. 'Said he'd come to take me to the station. I must have got out at the wrong stop.' She closed her eyes and sagged against the wing of the armchair.

'We got a call from Masons,' said the policewoman. 'It's that hardware store in that little shopping area where the station used to be. Seems she wandered in and started pulling stuff off the shelves. No damage – I think it was mostly plastic washing-up bowls, that sort of thing. All she could talk about was the taxi driver who collected her, said she was looking for him. We got her address from the driving licence in her purse.' She looked over at the woman dozing in the chair. 'I guess she hasn't used that in a while.' She handed over Ma's handbag; the two £10 notes were still inside, untouched.

Pav saw her to the door. 'I'm sorry for the trouble. We've been looking all morning, but it was almost impossible.'

'Your granddad's lucky to have you here.' Her radio crackled with static, but she ignored it.

'Father, actually. And the lady you found, she's my mother.' The other woman coloured and Pav felt guilty. 'Don't worry, it's an easy mistake.'

Back in the living room, Pa had pulled up another chair and was holding Ma's hand as she slept, slowly stroking her hair.

'We should get her washed and changed,' said Pav.

'Not now, pet. Let her be. I'll see to her later, when she's had a bit of a nap.' As if she'd just overdone it on the gardening. 'You get off now. You said this was a bad day and we've taken enough of your time. Get away with you – I'll phone later, tell you how she is.'

His shell had snapped back into place; she was the intruder now.

THE SEARCH for Ma had unsettled her. How could an old lady with the energy levels of a sloth make her way into the middle of town without spending any money, and still be able to trash a shop? And what about the taxi driver she seemed so keen to thank? Maybe he only existed in her imagination, but nothing seemed certain at the moment.

She decided to divert through Uskmouth on her way to the office and drove to the pathology lab, an anonymous Victorian mausoleum near the old Town Hall. Municipal, that was the only word to describe this area. Anachronistic might work too, part of the city that civilisation had left behind. There were no glass-fronted bars here, only decaying buildings like the ruins of empire inhabited by

164 · C. J. EMERSON

barbarians. What else are we, Pav thought as she left her car on a meter next to a dressed-stone doorway, still stuffed with the cardboard and newspaper from last night's tenant.

Gill Rossiter met her at the security desk, a sparse woman who seemed to grow more like her cadavers as the months passed.

'I heard you had a visitor yesterday,' Gill said, 'left a rather messy calling card at the neighbour's. Is it her you've come to see? The postmortem hasn't been done yet.'

'Not her. I wanted to check progress on the bodies we found in the basement.'

'Ah, those.' There were sunken ridges around her mouth, as if the jaw muscles had already begun to shrink and decay. 'I've been doing this job, or one like it, for over thirty years, but I've seen nothing like them. It took a while, you understand, for us to know what we were looking at. There were three sources: the dismembered bodies, the contents of the boiler and the pile of ash and bone in the far corner.'

Pav followed Gill through to her small office in the basement. 'That's what I couldn't get,' she said. 'Burning the bodies I understand, but I thought that left ash, nothing else.' Her brother's ashes, in the urn her parents kept hidden in the sideboard. She'd looked once, fascinated, and found nothing but a pale, soft powder, heavier than she'd expected.

The older woman sat in front of a monitor and brought up a picture of the boiler room at the derelict school, the floodlit pyre like the leavings of Genghis Khan. She pointed at a part of the screen. 'See there? That's the outline of part of a ribcage, there's a femur – and the skulls, of course. Some had been smashed when the ashes were raked out. The bone becomes very brittle after exposure to high temperatures, but it doesn't automatically disintegrate. The ashes from a crematorium result from the incinerated remains being put through a grinder. Cremains - never have liked that word.' She turned off the monitor. 'There was very little metal residue, and that's consistent with the unburned bodies; no hip replacements or pacemakers. Taking all that into account, and adding in the remains that hadn't yet been burned, we estimate that twenty-six people were disposed of there, all of them in their teens.'

A classroom of children, wiped away.

THE OFFICE FELT DESERTED; she felt deserted. Gus wouldn't be in again until Thursday, Rachel and Amir were tied up with their new day jobs, and with Finn embedded in CID for the day – keeping an eye on Spears – the grunt work would be down to her.

Sebastian: she said his name out loud, rolled it around. A martyr, the original Sebastian, a saint. She recalled paintings of his body pierced by arrows. In the name of the Father; who had this Sebastian called on as he buried the still-breathing boy?

He felt like the key, this missing man. They needed to find him and make him talk. Find the connections, weave the threads together. But it was all easier said than done; where to start? Hospitals were top of the list. If he'd handled the dying boy, as he must have done, then maybe he'd also picked up the infection. Of course, if he'd been strong enough to shake it off, then she was walking into a dead end, but if the infection had taken a hold...

There was so little to work on; a name which might not belong to him, a description which could have changed.

Only the infection would mark him out if he'd succumbed, and that was as good a starting point as any.

She began with the A&E departments radiating from Crouch End, but after an hour, there was no joy; this could take forever.

She thought again; time to apply a filter to focus the options. He was Welsh, from the Valleys if they weren't mistaken, and he'd already travelled down the M4 once in the past week. Why drive all the way from London to bury a body? Perhaps it was the call of home, perhaps he'd go back again.

So she made another list, hospitals en route from London to Uskmouth, and struck lucky after half an hour, talking to a doctor at the Royal Wiltshire who'd treated someone matching the description.

'He was delirious when the police brought him in,' the doctor told her. 'Yes, there was a lesion on his arm, probably some sort of infection; no, we didn't get a name. The police wanted to talk to him, but we're a hospital, not a prison. The antibiotics must have kicked in – broad spectrum, first port of call. Or the fluids - he was dehydrated. We took bloods but the results aren't back yet.'

'Where was he picked up?'

'Central reservation on the M4. Lucky the police got to him before an articulated lorry.'

Pav called the local police, but they couldn't add much. No abandoned car, no traffic cameras nearby. 'Could have been a hitchhiker – if he took a turn, the driver might have panicked and dumped him. Or he may have travelled across country, it happens. When we found him, he was walking west.'

Walking home.

She felt as if she'd reached another dead-end. He'd been

so near, almost in their hands; close her eyes and he was within reach. She could almost stretch out and touch this stranger who could bury a boy alive and yet place a crucifix in his hands.

She searched for a third time: Welsh, knew Tryleg, worked with wood; religious. Was that the way to track him? Catholic; '*Argued like a Jesuit,*' the priest had said. What if Sebastian was a failed priest, deserted by his faith? Religion could fuck people up at the best of times, but a fallen priest - that could explain a lot. He would have trained somewhere, and these days there couldn't be many young men processing through the seminaries.

An hour later, someone returned one of her calls. No Sebastian Evans in the past thirty years but a Sebastian Collier, born in Merthyr, ordained in 1995. The voice which told her sounded guarded. 'If you want to know more I'll not be your greatest help,' it said. 'I don't have all the details, but Father Mahoney in St Mary's Hazelbury is your best bet.'

She looked at the address; ninety minutes away at a push unless God had decided to remove every car and lorry from the roads, just for her. She could phone, but that didn't feel right. Although six o'clock was already in the rear-view mirror it had to be worth a trip, and she was halfway across the car park when Finn phoned.

'Boss? Sorry I didn't catch you before, busy day.'

'Any joy finding Ash?'

He ignored the question. 'We need to meet – now would be good if you're free.'

'Where are you?'

'Just coming up to the bridge, I could be at The Queen Bess in half an hour.'

'You can't tell me now? And why not meet at the office?'

'It's complicated. Sorry, I'm losing you, crap signal – see you later.'

And then he was gone. She could call him back, but what was the point? Whatever he had to tell her must be bad news, and why hurry that along?

THE AIR WAS STILL balmy from the afternoon sun, and she sat by the river with a half of opaque cider and a bowl of chips and ketchup. Comfort food, her first meal since breakfast with Finn this morning. The local kingfisher flashed blue amongst the branches that dipped into the water on the opposite bank; the leaves were just beginning to turn, with hints of gold and red breaking up the greens.

She watched a damp spaniel chase sticks into the water, retrieving them with ecstatic pride. A good job, well done; if only she could say the same for herself. She couldn't remember when she'd last felt this tired; perhaps it was just as well to leave the visit to Father Mahoney until the morning. Two priests in one week, not counting the errant Sebastian; more than she'd had contact with in the rest of her life, and it already felt like a surfeit.

She was about to go back to the bar for the third half when she heard footsteps crunching up behind her.

'Sorry I'm late.' Finn put a pint of bitter and a half of cider onto the table and slid onto the bench alongside her, facing out across the river. 'Callum told me what you were drinking and I could see the glass was getting low. How's your Ma? Bit of a scare, but nothing worse, I guess.'

'You didn't drive over here to ask me about my family. How did it go with Ash? I don't like secrets.'

'We still haven't traced him,' said Finn. 'Hasn't turned up for work, none of his colleagues know anything. We've been through the list of his friends you gave us, but nothing.' The spaniel dropped a stick at his feet and he threw it towards the river. 'I asked you earlier about the porn; you never answered.'

'What did you expect – my father was three feet away from me?'

'You want to tell me about it now? It would help, maybe.'

Perhaps it would at that. What was there to protect any more except her pride?

'He'd just got a new job in Avonport,' she said, 'something to do with reinsurance; he never quite got around to explaining it and I wasn't interested enough to push. That's when he started staying out at night – seeing clients, he said – and his new boss didn't seem like the best of influences. The first time I met the guy, he was wearing enough hair gel to get his entire head up someone's arse.

'A few weeks after that I stayed over at Ash's apartment one Friday night, and while he snored his way through the next morning, I decided to break the habit of a lifetime and clean up for him – the place was always a tip. Do it properly, I told myself, but when I moved the sofa to hoover underneath, I found a couple of DVDs in blank cases. Who uses those these days? I don't know whether I was curious or suspicious, but I put one into the player with the sound turned down. Ten seconds was all I needed, I promise. This was more than gynaecology, it was sadistic.'

It had made sense in a way. If that was what turned him on, no wonder they hadn't had sex for months, not that she'd cared. A blessing in disguise.

She took another sip of the cider, staring out across the river. 'I put the discs back in their hiding place and said nothing to Ash. Even now I'm not sure why, perhaps I didn't have the energy to listen to his lies. But after that day, nothing was the same. S&M porn plus coke – how much does it take to break a relationship? I should have known that being with a man was a crap idea.'

'We're not all bad. And you've seen enough broken relationships in your career; women who get abused, see their kids being abused but don't move out. For Christ's sake, some of them lose their children because of their loyalty.'

'Misplaced loyalty – what good is that?'

'They call it love,' said Finn.

'Love? That's a shifty word. I don't think I ever loved Ash. No, scratch that. I definitely never loved Ash, not even close. It was just that after Annie and then Jess, I wondered if something different would work better. I was wrong, but perhaps I was simply attached to him and didn't know how to break the thread. I'm not good at being by myself; it can be comforting to know there's another heartbeat in the house, someone to have a bit of banter with. Someone I can trust - not much to ask, is it?'

She turned to look at her friend; a late shaft of sun caught some silver in his dark hair and created hollows of shadow on his cheeks.

'And all this is because Ash saw Mrs Jenkins the night she got murdered,' said Pav. 'I'm no cheerleader for the guy, but I still can't believe he's a murderer. He wouldn't have a motive and he certainly hasn't got the balls.'

'I'm not so sure about that,' said Finn. 'We checked his computer – he'd been downloading some pretty unpleasant stuff, but the DVDs and the memory stick files were the worst.' He was sipping his drink more slowly than usual. 'You remember the original intelligence that kicked off Hexameter? There were rumours about snuff movies, but we discounted them, no evidence.' He paused. 'Sorry boss, I wish there was an easier way to say this.'

She felt the goosebumps on her arms. 'You're telling me that Ash owned a film of someone being murdered?'

'A teenage girl.' Finn looked away as he spoke, focusing on the tree across the river. 'I won't go into the details, but I'm sure you can imagine. Let's just say that death would have come as a relief after what they did to her.'

He kept his voice low even though no one else was nearby.

The sun was sliding behind the ridge, and the kingfisher had long since gone to his roost. Pav took another sip of cider, but it turned to vinegar in her gut.

'He could have sourced it from anywhere,' said Finn. 'It's even possible he didn't know what he'd got, but unlikely. Something like that would have cost him, and getting it on DVD means that there's no digital trace. Old school hard copies, makes our job so much harder.'

Her face felt numb. All this time she'd been searching for evidence and she'd been living with it, if only she'd known where to look.

Finn reached across the table as if to squeeze her hand, then withdrew it, finished his beer and stood up. 'I've arranged for Ash's computer and the DVDs to be transferred to us first thing tomorrow.'

'You got Spears to agree?'

'With a little persuasion. He wants in on the investigation, wants you to square it through Gus to make sure he gets assigned. We need to open this up now, and we could do worse.'

'It's not my call, but I'll do what I can.'

'One other thing, boss – I know you'll look at those movies tomorrow, but I promise you, they're in a different league from anything I've seen before. It's one thing seeing the end result, it's another watching it happen. And if Ash gets in touch with you, do yourself a favour and call me straight away, doesn't matter what time it is; you can't afford to compromise yourself any further for the sake of a fuckwit like him.'

She waited until he walked away, then threw the rest of the cider onto the ground and watched the puddle soak into the earth. A cloud of midges were hovering near the edge of the water, like a fragment of gauze caught in the air. What fantasies had Ash played out the few times they'd had sex, she wondered? Did he ever come close to realising them?

She walked back across the village green in the half light of dusk, shivering despite the warm evening air, and looked up at the sky. Although the sky was still light, the first stars were already shining as if impatient for the night to come.

CHAPTER
FOURTEEN

The Mission hadn't changed. Sebastian stood a couple of hundred metres down the street, looking at the large Victorian house on the corner plot. A high fence bordered the edge of the long back garden, but the tops of trees in a copse at the end were visible, waving slightly in the breeze. He pulled up the hood of his sweatshirt and slouched deliberately as he walked along the opposite side of the road, trying not to stare too obviously.

A woman walked past him, moving onto the edge of the pavement as if frightened of coming too close. And she's right, thought Sebastian; in my body and my soul I'm unclean. There was only one way to redemption now that confession had failed; to do what he came here for, to confront Bonetti. He crossed the road, waited with his hand on the gate for a moment, then walked quickly up the path and rang the bell.

The door opened to a man he didn't recognise; tall, thickset and unshaved, with a bloodstained plaster peeling from his right ear. Sebastian began to introduce himself, feeling like a stranger, but the other man stopped him.

'I know who you are – follow me.' Sebastian trailed behind him through to a familiar room at the back, overlooking the garden; his old office.

'Wait here,' said the man. 'I'll fetch Dr Bonetti.'

The bird feeders - empty now - were still there, hanging from the branches of the lilac tree close to the French windows, and the grass on the central lawn was yellow and waist high. Further down, a large branch from one of the plum trees had split from the trunk and dangled over the side fence into the street outside.

A voice called him back into the room. 'I have been expecting you, Sebastian! A little sooner would have been polite, perhaps, but there is always a welcome for the prodigal son, even one who has returned from the grave. I have to say, I did so admire your little ruse about drowning. So hard to prove it never happened.'

Bonetti stood in the doorway, looking as though he couldn't wait to slit the throat of a fatted calf. He held his arms wide with the invitation of an embrace, and there was no choice but to submit to the touch of the other man's cheek, the moist skin freshly shaved and anointed.

'Such sad news about the boy they found in the woods,' said Bonetti. 'You heard, of course. A tragedy, but no doubt the police will catch the perpetrator in time. Will that be a good thing, do you believe? And now, please, sit and relax. You've had a hard time, a long journey in many ways. Would I be right? As for the beard; most biblical, although you looked better before. And your hand – you have hurt yourself. Altogether, Sebastian, you have the look of someone who has fallen from his peak.'

The tall man reappeared with two mugs of coffee and then left them again. 'Two sugars,' said Bonetti, 'I believe I have remembered correctly. Such a long time you have been gone, and so suddenly you left us.'

They sat on opposite sides of the desk, two colleagues having a conversation. Listening to Lorenzo, Seb remembered, was like surrendering to a spell. He pushed the coffee aside.

'You know why I went.'

'A misunderstanding. If you had not been so precipitate, all would have become clear.' There was something about the way he spoke with the rhythm of a lullaby.

'There was no misunderstanding, just my wilful ignorance. I let you make a fool of me for long enough – not anymore. Cleaners, labourers; I must have been mad to believe that. Whorehouses, that's where my children went. All of them! And I sent them there while I smiled and told them God was on their side.'

The smile faded from Bonetti's eyes. 'Whorehouse? Such a strong word. You have evidence for such a wild allegation?'

Seb tried to stare him out, but failed. 'There was a boy,' he said, 'his name was Silviu. Remember him? You made a mistake when you brought him over. He remembered me from the orphanage in Bucharest and I gave him my mobile number, asked him to keep in touch.'

'You were given a strict exhortation not to do such a thing. Attachments bring pain.'

Seb ignored him. 'I told him, God help me, that this would be the start of a new life. That he'd be safe, that he'd have a real job and some self-respect. It was three weeks before he stole a phone from one of the men who paid to rape him every night, so that he could call me at last. And then he said sorry – to me! – for letting me down.'

Lorenzo moved the knot of his tie a fraction of a centimetre and adjusted his cuffs. 'We agreed, Sebastian, that there would be no contact with these young people, that they should be free to make new lives for themselves. You have brought this misery on yourself.'

Sebastian swiped the words away. 'Silviu told me he hadn't been good enough to be given a proper job, so you were punishing him – I was punishing him. He asked me how long would it take to prove himself.'

'Yes, I remember Silviu,' said Lorenzo, drawling the boy's name. 'A dim-witted boy, an inbred gypsy with the dumb loyalty of a dog. You believed his rantings? And if you did, why not discuss it with me instead of running away like a scared child yourself? Why not tell the authorities?'

'You know why!'

'Of course – the girl, Anca. She sends her regards, by the way. You have a good eye. She has grown into quite a handsome figure and is, I believe, quite safe for now.' He brushed some invisible dust from the sleeve of his jacket. 'You see, Sebastian, how I save you from temptation. But in return, all I get is curses instead of thanks. This is a burden to me, but I bear it out of regard for you.'

'Regard! Your only regard's for yourself. As for Anca; I agreed to help you for her sake, Bonetti, but I never agreed to what you've done.'

This was harder than he'd thought, pretending to be someone strong. 'Let me see Anca, let me take her somewhere safe. If you agree to stop this abominable business, you have my word that I'll keep my silence.'

The words sounded pathetic even as he said them. He'd been wrong to turn up here without a plan, Daniel and the lion's den. Except that Daniel had been saved because he was blameless in God's eyes. Who could possibly say that he, Sebastian, was blameless? No, he'd betrayed so many just to salve his conscience about what he'd done to Anca.

Bonetti broke into his thoughts. 'Keeping your silence; what would your God say to that, Sebastian?'

'There is no God, Bonetti – you've taught me that. There's only me, and I'll take my own chances.' Words, only words, but he could feel his body trembling with the effort. How could he possibly have thought that he could triumph over the man sitting opposite? The headache was back, and under the bandage on his hand, the skin was crawling and curling as if the edges of the wound were unwilling to meet and heal.

Lorenzo studied his fingernails and then shook his head. 'Your proposal is unacceptable, I am afraid. You want me to hand over my only guarantee of your cooperation – I think not. Bear in mind that I am not my own master – which of us is? I am merely a steward. I have to answer for my actions, I have to justify my decisions.' He turned to stare out at the garden. 'However, perhaps you can earn Anca's freedom in another way. Whatever you might think, I am not a vindictive man. Business comes first, and that requires a clear head. But, my dear Father, I dislike being crossed, I dislike being outmanoeuvred, and there is someone with whom I am currently annoyed, some unfinished business that needs to be tidied away. Prove yourself at that and I shall release the girl into your care, so that we may go our separate ways.'

'If I clear up this "unfinished business" for you, how will that guarantee my silence? What if I don't agree?'

Lorenzo sighed. 'I could have your tongue now, my friend. I could have your eyes and your ears. I could have your life and no one would be any wiser. You *will* agree, not just for yourself but for the girl. And afterwards, as I have promised, I shall set you both free. But your soul, Sebastian, in which you no longer profess belief – that will always belong to me, and that is all the guarantee I need.'

CHAPTER FIFTEEN

The opened case of Ash's MacBook stood eviscerated at the end of the workbench in the windowless room. 'We've rigged up his hard drive separately,' said the technician, a dark, round boy with an accent like wet coal. 'All we need are the files – I'll put them through to the monitor here, you won't miss much.' He pulled up a stool for Pav. 'Someone said he was your boyfriend, bloke who owned this.' The twist of his mouth was impossible to read; half smile, half sneer.

'"Was" is the operative word, Hawkeye. And no, I didn't have the faintest clue what he was downloading. Frankly, I'm not sure I want to know now.' She watched as the boy fiddled with the keyboard. 'How many videos are there?' she asked.

'Five, none of them very long. Four are standard S&M porn, but the other one, copied from the DVD... you sure you want to see it?'

'I've seen a lot of things in my time, and anyway, this is my case so I don't have much option.'

The boy shrugged, pressed a key, and the screen lit up. It was obvious, from the first shots, that this would be different. She'd seen enough porn to know what to expect, but these were no actors. The girl was spindle thin, with skin the colour of cheap wax. Her back was a lattice of red welts and her legs and arms were patchworked with bruises in every shade from yellow to deep purple. But as the camera panned around, there was something else.

'Freeze it there,' Pav ordered. 'Can you zoom in on that mark, the one on her neck?' She studied the screen. 'I need a better resolution.'

'I can sharpen it a little – there you go. Any more than that and you'll have to give me a while to work on the images.'

'No, it's fine.'

This mark was different, not a bruise or a cut. More like an ulcer, a weeping wound, a lesion. More like the marks on the bodies, the limbs in the basement, the boy with his crucifix. And Mira.

She signalled the boy to restart the film, a depressing sequence of depredations on the girl until finally – almost thankfully – a thin wire was wrapped around her neck and Pav watched her being strangled by a man, hooded like a terrorist. The girl barely struggled, and it was hard to know why; perhaps she had no strength left, or death felt like a welcome release, but with the final movement of one flailing arm, her fingers hooked the man's hood and pulled it aside for a second. The respite was short-lived; he let go with one hand to pull the camouflage back into place and then resumed twisting the wire.

The images stopped abruptly once the girl was still. 'You want to see the others?' asked the boy.

'Not yet,' she said. She looked away from the screen, feeling bone-weary. She'd known what to expect, but the reality had sucked away something inside. 'I want to look at the end of this one,' she said, pulling herself up straight. 'The man who strangled her, let me see him again.'

A few seconds later, she watched the man twisting the ligature into the girl's neck; even before his face was revealed, she recognised the bullet shape of his head, the heavy crooked nose. This was the man who'd tried to kidnap Mira from A&E, the man who'd whispered that she was a dead woman, the man she'd seen sitting on the village green the night Mrs Jenkins was killed. Even without seeing his face she'd know him now. She'd know him forever for the arrogant way he held himself, a self-appointed angel of death.

She stood up, flexing her shoulders. 'I've seen enough for now.'

'Was it any help?'

'Sadly, yes.' She had no doubts anymore; one way or another, something connected Ash to the people she was searching for. Traffickers, torturers, murderers.

'When were these downloaded?' she asked.

'The date stamps on the files have been altered, even those from the DVD - they all show the first of January 1900, which doesn't seem likely unless he discovered time travel. I'm still working on them. And the muppet didn't know how to shred a file, so I'll be able to reconstruct any data he thought he'd deleted. They never learn.'

BACK AT HER desk she watched again and again, looking for details. The room on the screen was like a naked stage set with bare walls and floor, plus a few props: the table over which the girl had been stretched, a single chair. Nothing extraneous, nothing to divert attention away from the main action. She'd wanted something identifiable but this was professionally anonymous, taking no chances.

At least there was the man. The cleaned up images were through now, on her monitor; she studied his face, caught in a moment of savage surprise as his victim pulled the hood aside, and then the girl before the coup de grâce. It was more than she could have hoped for, and she arranged to circulate stills of the two faces.

But there was another lead to follow up this morning, the one that she'd put off from last night. Father Mahoney, the man who knew something about Sebastian Collier. Was he their man? Within the next couple of hours, God willing, she might find out.

THE CHURCH APPEARED before Pav was ready for it. It sat on a small island surrounded by a labyrinth of streets, all within scent of the quays and malls of Hazelbury docks on the other side of Avonport. This wasn't tourist territory, though; the stonework on the building was as dark as wet slate, as if there had never been any funds to wash away the centuries of coal dust and smoke and God alone knew what else. She led Finn through the open door into the soft-spiced shadows. A woman in a headscarf was sitting in prayer halfway down, and as they walked towards the altar, Pav saw two pairs of men's shoes, one under each door of the confessional stalls.

They sat at the front and waited; after a while, Pav heard the woman behind as she creaked herself off her knees and echoed her way to the main doors, leaving them alone under the vault of the ceiling.

She closed her eyes, trying to ignore the incipient headache, waiting for the soft murmur of voices in the stalls to end. A long confession, she thought. How long did it take to bare a soul?

The sinner left first, a round man with frightened eyes that flicked to her face and away again in the time it took to blink. Whatever he'd confessed, the experience had left him no happier, not by the evidence of his stumbling trot down the side aisle. Half a minute later, as if he'd been sitting in solitude to digest the offloaded sins, the priest emerged from the other stall. For a moment the long, black vestments anonymised him, and then she registered the aquiline nose and elegant stoop, the knowing smile. Narziss come to life.

At first, the priest gave no more than a professional nod of acknowledgement as he walked towards the opposite side of the church. Then he stopped and turned, as if recognising that these were not the usual worshippers. 'I don't believe I've seen you here before.' A flinty voice that suited his frame, not quite hiding the Irish lilt. Not Sebastian, then, not their man. She'd half hoped, ever since last night; stranger things had happened.

'Someone at Ushaw Seminary gave me your name,' said Pav. 'They said you might know how we could find a Sebastian Collier.'

'And why might you be looking for such a man?'

'Do you know him?'

'That will depend upon who is asking and why. You will understand the need for confidentiality in some matters.'

Pav showed her ID. 'Regional Organised Crime Unit. We

really need to talk to him, and you'll appreciate that we too have a need for confidentiality.'

She turned around for a second at a noise from the back of the church as an elderly couple supported each other to the nearest pew. 'If we could just have a few minutes of your time,' said Pav. 'This might sound like a cliché, but there really are lives at stake.'

The priest led them into a small side room and found three chairs. 'This is a busy time for me. I came back last week from a three-month sabbatical and it seems that many of my parishioners preferred to store their sins for my delectation, rather than soil the ears of my young replacement. Some may say that was a wise choice, but it's left me with little spare time.'

'Sebastian Collier, Father, he might need help. We believe he might be seriously unwell.'

The priest's face lost its colour. 'Unwell, you say. Wait here a moment.' He returned within a minute, his face like marble against the black vestments. He handed Pav a folded leaflet. 'Sebastian Collier, that was his name. Father Sebastian – we trained together at Ushaw seminary and that is the order of service for his funeral last February. A cold day it was, too. Bitter. Never liked the cold, Sebastian. Why he chose the sea, I could never fathom.'

Pav looked up from the leaflet. 'The sea?'

'His clothes were found on a beach on the Gower peninsular. And the note; I never saw it, but I'm told it was nothing more than the usual apologies. A crying shame; he was a decent man at heart, and I shudder to think of his soul in hell.'

'You're saying he killed himself,' said Finn.

'A mortal sin. I knew he was troubled after he came back from Romania for the last time.' He examined the palms of his hands, meant to be stained with earth. 'Are either of you religious?' he asked. 'One of the greatest gifts from faith, true faith, is certainty. No need for questions, just belief. Life is simpler that way, and a simple life is what most people crave. We give them that. But for Sebastian – whether it was his father's influence or something else, I don't know – the questions never ceased. How many times did I tell him, the recipe for happiness is to put your faith in God, with a little help from whiskey on the really bad days. But he was always searching for answers. If I were honest, I would say he lost his faith years ago, and had been searching for a substitute ever since.'

'You mentioned Romania,' said Pav. 'What was he doing there?'

Mahoney smiled. 'For a while he thought that might be the solution. Leave ideas behind and work with the poor and dispossessed, just like our Lord. He helped to build a school, by all accounts, and became a dab hand with a hammer and chisel.'

'When was that?' asked Pav.

The priest thought for a moment. 'Must be getting on for eight years ago that he first went out there. All his time at home was spent raising money so that he could go back.'

'But something happened,' said Finn.

'You're talking to the wrong man. I saw him only once after he returned last time; I think I made him uncomfortable. There was a light in his eyes, but it was the unhealthy, febrile glow of a fanatic. He made no sense to me; all he could talk about was his mission to help these orphans. We lost contact over eighteen months ago – I have no idea where he went, so it will do you no good to ask – and the next I heard was of his death.'

'Was the body ever found?'

'I believe not, but that would be a question for the police; my care is the soul, not the flesh. And now, if you will excuse me, I must leave the dead to their own devices and attend to the living.'

THEY STOPPED for fuel and coffee at the motorway services, on the English side of the old bridge overlooking the estuary. The ham in her sandwich tasted like plastic as Pav waited for Finn to finish his call.

'As you suspected, no body was ever found,' he said. 'Not that it's surprising. With the current around there, he could easily have been washed out to sea, and a body doesn't float forever once the gases from decomposition have dissipated. On the other hand, he could have weighed himself down and not floated at all.'

'Or he didn't drown. What about the suicide note?'

'There should be a copy waiting for us at the office by the time we get back, but from what Mahoney said, it won't shed much light.'

'I think we'll be the judge of that.' She pushed the remainder of the sandwich away. 'Why is it whenever I eat something in your company it tastes like industrial effluent?'

'This from the gourmand of Blackbrook?' Finn got to his feet. 'You want me to get you something else?'

'Sit down! I know you work for me, but you're not a bloody servant. I don't treat you like a servant, do I?'

'Only when the moon's in Virgo.'

'In that case, I'll have a slice of pizza to go and another of their hot brown drinks. With sugar.'

· · ·

HALFWAY ACROSS THE BRIDGE, she took a call from the laboratory in Mill Hill. 'I can't believe it,' she said to Finn. 'We have good news for a change. It seems that our man with the rats has found something that attacks the infection. A combination of anti-fungal and antibiotic; don't ask me for details.'

'Sounds like something for athlete's foot. They'll give this to Mira?'

'It works in a Petri dish or whatever these guys use. But it's a step forward, which is more than we can say for our disappearing priest. Every time it looks like we're getting somewhere, we hit another roadblock. His whole identity could be a fabrication and we could be looking in entirely the wrong direction.'

'Or the whole thing was an amateur attempt to fake a suicide.'

'Not so amateur; he got away with it up to now.' She indicated for the turnoff to Uskmouth. 'Priests; why can't these people marry and leave a family behind for us to interrogate?'

'Look who's talking. Sorry, boss, bad joke. I'll do some more digging when we get back, but there was no mention of any living parents or siblings when he disappeared. Or died.'

SHE DIDN'T ARRIVE HOME until nearly 6:30 p.m.; the afternoon had been a waste of time and she felt as though she was clutching at mist. The man she wanted had been so close, and now he was drifting away again. It happened, she knew that. Sometimes there were no happy endings – most times, if she was honest. Sometimes the gap was just too big to jump. And if Sebastian, or whatever his name was, stayed dead, then the only chance was Mira. She'd have to pray that the drugs worked and they could get to her in time.

Coming back to Mill Terrace felt strange; she'd never realised before how keenly an absence could be felt. She parked opposite the cottage, took her bag from the passenger seat, rested it on the bonnet and then realised that she'd left the house keys in the glove compartment. A cat, somewhere, was wailing. A painful love life, cats, she'd read once; no wonder they shouted so much.

On days like this, she regretted the end of the summer; it could be June, not September. The leaves looked washed and fresh, not yet ready for their chameleon moments, and there was a softness in the air, a perfume from some flowers that she couldn't see.

With the keys in one hand, she walked up to the front door and stopped. Not again. The door was slightly open, although there was no sign of broken glass this time. She dropped the bag on the path beside her, feeling the rush of adrenaline. He must have come for her, the man who'd tried to take Mira.

The decision was simple this time; no more heroics, not somewhere so isolated. She backed slowly down the path, wondering if he was watching her from inside, wondering if she had time to reach her car and lock herself in safely; some risks weren't worth taking. She was almost at the gate when the door opened a little more widely.

'Babe, it's me!' And now she could see him in the shadows; Ash, keeping out of sight and beckoning her. His voice was hoarse and low, as if someone else might hear. 'I need to talk to you, babe. Please.'

There was no doubt about what she should do. Go to the car, lock herself in, call for backup, and keep eyes on Ash. That's what she should do, that's what protocol said.

She glanced over her shoulder; at her car, at the lane leading down to the main road, at the trees. And then she took a deep breath of the soft air and walked towards the cottage.

Inside, with the door shut, Ash kept his distance. He hadn't washed in days, or changed his clothes, if the smell was anything to go by. He seemed smaller than ever, like a soft balloon, as if something was missing.

'How did you get in?' Pav asked.

'I lied about losing your key. Sorry. Insurance, you know how it is.'

'The police are looking for you. I was looking for you.'

He was finding it hard to look at her, and didn't say anything.

'You're a stupid bastard,' Pav said. 'They found the DVDs and the shit on your computer.'

'It isn't what you think.'

'You have no idea what I think. And do you really believe I've not seen those videos, Ash? I already knew what you were like when I found some fucking violent porn at your apartment months ago. Trust me, I wish I'd said something then. But snuff movies are a different league. Stranglings? Beheadings? You're a psycho, you know that. You should be inside. You will be.'

There was a frantic look about him. 'I don't suppose you got any stuff, babe? Just a bit to see me through.'

She couldn't believe it. 'Are you mad - when have you ever seen me do drugs? I think you're confusing me with one of your slags.'

'No, I promise. I just wondered. It's been a bad few days.'

'Tell me about it. And you know you're in the frame after what happened to Mrs Jenkins?'

He ignored her. 'I came to say sorry, been a bit of a prick.'

'What, the great Ashkan Godivala apologising? This must be a dream. No, sorry, more like a nightmare.'

His clothes were stained as if he'd been sleeping on damp grass. 'I could do with some money, babe. Can't use my cards, need a little cash. Fifty, a hundred - a grand if you got it. Anything.'

'You think I wander around with a thousand quid in my purse? Dream on, Ash, I'm a government employee, not a fucking drug dealer.'

'You don't understand. I really need your help. There are people who want me out of the way, permanently, but if I can just get over to France I could make my way from there.'

Ducking and diving, business as usual. 'What are you trying to do, Ash, use emotional blackmail on me? It won't work, I know you too well.'

She'd never seen him like this. He'd been brought up as a little Persian princeling, by a mother who barely escaped with her life when the mullahs took over. As far as Ash was concerned, the world owed him a living.

'Who are these mysterious people?' Pav asked. 'Running away won't solve anything. Whatever you're mixed up in, you should let me take you in just to keep you safe. We'll find you in the end, or the people you're running from will, and we both know what they're capable of. Do you understand what I'm saying?'

He laughed, as if at a bad joke. 'You think your people can keep me safe? Do me a favour. I need to get away, babe. You gotta believe me, it's the only way.'

All this time he'd been standing like a chastened child, but now he lunged forward and tried to grab her, even though there was no strength in his movements. As she pushed him away, he sank to his knees and started to cry.

'It's no good, Ash, it doesn't work. This is your problem and you can't make it mine. I'm telling you, for the last time – turn yourself in, give yourself a break. If you don't, I will.'

He shook his head slowly from side to side, as if trying to shake away the words. 'I can't, babe, I can't...'

She reached down and pulled him upright; his whole body was shaking. 'Ash, listen to me. No money, no drugs, nothing. I'll give you one break; turn yourself in and earn yourself a few brownie points. Use my phone, call now.' She handed him her mobile, but he brushed it aside and stared into her eyes, a stranger at last. 'You want me to call?' she asked.

He shook his head. 'I'll do it, babe, promise. But I don't want to wait here. I'll go into town, go to the police station...'

'How? I didn't see your car outside. I'll drive you.'

He pushed past her and made for the door. 'A few minutes, babe, for the old days. Not so much to ask.'

'I can't do that, Ash, I can't let you leave.' She moved in front of him, blocking his way. His nose was running, but he didn't seem to have noticed, and he mumbled something, but she couldn't catch the words.

'I'm going to call my people now,' she said. 'Trust me, you'll feel better when it's over.'

'Sorry babe, can't let you do that.' With an energy that took her by surprise, he knocked the phone out of her hands; it bounced once and skittered across the floor-boards. Pav swore, bent to pick it up and stood upright to see Ash with one of her kitchen knives in his hands. Unsteady hands, the point of the knife describing small, random patterns in the air.

He'd moved between her and the door. 'Have you used a knife before?' she asked, keeping her voice low and even. 'It's not as easy as you think. You don't want to hurt me, and I don't want to hurt you. Drop it, now. Please don't make this even worse.'

He shook his head slowly.' I didn't want this, it wasn't meant to happen this way. You don't know what they're like.'

'They? Who are they? C'mon Ash, tell me and I can help you. Whatever you think, we can protect you.'

'It was just business,' he said, 'you have to believe me. I didn't know what they were doing, not at first, and by then it was too late.'

'I'm not a mind reader, Ash. Help me here, tell me who "they" are, what they were doing.' She'd kept her voice calm, trying to lower the temperature, but it had no effect.

'The fucking movies! You've seen them, you know what I'm talking about.' He was crying openly now, his whole body shuddering, but the knife was still pointed at her. 'I just want to get away, leave this whole shit heap behind. Come with me babe, we'll go abroad, start again. I'll stay clean, promise.'

Still the fantasist. Still thinking that by ignoring reality it would go away. 'You know I can't do that. Drop the knife, Ash. Let me call someone and we'll put an end to this.'

He sniffed, wiped his nose on his sleeve and pulled himself upright. 'You always were a self-righteous little bitch. Now you can go fuck yourself.'

As he half turned towards the door, she threw herself forward, but he twisted and slashed with the knife, catching her arm just above the wrist. For a second she wondered if he'd missed, and then she felt the burning pain and saw thick blood welling along the arc of the cut. She tensed, waiting for the next attack, but Ash was already gone.

She thought of following and trying to restrain him, but in the state he was in, anything could happen, and she wasn't ready to become a statistic. One cut was enough, but thankfully it wasn't too deep. The blood was flowing freely, but not pumping, so he hadn't damaged an artery. She used an entire box of elastoplasts and then called Finn on the landline.

'I'll take the car,' she said, 'try to track him.'

'Don't be daft – you should go to A&E.'

'Not a luxury I can afford. I screwed up, not calling it in as soon as I saw him. And if I think I'm going to collapse, I'll let you know; in the meantime, put out an alert. You'll need to organise a helicopter, and dogs for the woods. And don't forget a house-to-house in Blackbrook. He's already over the edge and the last thing we want is him trying to buy his way out with a kidnap.'

AFTER THREE MILES on the road to town, she turned around and drove back through the village towards Gwenstow, but there was no sign of him. He could have cut across the fields and taken the riverside path down to Smallweir Bridge; from there he could cross the river and then climb up through the woods towards Tryleg. Not really Ash's style, cross-country hiking, but this was an Ash she didn't know.

She returned home and checked the house carefully in case he'd slipped back while she was out, but the place was undisturbed. What a mistake, letting him get away. She should have tackled him harder, knife or no knife. If it had been anyone else, a stranger, would she have let him go so easily? Of course not, she knew that, and it wasn't fear that held her back. No, it was shared history, memories, pretending to herself that somewhere inside him was the man he used to be; a selfish, arrogant prick, but not a murderer. A weakness on her part; he wouldn't catch her like that again.

She stood in the middle of the living room and listened; there was nothing left but the echoes of their argument seeping into the walls and she thought, some things can't be cleaned away.

CHAPTER
SIXTEEN

The road had been climbing for a while now, following the stream that glittered through the trees lining the slopes. Autumn was coming. At this height, the leaves were already turning, and the air outside the car was cool and fresh. Bonetti had barely spoken since they started the journey, driving like an old man with both hands on the wheel. He was worried. Anyone could see that. No, more than worried; scared. Somehow, that didn't make Seb feel any better.

'*I am not my own master,*' Lorenzo had said at the Mission, the day that Sebastian confronted him; but today Bonetti's master was about to be revealed, and Sebastian couldn't help feeling this was an experience he'd rather skip.

Another few minutes of driving and they'd be above the tree line and onto the moor. From there, the road climbed still higher until it bridged the crest between two peaks and then fell down to the plain below, stretching north and away from the hills. It was years since Sebastian had been here, not since he was a teenager crashing the gears on a friend's Ford as they drove too fast on the mountain roads, getting their kicks where they could. Innocent times, forever out of reach.

They didn't get that far. A few seconds later Bonetti slowed down as they turned left up a track that Sebastian didn't remember from the old days. A few more minutes, and they arrived at a pair of unlikely security gates set into a high fence. Most of the manmade structures around here were barns or bothys, or isolated houses that looked as if they couldn't offer more than cold comfort. But this looked official, almost corporate; not at all what he was expecting. Bonetti punched a code into the keypad. The gates swung open, and they drove towards a converted farmhouse on one side of a courtyard peppered with small outbuildings. But this wasn't a working farm; there were no signs or smells of any animals, no farm machinery. There was, though, an air of watchfulness, as if they were being tracked by unseen eyes.

The farmhouse door opened as Bonetti locked the car behind them, but whoever was inside remained in the shadows. It was only when they moved into the hallway that Sebastian saw the woman who'd been waiting for them; as tall and lean as him but older, in her late 40s or early 50s. Dressed in designer jeans and a sweatshirt, her long black hair was pulled tight into a flamenco bun. She nodded at Bonetti, ignored Sebastian and led the way down the corridor to a large kitchen with windows overshadowed by the hill above.

There was no small talk; as soon as they were sitting around the table, she started.

'When I give you instructions, I expect them to be carried out. I do not pay for initiative, do you understand? So which of you was it? You, Bonetti – do not give me any crap. Did you do it yourself or did you get your new best friend to do your dirty work?'

Sebastian looked from one to the other, wondering what the hell she was talking about. At least she wasn't expecting him to say anything, not yet. The warm smell of sweat rising from Bonetti, sitting next to him, was strangely reassuring.

'If you would let me explain...' It was interesting to hear how easily the man's confidence had been sucked away.

'If I wanted excuses, I would ask for them,' said the woman. 'Just answer my question, as if I do not already know the answer. Were you the one messing about with that woman from the crime unit? Find the girl, I said. Do it carefully, I said. I did not tell you to screw around for your own entertainment.'

'Mess about? Screw around?' Bonetti drew himself up in his chair, the small moustache bristling. 'I know how important this woman is – please, madam, do not take me for a fool. She is strong willed; I see that in her eyes the day outside the school. To make her talk will not be easy. She needs to be broken down, to be afraid. I am a psychologist, I know these things. I am preparing her, I am softening her like *osso bucco* for the oven, and when she is ready, she will tell us how to find the girl, she will tell us everything else she has discovered about our operation. And when she is ready, all she will need is a priest to hear her confession.' He turned to Sebastian, smiled and then sat back, looking pleased with himself.

'Watch your tongue with me, Bonetti, you self-satisfied little prick,' said the woman. 'If you had done your job properly in the first place, we would not be in this position. Sangre de Dios, how could you leave the girl alive in that basement? How did your factotum let the other one escape from the house in the first place? We are on a knife edge here, you realise that? Unless the girl has lost her wits, she will start talking before too long, as soon as she recovers, and it will not be me in the spotlight.'

Bonetti stopped smiling. 'Trust me madam, mistakes will not happen again. As you know, I have already arranged for Defrim – my "factotum", as you delight in calling him – to pay the price for his error.'

'And a damned good thing, too. It is bad enough having the girl on the loose. Trust me, Bonetti, if I have to shut down this operation because of your infantile mistakes, I am going to have a nice new star for one of the films, and you will not be around for a repeat performance.' She turned to take in Sebastian for the first time, looking at him the way she might with an annoying insect. 'You have thirty-six hours, both of you. If you have not found out where the girl is by then, and made sure she keeps any secrets, we shall have to do things the hard way and I shall be most annoyed. You do not want me to be annoyed. Parvati McNeil is my friend and friends are rather hard to come by. When I waste them, it has to be for a very good reason.'

From the window of his rented bedsit in Abertrothy, Sebastian watched the Italian drive away. The room was small but functional, better than his bolthole in London. Bonetti had put up the deposit, hired a car and given him a couple of hundred pounds as a float. Apart from that, he had nothing, not even his pride. He made himself a mug of bitter coffee and wandered back to the window, looking out at the builder's yard on the other side of the street.

He'd seen her before, of course. It had taken a few

minutes, sitting down earlier at the table in the farmhouse, but then he'd remembered. It was soon after Bonetti's trips to Vietnam and Thailand, a few months after the Mission began operations.

'Why should we limit ourselves to white Europeans?' Bonetti had said. 'Discrimination, Sebastian, it is the evil of our times.' But nothing had come of the trips apart from a short-lived influx of thin, consumptive teenagers with haunted eyes. They soon stopped arriving and Sebastian had carried on with his fundraising for the Mission. Every couple of weeks, another small group of young people would arrive from the old favourites; Romania, Ukraine, Bulgaria. A few nights at the house in Uskmouth and then they'd disappear on to their new jobs and their new lives. That, he'd believed, was the plan.

Thinking about it now, the day the woman turned up was the day he allowed himself suspicions for the first time. 'Some of our charges are not adapting so well,' Bonetti had said. 'The dear lady I met this afternoon, she runs a hostel, she will help them get back on their feet.'

'Why can't they come back here?' Sebastian said. 'There won't be that many, and if they're in trouble I can help them.'

Bonetti's smile would have shattered at a touch. 'Your heart does you credit, Sebastian, but you have a gift for raising money. You are our public face, you play the part to perfection. No, I cannot allow you to be distracted. This lady and her hostel, they are a valuable addition to our services. To everything – and everyone – there is a season. God gave you skills, Father, use them, and let others use theirs.' He'd put his arm around Sebastian's shoulders. 'And now you can see, perhaps, that your misgivings are mistaken.'

And instead, Sebastian remembered, he'd seen one more secret. One too many.

He watched a couple of men in the yard opposite, loading a pickup with lengths of wood. He would swap places with either of them in a second; simple lives, without deception. Playing the part, that's what Bonetti had said about him, and he was right. Perhaps his whole life had been an act; perhaps that's what you do, he thought, when you're too weak to be yourself. You try other lives for size; priest, celibate, missionary. Until one day you no longer recognise your own face in the mirror and you wonder who you are.

CHAPTER
SEVENTEEN

T wo hours had passed since Ash disappeared and there was still no news. The only sound was the helicopter quartering the valley, and even that had faded now. They'd lost him, she could feel it. Maybe he'd hidden a car nearby and wasn't as helpless as he seemed. Wherever he was, though, he wouldn't be back. That was knowledge, not a belief or a feeling. Even Ash couldn't keep the mask on after what happened today.

Her arm ached even though the cut no longer burned, and she searched in vain for painkillers. Food, then, but even there she drew a blank. The burgers from the back of the freezer compartment look like the flesh of an ice age hunter preserved in a glacier, and the furry surface on the last pot of yoghurt seemed to be moving of its own accord. As for the remains of last week's loaf...

She checked the time; half an hour before Waitrose in Abertrothy shut, enough time to pick up plasters, paracetamol and something microwaveable. Forty minutes later, she was halfway out of the parking space at the supermarket when she felt a slight jolt and heard someone cry out. She could have sworn there was nothing behind the car when she checked the mirror a second before, but a man was there now, staring at her through the rear window and rubbing his thigh. At least he wasn't stretched out on the ground, bleeding. She pulled forward again, then went over to see how much damage had been done.

'I can't believe I just did that – are you okay? I swear I checked in the mirror – I didn't see anyone.'

He straightened up and flexed his knee. 'No permanent damage. I'll have a spectacular bruise for a few days, but that's all. And it was probably my fault – I should have looked where I was walking, but it's been a long day.' He held out his hand. 'Michael, Michael Rees. When you move to a new area, you hope you'll meet people quickly, but not quite like this.'

'I am really, really sorry. Are you sure you're okay? Will you be able to drive?'

'I'm fine, seriously. Nothing that a pair of crutches can't fix.' He saw the look on her face. 'Only kidding. On the other hand, a decent glass of wine wouldn't go amiss. Self-medication isn't always bad. I don't know Abertrothy that well – is there somewhere nearby? It'll be my treat; from the look on your face, you feel worse than I do.'

She was about to refuse; when it came to bad days, her luck beat his any time. She should count her blessings and get away before his bruise began to throb, and he revealed himself as a hot-shot litigation lawyer; that would be the clever thing to do. But then she looked again. The corners of his down-turned eyes radiated into too many lines, the utilitarian haircut would get a thumbs down from any significant other in his life, and the little wince of pain as he shifted his weight pushed her guilt button.

'The pubs in town are rubbish,' she said. 'But if you

fancy a village local, you could do a lot worse than the Queen Bess in Blackbrook. It's ten minutes down the valley road; I'll probably be there in an hour or so, and I definitely think the drinks should be on me.'

WHEN SHE ARRIVED, the place was empty except for Rafe and his dog, a waist-high bull mastiff.

'You spoil that dog,' said Rafe as he watched Pav empty most of a packet of crisps on to the floor. He drained the glass that was already on the table and started on the new one she brought over. 'You're looking different; don't make an old man guess – what is it? Hair, clothes, makeup?'

'You're the same age as my Pa and anyway, you complain if I don't feed your damned dog.'

'It's for your own good, helps you stay on his right side.' He studied her again. 'You've lost weight.'

'Is that a compliment or a complaint?'

'When have I ever complained about you? So, did you come here just to make me happy?'

'Always, Rafe. But as it happens, I might be meeting someone – if he bothers to turn up.'

'Not that Ash, is it? I thought you told him to piss off, like I suggested months ago. Anyone could see that someone like Jess is more your type.'

'Sadly, Jess didn't feel the same.'

Detta, the Ferry's version of a chef, came out from the kitchens, trailing the smell of overcooked chips. 'You heard any more about Mrs J, Pav? I ain't been back to the house since it all kicked off, can't believe you're still sleeping next door!'

A break-in at the Mill Terrace and Mrs Jenkins killed by a burglar, that was the story put out for public consumption. It had seemed better that way, they'd decided, to keep it simple. No incurable diseases, no links to a serial killer or human trafficking. A nice, straightforward murder, more than enough gossip for a small village.

Pav shrugged. 'Sorry Detta, I don't know any more than you guys.'

'Well, it's done for me, this business. Staying with Darren, I am, till I find a new gaff. I told the landlord, a blood-soaked place like that ain't fit for proper people, not anymore.'

The mastiff nuzzled Pav's hand, wanting more crisps, and she emptied the rest of the packet onto the stone flagstones, watching the dog flick them up with one sweep of his tongue.

'So what do you think would happen if you stayed?' Pav asked.

'When people's murdered, they come back to where it was done. Everyone knows that. They're trapped, desperate for the warmth of the living.'

'But if Mrs J came back, surely she'd haunt her own house, not yours.'

'I'm not taking no chances. What if she got it wrong and went in my front door instead of hers? No way I'm waking up to her hovering at the end of the bed, moaning at me. No, I'm off. You would be too, if you had any sense.'

Detta downed the rest of her cider. 'I'd better get back to the kitchen or Callum'll start whingeing – there's homemade prawn curry on the specials board tonight and he goes mental if I use one that's gone past its sell-by date.'

Pav checked the time. As pubs went, the Queen Bess wouldn't be everybody's first choice. Stone floors, walls covered with plaster that always seemed to be bubbling with the damp that migrated from the slopes behind the building, upholstery on the chairs and benches whose original colours and patterns had been obliterated by beer stains. On the other hand, it had mercifully escaped the depredations of a corporate chain, the beer and cider were excellent, and no-one asked too many questions. Live and let live in the good Queen Bess.

Another ten minutes passed before she saw Michael through the window, manoeuvring his way through the blockade of smokers on the terrace.

'He hasn't let you down, then,' said Rafe as he snapped the lead onto the dog's collar and stood to go. 'Never let it be said that I cramped the style of a pretty lady.'

'You're cruisin' Rafe, you know that.'

'I know. That's why you love me.'

Michael, his pint, and a large glass of Shiraz slipped into the space that Rafe had left at the end of the bench. His faux-leather jacket smelled as if he'd bought it that afternoon – Pav could almost hear it creaking as he moved his arms. She felt a twinge of guilt; the poor boy probably thought he was on some kind of date. He'd learn soon enough.

'This is different,' he said, looking around.

'Not what you expected?'

'Oh, better. The chap behind the bar already gave me five minutes on the problems with his bees. I think he mistook me for someone else.'

'No – he does that to everyone. Very non-discriminating is Callum.'

She felt dislocated, and the cut Ash had given her was throbbing again. This was a mistake, for sure. Michael would want to ask her questions for which she had no answers; at least, none that she was prepared to give, and she didn't have the energy for someone new and his expectations.

'I didn't notice any crutches,' she said.

'I'll live. Like I said, the whole thing was my fault. I should have looked where I was going.'

The conversation faltered as the noise of the bar flowed around their table. A listener, Michael, not a talker; this would be harder than she'd thought. One more glass and then she could call it a night with all the proprieties observed.

They both started speaking at the same time. 'Sorry,' he said, 'you first.'

'You said you hadn't been long in the area – I wondered what brought you here.'

'I'm a counsellor, newly qualified. Abertrothy seemed like a good place to open a new practice. I'm negotiating on somewhere in town to work from, and tomorrow I start looking for a place to live.'

'Not above the shop?'

'Not in my line of work; it helps to have a little distance between you and your clients. What's your story?'

She gave the stock answer. 'Civil servant, very boring and not worth talking about.'

'That usually means you're dying to tell someone.'

'Sorry counsellor, not this time. Sometimes, Dr Freud, boring means dry as dust.'

'Touché. So what about home – is there a Mr Pav waiting at for you with a cup of cocoa when you leave here?'

'Trust me, you're in no danger there. It's a touchy subject.'

'If you want to talk about it...'

'No, Ash is history, if not exactly ancient. He's gone, and good riddance to the bastard.'

'Remind me to stay on your good side. I'm glad I wasn't in his shoes when you took against him.'

'You'd never have squeezed into them.' The crowd in the small bar had grown, and she slipped off her jacket.

Michael noticed the plasters decorating her arm. 'Wow! That doesn't look like a little scratch. You should have that dressed properly.'

'Don't worry, I'm not into self harm. An accident with a bread knife, looks worse than it feels. To be honest, I had an argument with my ex. He had the knife, though I don't think he meant to hurt me.'

'Wow again! Did you call the police?'

'He got away and they haven't found him so far. I have no idea where he is now. To be honest, the whole relationship was a short-lived mistake I won't make again. Men aren't really my style, so I'm putting Ash into the category of the exception that proves the rule.'

Michael smiled. 'You're managing my expectations.'

'Just being honest. I've been through a few relationships, and by now I know what works and what doesn't. What did that philosopher say? Something like "Those who don't learn from history are doomed to repeat it".'

Pav watched as Michael drew his fingernail through a bead of liquid on the table, making a comet's tail, and then looked up. 'I've never been sure about history,' he said. 'Why look back at things you can't change? The starting line is where we are right now, the present. To think anything else is a waste of effort.' He rubbed the comet away into a smear and smiled. 'And now the counsellor has shut up shop for the evening! Buy you another?'

. . .

BEFORE THEY LEFT, Pav poked her head into the kitchen and called Detta over. 'Your place,' she said, 'are you serious about moving?'

'Already gone – me, I mean, not the cottage. Darren's picking up the rest of my gear tomorrow, what there is of it. Why?'

'The guy I was having a drink with has just moved to the area and he's looking for somewhere to live around here. I thought maybe he could check out the cottage.'

Detta took a key from a bunch that must have doubled her weight. 'It's a spare – give him the tour whenever.'

Michael walked across the old footbridge with her, but stopped on the other side. 'This is me - I left my car on the main road. It's been a great evening, Pav. Loved the pub, loved the people.'

'Do you want a coffee or something? I could show you Detta's place now, but knowing her it won't be at its best.'

'Tempting,' he said, 'but my expectations have been well and truly managed, and I hadn't planned on being out at all this evening. There are case notes I should have written up days ago.'

'Sure – whatever.' She found an old receipt in her bag and scribbled her mobile number. 'A place like this is probably too small for you, anyway. But if you change your mind and want to look around...' She handed him the scrap of paper.

He took the pen from her, tore the paper in half and wrote his number on the back. 'Fair exchange. But don't worry, I'll call you tomorrow if that's okay – somewhere in a village like this would be perfect.'

Pav watched him walk to the end of the lane, where it curled round and down to join the main road. A strange man, a tad nervous for a counsellor. But there was something about him. Needy? Sad? Lost, maybe? The last street-lamp caught him in a pool of light and she wondered if he'd turn and wave, but his dark figure carried on walking and merged into the shadows.

INSIDE THE COTTAGE, alone, she treated herself to a mug of black Costa Rican; perhaps the caffeine and alcohol would cancel each other out. She slumped on the sofa and stared at a dusty cobweb hanging from the ceiling behind the dead screen of the TV. She must have missed it in her desultory cleaning the other day, after the break-in.

She was missing Jess tonight, the comforting warmth of her body in the dark, the softness of her skin, the way she used to murmur in her sleep, and the riot of her hair when she woke in the morning. She missed the sound of her voice, singing while she scrambled eggs for their breakfasts. But most of all, she missed that deep, anchored feeling of being loved.

EIGHTEEN

S he'd barely left the village the next morning when Finn called. 'We found a body,' he said as soon as he heard her voice, 'washed up on the estuary.' He paused, as if waiting for her to make the connection. 'I'm sorry, boss – it's possible we've found Ash. We need someone to help us with identification.' Another pause.

It felt as if a void had opened up inside her. 'Are you sure?' she said. 'You met him, Finn, you know what he looks like.'

'We're pretty certain, just need confirmation. I'll meet you there; drive safely.'

FORTY MINUTES later she parked easily enough near the mortuary, a slab of concrete with small, high windows like slitted eyes. She must have driven past it a hundred times and not cared about what happened inside. Finn met her in reception and as they moved further into the building, the smell reminded her of the laboratories in Mill Hill, sweet and acrid at the same time. Unnatural.

She'd imagined something different, something more respectful. A chapel of rest, perhaps, a body prepared for public consumption and public grief, but this was the bureaucracy of death with corridors of finished lives waiting to be archived. They brought the body to her on a trolley.

'Are you sure you're okay with this?' asked Finn. 'It's one thing with strangers, but someone you know...' His voice trailed into silence.

'Whatever it takes. And you called me, remember? Let me see him.'

Finn hesitated. 'They've tidied him up a bit, but the body was in the water for a while – I'm just saying.' They pulled the covering back from his face and she looked down at her ex-lover, not that love had ever been part of the equation. His once-olive skin was crisscrossed with marks like the raking of nails, and part of the top lip was missing, a soft, ragged fading of the flesh.

'Where was he, exactly?' she asked, speaking through cotton wool.

'On the mud flats in the main estuary. We don't know if the body was carried down by the river or washed in by the sea. The post-mortem may give us more of a clue as to where he went in; there was a bit of damage so he probably got knocked about in the water – rocks, that kind of thing.'

The body in front of her had been Ash once, but now it was nothing. She tried to feel something for him, something for the old days, but the only sensation was numbness, as if she were almost as dead as the flesh on the trolley. She nodded at Finn, watched as they covered the face and wheeled the body away.

'Thanks,' she said, and she meant it. Seeing the body

had made it real. There was no mistake; Ash really had gone. 'When did it happen?'

'Yesterday, from what we can tell,' said Finn. 'It must have happened soon after he left your place, and there was no sign of violence in case you were wondering. I'm betting on suicide. Coming to see you was probably a last act of desperation; he must have known we'd catch up with him in the end.'

Pav shook her head; this felt wrong in so many ways. 'I still don't understand how he could have become so mixed up in this. Ash was weak, he was...'

He was what – a nearly man who walked a fine line and fell the wrong way? Perhaps she should have noticed the changes sooner, but they'd crept upon Ash like an insidious illness that hobbled and hunched by imperceptible degrees, until there was no trace left of the original person. Once, maybe, she could have saved him, but now it would always be too late.

She shrugged the memories away. As Michael had said, why look back on things you can't change?

'We'll need a DNA analysis,' she said, 'to see if there are any links to the bodies.'

They walked back outside and stood in the soft drizzle; the air smelled of mud from the distant estuary, and a pair of seagulls circled overhead, shouting into the breeze.

'You should take some time to yourself,' said Finn. 'This can't have been the easiest of days.'

'You'll be telling me I need a welfare officer next.'

'I value my health more than that. Seriously, boss; whatever happened between you, whatever made you kick him out, you can't pretend the past never happened. I know you're tough, but he used to be your partner.'

' "Used to be" being the operative words. He was one of

the worst mistakes of my life, and one I don't intend to make again. I would never have wished this on him, but in the end, he was responsible for the choices he made. Just like we all are.'

'It's not just Ash,' said Finn, slowly. 'I have a nasty feeling you're in someone's sights. The murder of your neighbour, the man on the village green, Ash turning up like that. Doesn't feel right.'

'I'll be careful.' But it wasn't right. Someone, some-where, was sending her a message.

SHE WAS HALFWAY home when a call came in from the tech who'd been looking at the files they retrieved from Ash. 'I reconstructed some of the files he thought he'd deleted. Wish I hadn't if I'm honest. But there's one you need to know about. The girl who ran away after you got her that placement? I ran facial recognition, as per, and she's in one of the videos.'

'Are you sure?'

'One hundred per cent. I double checked; it's Eva. I'm really sorry she didn't make it. I guess whoever she was running from caught up with her again.'

SHE WAITED until she was home to make the courtesy call to Bella. It was still hard to credit that the woman had taken Eva out in public, less than twenty-four hours after arriving at The Swallows, and then been careless enough to let her run off again. All the same, it would be far better to hear the bad news from a friend, than discover what happened on the grapevine. Another breach of the rules, but what the hell?

She let the other woman prattle on for a few moments, vaguely hearing an invitation to dinner. 'Pav, are you okay? The nineteenth, I asked if you are free in the evening. If my food is so bad, you must not be afraid to tell me.'

'It's not that.' She paused, wishing she'd taken the time to choose the right words. 'I'm sorry, Bella, but it's Eva. She's dead.' She'd expected some reaction, but not this silence. 'Bella – are you there? Whoever was keeping Eva before must have caught up with her. We have it on a video, her being murdered.'

Bella was breathing at the other end of the line, but not speaking.

'We retrieved some images, some videos,' Pav said. 'I've seen what they did to her.'

At last, there was a reaction from the other woman. 'That poor, poor girl. I shall never forgive myself.'

'She ran off, Bella, her choice. It isn't as if you delivered her back to the bastards who were using her. And there's something else. I think... I think Ash was involved.'

'Ash? Why do you say this?'

'I can't go into the details, sorry. But there's been another incident; someone murdered my neighbour in her own home. Ash was there at around the same time, and the police found evidence at his apartment.'

'Evidence? What, like a gun or a knife?'

'No, but he's been involved in some very unpleasant activities. Enough to put him away for a long time.'

'I don't believe this. Ash? The way you always described him, he had no balls for such a thing.'

'That's what I thought until he came to my house yesterday and took a knife to me. The police are still looking for him.'

'Not Ash, no.' Pav could almost see the head shaking.

'This must be the work of someone else. I know it. If I meet these people, I will make them pay, I swear. Listen, I shall go now. You have things to do, but I shall call you later and we shall talk more. Have strength, my friend.'

———

WHILE SHE WAS SPEAKING to Bella, Gus tried to contact her, then sent a text asking her to get back to him. He answered within a couple of rings. 'It's for your own good, Pav. You're on sick leave, effective immediately, and you'd do the same if you were in my shoes, lassie. You're too close, I need someone objective. Finn will hold the reins for you, insulate you. Go for a run, eat chocolate, watch Oprah, do whatever you do to relax. If anything happens, we'll let you know.'

CHAPTER
NINETEEN

In her heart she knew Gus was right, but it didn't help now, sitting in her desecrated house and feeling empty. Even her mobile was complaining, a low soulful grizzle from her bag, and she plugged it in to recharge next to the TV. She looked around the small living room as if seeing it for the first time. It seemed incomprehensible that Ash had been here only yesterday, begging for help. But no matter what he was running from, he wasn't the type to kill himself; too selfish, for a start. And now he was just another unexplained mystery to add to the others, and she was off the case. Helpless.

Home was supposed to be a place of safety, but now it felt more like a cage. She would have to move away, she realised that now. From the village, maybe, but from the cottage for sure. She'd become an intruder in her own home. She thought back on what Gus had said when he condemned her to being an observer, not a participant. Watch daytime TV? A hard no to that one. Or go for a run; definitely a more attractive option. She changed into joggers, trainers and a tee shirt, and grabbed a couple of notes from her bag; an old habit, never to go out without cash, one of Pa's exhortations that she'd never shaken off.

She paused by the back door, having second thoughts. A run would still feel like staying on home turf, even if she took a different route from her usual circuit. No, she wanted to leave the cottage and the village behind for a while, and even if she was off the case, no-one could stop her from doing a drive-by of the house in Uskmouth where Eva had been imprisoned. The place would be deserted now, after the raid, but just being back at the location might spark an idea. It was better than accepting defeat.

FORTY MINUTES later she cruised slowly towards the house, hoping for a space to park. It looked the same as on the morning of the raid, except for the curtains in the upstairs windows that someone had pulled back. And then she braked suddenly, lucky that no-one was behind her. She'd seen something, a moving shadow in the house. Someone was there. Police? No, they'd have finished their searches long since. Surely Defrim's employers weren't setting up shop there again? Whatever. Whoever was in there would be up to no good, and it was her job to do something about it, whether or not Gus liked it.

She pulled in to a spot a couple of hundred metres down the street; time to call this in and get some backup. She reached into her bag for her phone, then swore to herself as she remembered it was still sitting by the TV at home, recharging. Definitely not thinking straight; that phone was usually like a fifth limb. She checked her side mirror; the house was just visible and the front door opened as she watched. A man came out, head down, climbed into a black Merc that had been parked outside, and drove off in the opposite direction. A man she recognised; bullet head, bulldog build, and although she couldn't see from where she was, he probably had a chunk of ear missing, too. Thank God he hadn't looked down the street and seen her car, which stuck out here like a parrot in a flock of sparrows.

This time, he wouldn't get away from her. The Merc had driven off in the opposite direction, and after a five-point turn, she set off in pursuit. At the end of the street, she had to make a call - left or right. There was no time to deliberate, so left it was. She struck lucky; despite the delay, the Merc was only a few cars in front of her, held up in a small queue behind a campervan with German plates that seemed completely out of place in the urban streets. Without a phone to mobilise the cavalry, all she could do was track him at a distance; tailing a suspect 101. From time to time he nearly gave her the slip, but her karma account seemed, unusually, to be in credit and she always found him again. The luck ran out, as per, when a small van insinuated itself in front of her and then decided to park in a space at least six inches too short. By the time she was moving again the Merc had disappeared.

She gradually left behind the narrow streets of terraces and semis, and cruised slowly past the late-Victorian villas fronted by small gardens and large cars. One bell per house here, not an area she knew too well. When she was still with the regular police, most of her work had been with people who'd grown up in the estates of east London, or the tightly packed streets closer to the docks in Uskmouth. This was different; the kids around here would no more go to a state school than their parents would spend Saturday nights playing bingo.

After fifteen minutes, she was ready to give in. She needed to make that call, but phone boxes had gone the way of the dinosaurs long since. She turned the last corner, about to put on speed and head for the motorway, and saw the black Mercedes. It was parked outside a large corner house, three storeys high, with a faux-chateau turret.

She pulled onto the side of the road. The driver might have thought that he'd lost her, always assuming he knew she was following. And now what? For all she knew, this wasn't even the right house; he could have parked his car in the nearest space and gone anywhere. But there was no point in wondering when all she had to do was look for herself. A few minutes, she told herself, enough to make sure, and then she'd find a phone.

She turned the car and drove around the block, parking in the side street next to the high wooden fence that ran the length of the rear garden. Towards the far end of the fence, at least a hundred feet from the back of the house, a branch from one of the trees was hanging over into the street. She wasn't that heavy; if the branch could hold her weight, she could use it to pull herself up and get over the fence into the back garden. On balance, it was a good thing Finn wasn't around. Although he tried, the protective male instinct had a tendency to intrude when it wasn't needed, which was always. Add in his annoying penchant for following rules... no, this was a one-woman job. A quick recce, to see if the place was worth a better look, and she'd be back in the Porsche and heading home.

She waited in the car until she was sure the streets were clear and then ran down towards the branch. After a couple of exploratory tugs, it seemed secure enough. She braced her feet against the fence, then walked herself up by using the branch as a support. She glanced over the top. The garden seemed deserted from what she could see through the overgrown shrubs, so she jumped down, avoiding a patch of ancient raspberry canes, and stayed in a crouch. So far, so lucky.

There was another tree further back with lower branches; it would be easy enough to use that as a ladder to get herself back out onto the street when she needed to. All that training had come in useful after all. She stayed in the crouch for a couple more minutes, peering through the leaves of some variegated bush, but couldn't make out any movement. Apart from the occasional car passing and a blackbird singing overhead, no sound appeared to be coming from the house; no voices, no radio. Maybe this was the wrong place after all. One thing was for sure, though – whoever owned this place wasn't a fan of garden makeovers. But today the neglect could work to her advantage.

With a little care, staying low, she made her way around the edge of the garden until she reached the stone patio outside the French windows. A wooden bird table had toppled onto its side, cushioned by the long grass. Another couple of feeders, hanging from the branch of a lilac tree, were empty and covered in mouldy white droppings. The place looked abandoned, as if some distressed gentle-woman had grown old here, widowed and abandoned by her children, unable to keep the place going. The paintwork on the back windows was scarred and flaking, and the putty around the bottom of one of the French windows had fallen away, leaving the soft wood to rot and crumble. Along the back wall of the house, a line of giant flowerpots was overflowing with dandelions, and the plastic downpipe at the corner had fallen away from the gutter, its open end pointing vacantly at the sky like an over-long mortar.

The windows in the two top stories were blind, with thin curtains pulled tight. From here, it looked like a cheap lodging house and she wasn't sure if she felt relief or disappointment. It didn't seem as if anyone lived here now, noone who would match the neighbourhood, but it wouldn't hurt to look inside. Still in a half crouch, she scuttled to the back wall of the house, and then sidled across to the French windows and peered through into the shadow of the room. As her eyes adjusted, she made out a desk, a couple of chairs, and a metal filing cabinet in the far corner – not exactly old lady furniture, but nothing sinister.

On the other side of the patio, an outhouse ran out from the main building. An old wash house, perhaps, from a time when places like this had servants for the dirty work? She tried the door; it swung open easily into a narrow room with a concrete floor, and the shelves around the walls were full of faded tins and jars. At the far end, an antique lawnmower nestled against a selection of spades and forks covered with cobwebs. She was right; no-one had touched the garden in years. On the opposite wall adjoining the house, another narrow door stood slightly ajar. She pulled it open, slowly. There was nothing inside but a flight of stairs going down into the gloom, the entrance to a cellar. If only she hadn't left her mobile behind; with the torch on her phone, she could have gone down to investigate, but on first sight nothing seemed awry. And this was, after all, just an initial recce. Off the books.

She was about to go back into the garden when she heard a sound from outside, like squeaking wheels making their way across the patio. Shit and double shit. There was nowhere to hide in this narrow room, only the cellar, but now she had no choice. She pulled open the narrow door again, but with only one foot on the first step, she sensed movement below; someone was already down there and about to climb up.

She lunged towards the outside door but before she reached it someone was standing there, holding the handle of a trolley piled with cardboard boxes, the same man who'd photographed her outside the school on the day she found Mira and the bodies. There was no surprise on his pinched face, just an unnaturally white smile under the clipped moustache.

'How delightful to see you, Detective Inspector, although not unexpected. But sneaking around like this, I think this is not very professional for a lady of your high standing. And how very uncomfortable you must be in these spartan accommodations – please, come into the house. I insist.'

As if she had a choice. She walked between them, back into the garden and through the French windows, into the study. The smaller man perched on the edge of the desk, looking at her quizzically.

'I told my colleagues that you were resourceful, but you have excelled yourself. My congratulations on finding us. Mitchell saw you outside the house we used for some of our activities - you really should choose a less noticeable car. He worried that he had been too successful in getting away from you, but I knew better. Tenacity, a wonderful trait in a woman. The quarry hunts the hunter; you English, you always have to be different.'

He slid off the desk and studied her as if she were some slave up for auction. 'You are better looking than I remembered; some of our customers prefer experience to youth, and that charming scar on your face adds just a hint of spice. How old are you – thirty-one, thirty-two? Perhaps a little older, but you hide it well. I am an excellent judge, no? Practice makes perfect, that is one of your sayings, I believe. But before we plan your future, I need some information.' He took a tissue from the box on the desk and dabbed at the side of his mouth, as if he'd just finished a satisfying meal. 'The girl, Mira, she belongs to me and I need to get her back. No, no protests, please. We are not negotiating.'

Recriminations could come later, Pav told herself. Right now, she just needed to stay alive. 'Even if I wanted to, I couldn't help you,' she said. 'I don't know where she is.'

The smile didn't shift. 'A good opening gambit and I expected nothing less. But, unfortunately, our time is limited and there is no time for a long game. You have brought this sadness upon yourself, you understand, with your pride in your own abilities and your arrogance. I understand, I see into your mind.'

'If you're that fucking clever, find out where she is for yourself.'

The carpet burned the skin of her cheek as she fell, feeling sick from the punch to her kidneys. Breathing was hard enough now, let alone talking.

'It is in my gift to make things hard or easy for you,' said the man at the desk. 'A cliché used by every interrogator, but true nonetheless. And you will tell us what you know, that is my promise. Someone else questioned my methods today, and I will not have you make me a liar.'

As the second man hauled her upright, Pav tensed, waiting for another punch, but the sound of the front door-bell interrupted them.

The little man checked his watch and frowned. 'Everyone is early today, no sense of courtesy; do they have no understanding? I say to them, every time, no consignments until after dark, but I am surrounded by fools.' He nodded at the other man. 'It is impossible for her to stay here, Mitchell. Wait until tonight, then take her to the river.'

The bodybuilder spoke for the first time, ignoring Pav. 'We shouldn't be using that place. It's too dangerous.'

'Of course it is too dangerous! But now that the school has been compromised, we need to use the old site again, at least until we find somewhere more permanent.'

Was this what they'd done with Ash, taken him to the river? Whatever they were talking about, it didn't sound as if she had much future, and if that was the case, what did she have to lose? With the little man already halfway across the room to the door, she made a dash for the French windows, betting on her speed against Mitchell's strength. But she needn't have bothered. She managed a couple of steps, no more, and then something hit her from behind and the world had turned black before she hit the floor.

CHAPTER
TWENTY

Had night fallen while she was unconscious? Her eyes gradually became accustomed to the darkness as she noticed slivers of light creeping in through the edges of the windows. Badly fitting shutters outside, probably, loose enough for her to make out some details in the room. The headache was back with a vengeance. She tried to move, then realised that they'd fastened her hands behind her back, probably with the same tape they'd used on her ankles. And across her mouth.

She managed to sidewind her way across the floor until she reached the nearest wall and levered herself into a sitting position. This was no ordinary house, that much was obvious. The walls were fabricated from stained and slatted wood, and there was no ceiling between her and the pitched roof. Some kind of hut, then; too big for a garden shed – a summerhouse, perhaps? The few tattered, peeling posters on the back wall were covered with faded diagrams of various fish, and then Pav realised where she was. Years ago, soon after he moved down from Edinburgh, Pa had joined a fishing club. At weekends, three or four of the guys would rent a fisherman's hut for the day. Most of the places they used were set back a few yards from the river, at the edge of the woods; somewhere for the lads to stow their gear, eat their sandwiches, and drink their beer. He'd taken her once for a bit of father-daughter bonding, but spending a day watching nothing happen had never been her idea of a good time.

Maybe this wasn't the same hut, but it was similar. The small wooden table and a couple of chairs, the grimy rug on the floor with a pattern that could be anything. One thing was different, though; the smell. She couldn't remember if Pa and his friends ever caught a fish, but this place stank like the hold of a Grimsby trawler on a hot, airless day.

She only had one thing on her mind right now, to rip the tape away from her mouth so that she could suck some air into her lungs – even this miasma – and for that she needed to free her hands. Looking down at her ankles, she saw they'd used silver duct tape. Cheap and effective. She tried flexing her wrists, hoping to stretch the tape, but it was wrapped too tightly.

Lying on the floor wouldn't solve anything. With her back to the wall and using it as a support, she levered herself to her feet. Now she needed something to help her cut through the tape, but the hut was almost empty. The table and chairs were no use and there was nothing else; no cupboards, no tools.

No matter. She started in one corner, taking in a section of the hut at a time, aiming to exhaust every possibility before moving on. Focus, she told herself, take control. Now that her eyes had adjusted, she noticed the head of a screw sticking out from the wall, just above the highest poster. Walking was impossible, but with a series of small, balanced hops, she worked her way round until she was standing underneath the poster. The screw was higher than the top of her head, and there was no way she could get her wrists that high. Now she was this close, though, nothing was going to beat her.

She hopped over to the small table and managed – inch by inch – to push it across the rug until it was underneath the poster. Now all she had to do was clamber onto the table somehow, stand upright and use the screw head as a blade to cut through the tape. Either that, or die of asphyxiation.

Getting onto the table was easier than she'd thought, although from the way it began to creak she wondered if it would hold her weight. It shifted slightly, and she struggled to keep her balance as she pushed herself against the wall until she was standing upright again, but two and a half feet taller than before. She could feel the screw now, pressing into her left shoulder blade and she bent forward, lifted her arms behind her back as far as they would go, and started to saw away. The screw couldn't have been more than a quarter of an inch out of the wall, and she kept missing the tape and catching her skin. Her wrists were soon sticky with blood, but after the first couple of minutes, the first sharp pains retreated into a dull soreness that muted the individual cuts. And then she felt something give, a slight movement; at last that damned tape was beginning to fray. Adrenaline was her friend, masking any pain, until a last frantic attack on the screw head succeeded and her hands were free.

The muscles in her shoulders and chest were burning, and it was all she could do to keep her breathing even. She looked at her wrists for the first time – a mess, for sure, but as far as she could see the cuts were superficial. And what did that matter now that she could rip the tape off her lips and gulp in air?

Freeing her ankles was easier; once the feeling was back into her fingers, she peeled the tape away, layer by layer, until her legs could move freely again. Slowly and carefully, conscious of muscles that were as hard as rocks and joints injected with superglue, she climbed down from the table and forced her body into a few warm-up stretches. Part one completed. At least now she could move and breathe, but she still had to break out of this prison. She had no idea how long she'd been in the hut; they'd taken her watch. Long enough, though, for them to move her from a house in the middle of town to a hut by the river, if that's where she was. And unless she was mistaken, it was finally getting dark outside.

She tried to remember what had happened, how she'd ended up here. The screw-up at the house in Uskmouth, of course, then the front doorbell ringing and that small blonde bastard telling Lurch to take her to the river. After that, nothing until she woke up.

She checked her pockets for anything that might help, but all she found was the handful of papers she'd scooped from her bag earlier before the aborted run; the fragments of a three-week old tissue, a couple of crumpled five-pound notes and the half-receipt with Michael's number scribbled in green ink. Not much use to her now, unless she could make an origami escape kit.

Not that it mattered. They wouldn't leave her here for long. She tried the door, just in case, but it was locked tight, and if it was anything like Pa's hut there would be a padlock on the outside to keep out the riffraff in the close season. The windows were useless. As well as external shutters, the glass had been reinforced with wire mesh. She tried to smash one of them with a chair which fell to pieces in her hands while the window barely trembled. She tried the door again, using her shoulder, but the shock jarred her head so badly that for a moment she thought she was going to lose consciousness again.

The smell had insinuated itself into her senses. She'd forgotten about it while she was working on her wrists, but now it was inescapable. Something, somewhere, was rotting, but she couldn't see what. Maybe something outside the hut? Perhaps, but her senses told her that the source of the stench was closer. Inside. With her. She crept around the room, sniffing every couple of seconds, and then isolated the strongest hit in one corner, at the back of the hut where the table had been standing before she moved it.

She couldn't see anything obvious at first, but then she bent down and the smell almost overpowered her, a sweet mixture of rotting meat and vomit. The edge of the carpet had rucked up when she moved the table, and now that she was close to the floor she saw what looked like the edge of a trapdoor. Maybe there was a cellar, although much good that would do her. Strange, though. Who built cellars in fishermen's huts? And she needed to get out, not find somewhere to hide. On the other hand, maybe there was something down there she could use to help her escape. She pulled back the rug, levered open the trapdoor and looked down into the source of the sickly stench.

Whoever dug the cellar hadn't been an expert at house conversion; a short ladder dropped into the darkness on one side with a torch hanging from a rusty hook beside it; one bonus point – at least now she had light for when it got properly dark, and a weapon of sorts. It probably wouldn't be much use against whoever had put her there, but a psychological prop was better than nothing. She turned the torch on, glad to find that the batteries weren't dead even if the beam wasn't exactly a searchlight. A tunnel led from the bottom of the hole for as far as she could see, but the whole construction looked raw and ramshackle, like some mediaeval mineshaft. On the positive side, a tunnel rather than a cellar was good news; cellars went nowhere, tunnels did. If you were lucky.

She took the ladder carefully, feeling as if she was climbing into her grave; the entrance to the tunnel was less than four feet high and she was forced to crouch close to the ground. The smell of rotting meat mingled with the scent of damp clay as she played the torch beam onto the floor of the tunnel, and then wished she hadn't. Seeing Ash in the mortuary had been one thing, but the bodies of three teenage girls, laid end to end in the tunnel, was something else. She turned away for a second and then looked back; one of them was naked, the other two were still dressed, all three of them had started to decompose. In the torchlight, the bare skin was mottled; it took a few moments before she realised that the body in the middle was missing its head, and the naked body furthest from her had swollen in some bizarre parody of a pregnancy. She found a tissue in the pocket of her joggers and held it over her nose and mouth, but nothing could stop her breathing in this scent of death.

Now she understood what the man had meant, back at the house. This must be where they'd brought the bodies before they started using the incinerator in the school basement. But there were only three, and they couldn't have been here that long. If there were others, where were they now? The tunnel stretched on until it was lost in darkness. As far as she could see, the rest of it was empty, but it had to lead somewhere. These poor souls were long past any help that she could give, and if she stayed here for much longer she'd be joining them. She did her best to sidle past without touching, still in a half crouch, and it was only as she reached the third body, the naked girl, that she recognised the bloated moon-face as Eva's.

'Oh Jesus!' the sound of her own voice surprised her, forcing her on. The yellow torch beam barely reached twenty feet in front; for all she knew, the tunnel might go on for miles. The surfaces were mostly red, raw clay with rough wooden supports at intervals; in a couple of places, the walls had crumbled slightly in small landslips, and a hundred metres further down one of the roof props had fallen away completely. This had been dug out quickly, with no thought for permanence.

As she moved forward, her shoulder brushed against the roof and a clump of the earth fell onto the ground behind her. She stopped, listening for the sound of any other movement. For all she knew, the vibrations of her steps were about to set off a collapse and at any moment now she'd be lying there with damp clay in her mouth and her nostrils, instead of air. Like the boy in the woods.

She started shuffling forward again, convinced that the roof of the tunnel was getting lower the further in she travelled. Her shoulders and thighs were aching from the constant crouch and then, almost without noticing, she reached the end. In front of her was another ladder, fixed to the end of the tunnel, although this one was around three times the height of the one she'd come down at the other end. She shone the torch onto the bottom of another trap-door, and tried to work out how far she'd walked – a quarter of a mile, maybe, but in those conditions who could judge? Not that it mattered. There weren't many choices left.

She looped the torch over her wrist, climbed the ladder and pushed at the trapdoor, but it seemed stuck fast. She tried again and then rested, hanging on to the ladder. Perhaps it was padlocked shut, or covered with a heavy piece of furniture. For all she knew, the trapdoor might open into another hut with people at the top waiting for her, but even that would be better than staying in a dark tunnel with three rotting corpses. She climbed another couple of rungs until her shoulder rested against the trapdoor, and then pushed again, using all her strength. This time it moved slightly; another shove and there was enough of a gap for her to get her fingers around the edge of the door and push it to one side.

Immediately something cold and damp fell onto her face and she nearly lost her grip on the ladder until she realised it was wet leaf mould and earth.

She clambered out into a small clearing surrounded by trees; this had to be the woodland running back from the river. That would fit, the tunnel leading away from the hut and the water into the slope behind. And she'd been right about the time; the sun had long since gone down, leaving a pale orange afterglow in the sky. The trees were little more than silhouettes and the undergrowth had dissolved into shadows, but none of that mattered; she was free.

The trapdoor had been set into a wooden frame and hidden by a covering of leaves. She could see why pushing it open had been so difficult; the rotting trunk of a small, fallen tree had rolled away to one side as she pushed the door open. There was something else a short distance away; a pit lined with stone and protected by wooden railings. She'd seen these constructions before, dotted about in the woods behind her cottage; old lime kilns. She remembered finding one with Jess on one of their walks. '*You want to keep away from those,'* she'd said. *'When people died in the plague they were thrown into grave pits and sprinkled with quicklime to decompose the bodies and keep disease at bay. Nasty stuff.'*

As she looked into the kiln, so handily close to the end of the tunnel, Pav realised what might have happened to the other bodies. The estuary was just visible through the trees – at least a mile wide at this point – so at a rough guess she was five miles, give or take, from Uskmouth. The slope behind her rose in a steep mixture of trees and rocky outcrops made for birds and animals, not people. This wasn't natural walking country – there were prettier woods further upriver in tourist territory. And fishermen stuck close to the water, so any number of bodies could be hidden up here in shallow pits, quicklime or no; the likelihood of them being found was close to zero. With the tunnel hidden, there would be no giveaway tracks leading up from the hut; she was probably standing in the middle of a graveyard.

She kicked tentatively at the layers of dead leaves, scraping them away from the surface of the earth, then moved a few feet further on and tried again. She couldn't leave until she was sure. After a few minutes, she found a line, a border; packed earth on one side, loose on the other. She used a large stick to dig, gently at first and then with more effort until, with a shiver of disgust, she felt the stick catch on something. Like an archaeologist, she knelt closer, wielding the tip of the stick like a surgeon's instrument, flicking aside small lumps of clay and clods of humus. Gradually, millimetre by millimetre, the shape of a hand emerged. She stopped and sat back on her heels. There was no need to dig further. If she got out of this alive, there would be time enough to come back with a team to excavate the dead. For now, she used her feet to cover the traces of her excavation with the earth and leaves that she'd scraped away. Someone, she promised herself, was going to pay.

That was for the future. Surrounded by death, there was only one thing to do now; push on up the slope and away from the hut and the track that led to it, away from this grave pit. As she picked her way across the piles of leaves and broken branches, a half-remembered line played through her mind – *tread softly, because you tread on my dreams*.

More like nightmares.

CHAPTER
TWENTY-ONE

She moved through the undergrowth as quickly as possible, not sure how much of a lead she had, but the headache was getting worse and at one point she stopped to throw up a thin, yellow bile over a pile of leaves. Her memory of being at the house in Uskmouth was foggy, and she recognised the signs; they'd drugged her, for sure, getting her to take roofies or GHB. The adrenaline hit from escaping the hut was already dissipating, and she felt an almost irresistible urge to lie on a mattress of leaves and close her eyes. Bad idea; that would be a postponement at best, more likely a speedy recapture.

She had to move quickly; the men from the house might have planned to leave her in the hut overnight, but if not, someone could be coming down the track now. Once he was inside the hut, he'd see immediately what had happened. No crawling through a tunnel for him, he'd come straight to the graveyard in the woods. Mitchell, probably, looking for revenge.

At first she used the torch, before realising that the beam might give her away. Damned brain, definitely working on little more than standby power. And she needed both hands to help her climb the steeper parts of the slope through the woods; the torch had already become more of a hindrance than a help. She left it in a crevice of rock, covered with leaves in case any pursuers should find it and guess which direction she'd taken. Ridiculous, of course – she must have been leaving a trail you could see from space. As for direction, she had no idea where she was going, only what she was running from.

The cuts on her wrists were aching now, and the wound from Ash's knife had re-opened. Blood mingled with dirt as she scrabbled her way up one of the steeper sections of damp, slippery earth, and as she grabbed the trunk of a sapling to help pull herself along it snapped off in her hand and she tumbled backwards, rolling twenty feet down the slope. One of the bigger trees broke her fall, and she lay on her back for a few moments, unable to move; a rock or a root had dug into her kidneys on the way down, just where Lurch had punched her earlier, and it felt as if someone had stuck a knife through her side. Nothing broken though, just a few more bruises and cuts, and she was getting used to those. At least there were no sounds of of a search party coming through the trees. Whatever noise she'd made in her fall had been heard by her and the night animals, no-one else.

Her sense of time was still awry, but she guessed it must have been an hour or more since she'd come out of the tunnel. The slope eventually levelled off, and she reached the edge of the trees. The ground fell away in front of her on the other side of the ridge; this time the panorama was of moonlit fields and hedges, and in the distance the orange glow of Uskmouth lightened the sky. Still no sign of a road.

She had another problem. Until now, she'd benefited

from the cover of the trees, but the gibbous moon would give more than enough light for anyone to see her if she scurried across the middle of an empty field like a frightened rabbit.

She looked out across the patterned countryside, trying to think clearly. She was tired. God alone knew what she looked like; the moonlight showed tracksuit bottoms stained with mud and leaf mould, with a tear just below her left knee, damp with blood. That would explain the limp.

She forced herself to focus on her options. Follow the line of trees either left or right - more cover but in the wrong direction - or go straight towards the distant town, cutting across the fields. Risky, but that was what her heart told her to do; get as much space as possible between her and the hut. Stay low, by the hedges, and she should be okay.

Despite the exercise, she was shivering uncontrollably, still wearing the joggers and tee-shirt. As days went, this had been a doozy, and the future wasn't looking especially bright. With a combination of stress, drugs and nothing to eat since breakfast, she knew her energy levels were falling dangerously low as she dropped down towards the open countryside.

At least Uskmouth was a waypoint in the distance; she lost count of the number of times she was forced to change direction, trying to find a gate or stile in the hedges around the fields. If it hadn't been for the glow in the sky, she might easily have found herself back in the woods.

It wasn't only hunger and tiredness making her feel cold. The wind had started to blow more strongly from the north, and outriders from a bank of dark cloud were already dimming the moon. Ten minutes later the rain began, cold and heavy, every drop seeping through her clothes to the skin.

Something inside her head was trying to prise the two halves of her brain apart, and there was a strange taste at the back of her mouth. She was finding it harder to think clearly, and she voiced her thoughts in a subdued, private muttering until she reached a final gate at the edge of a field and found herself on a road. A narrow road, for sure, little more than a country lane, but it was surfaced with tarmac, not earth. For the first time since she escaped from the hut, she felt as though she was on her way home.

She walked a mile at least before the first car passed her, ignoring her frantic waving for it to stop. And then she realised; for all she knew, this could be the road towards the fishermen's hut. The next car might be people searching for her, and this time she'd have nowhere to hide. Whatever drugs they'd given her were still practising their malign magic in her brain, and though a double espresso might knock her back on track, there was fat chance of one here. She'd just have to focus; take it slow, think before acting.

She remembered passing a stile into one of the fields a couple of hundred metres back, just after a bend in the road. She started to half jog, half shamble back, staying close to the hedge for the illusion of safety. What other options did she have?

Almost at the stile, and then she heard an engine. She broke into the semblance of a run, knowing that she wouldn't make it to the opening in time. Then, like Sancho Panza on a motorised donkey, a man on a moped wobbled round the bend towards her. If this was one of her pursuers, they'd definitely changed their style. She walked out into the middle of the road as the moped approached, trying to look more like a damsel in distress than a mad woman, and forced him to stop.

The boy under the helmet was a frightened mouse, seventeen years old at best, with L-plates that looked like permanent fixtures. Pav reached over and turned off the engine; he seemed spooked enough already and she didn't want him panicking and making a dash for freedom. At first she thought of asking for a lift, but there was no way the machine could carry the two of them. Steal the bike? A possibility, but she wasn't on her best form and the boy might have hidden strengths. Unlikely, but still.

The headache was so bad now that she was finding it hard to think clearly, but the boy looked increasingly edgy, and so she fumbled a story about being dumped out of the car by her boyfriend after an argument. 'He drove off with my bag, my phone – everything,' she said. It wasn't hard to be convincing, the desperation in her voice was genuine. 'I need to make a phone call, get a friend to pick me up. If I could use your mobile, please, just one call...'

Her first thought was Finn, but the phone was answered by a voice she didn't recognise; who needed to remember phone numbers these days? She tried again with the same result, and then called her office, but that was the wrong number too. It was no good, everything seemed scrambled in her brain. There was always 999, of course, she couldn't get that wrong. But for a senior ROCU officer to need rescuing by the local police would be something she'd never live down, not to mention the ammunition it would give the Chief Constable in his fight to keep ROCU out of his hair. Gus would have her transfer signed in a heartbeat, especially as she was off the case.

All she wanted right now was a friendly face, and then

she remembered the torn piece of paper with the number that Michael had scribbled – was that only last night?

The boy on the bike was fidgeting. 'I gotta be getting on, me Mam'll have tea waiting. She'll have me bollocks for breakfast if I'm late back.'

'One more call, promise – if your Mam says anything you can tell her it was my fault.'

From the look on his face, that wasn't a helpful suggestion. Pav punched Michael's number carefully, using the light of the boy's headlamp to read by and checking after every digit, saying a prayer just in case.

Michael answered so quickly, he must have been holding his phone. 'Pav? Sorry, I didn't think it was you – your name didn't come up. Have you changed your number?' She'd caught him at a bad time; he sounded like a stranger, distant.

'Please Michael, just listen to me. Something's happened – I can't explain right now – I need you to pick me up. I'm...'

Fuck! She had no idea where she was other than between the river and Uskmouth. She asked the boy and managed to get enough of an idea to tell Michael. 'Drive slowly,' she said. 'I'll keep out of sight until I see you.'

'Are you sure you're okay?' he said, with a tremor in his voice. 'You sound... strange.'

'Understatement of the year. I'm cold and I'm wet and I'm hungry. Please, Michael, just drive. And be quick.'

As soon as the moped disappeared, Pav climbed over the stile and crouched behind the hedge. At least the rain had blown itself out, but she was soaked and shivering, and the pains in her head and kidneys were spreading. The bandage over the wound from Ash's knife had long since disappeared, ripped away in one of her falls, and her arms were streaked with blood and dirt. Twenty minutes, Michael had said; the only difficulty was judging how much time had passed. A car sped by after a while, but it had to be pushing sixty and anyway, it was too soon for Michael to reach her.

Her body was shutting down. She didn't feel cold anymore, just distant, as if her mind was becoming disconnected. Her body belonged to someone else. She lost herself in a dream about waiting for a train on an empty, wet platform, hearing it pulling slowly into the station, when the sound of a car engine broke through. She crept along to the stile and peered through the bars; an Aygo was crawling along the road at little more than walking pace. Her legs were so stiff that she barely managed to stand in time to wave him down.

'I won't ask what happened,' he said. 'That can wait. You need a bath and some dry clothes.'

'How far are we from home?' she asked, as he settled her into the passenger seat.

'Twenty minutes if I put my foot down, but you should stay with me tonight – I'll sleep on some cushions, you have the bed.'

She tried to protest, but he refused to listen. 'Whatever trouble you're in, you shouldn't be on your own. Not in the state you're in. No arguments, you're coming back with me.'

She realised the car had stopped only when he shook her awake. She recognised the street, part of the old town near the edge of Abertrothy, with a builder's yard opposite. Not somewhere she'd choose to live if she could afford anywhere else; a strange choice for a therapist. Even Detta's cottage would be an improvement. She let him shepherd her up two flights of uncarpeted stairs to a small bedsit; a round table with one leg propped up on a paperback, two chairs with dull orange cushions, and an unmade sofa bed by the window.

Michael rummaged in an open suitcase at the foot of the bed and pulled out a pair of jeans and a sweatshirt.

'I know you'll be swamped, but it's only for tonight.'

At first she thought he was going to watch her undress, but then he coloured and went to the door.

'I'll wait outside – shout when you're finished.'

She should have gone home, but would that have been safer? Perhaps there was no 'home' any more, not for her. Eva, Mira, even Ash – she'd failed them all. At least here she'd be invisible to anyone trying to find her.

She dried herself with a towel that Michael had left, glad of its cheap harshness on her skin, and pulled on the clothes, turning up the sleeves and legs in heavy rolls of fabric. As she finished, the door opened slightly.

'Are you okay? I thought you might have fallen asleep.' He collected her wet clothes from the floor and bundled them into a plastic bag. 'No washing machine, sorry.'

'I need a phone,' she said, 'I have to call someone.'

'You need something to warm you up first.' He came back from the curtained-off kitchenette with a glass of brandy. 'No arguments, drink this.'

She took the glass, lifted it to her lips and then handed it back, untouched. 'I can't. Do you have coffee? Strong, black. And that phone, I really need to call Finn.'

'Finn? You said you didn't have a boyfriend.' He laughed nervously.

'A colleague,' she said. 'he'll know what to do, get the right people involved.'

Michael handed her the glass again. 'I'm sorry Pav. I never had a landline installed, and I left the mobile in my car. Go on, knock this back while I go downstairs – you'll feel much better, I promise. Then I'll make us some coffee.'

Why not? It wasn't as if she was going anywhere, and he looked so worried and nervous that she took the glass and drank the brandy in one gulp. 'Happy now?'

'You stay here – I'll be back in a moment.'

The alcohol filled her body with its sweet vapours and she fell back into the chair. He was right. The dark cloud that enveloped her only a few moments ago had already shredded and blown away. 'I'm going nowhere, my friend. Take all the time you want.'

CHAPTER
TWENTY-TWO

It was a dream she hadn't relived for years. She was flying, a child sitting on someone's shoulders. When she was young, Pa would walk her up and down the garden and she would stretch her arms out and pretend to be a plane. And now she was inside the cabin, flying somewhere, hitting turbulence – air pockets – bouncing her around, making her afraid. And then blurred shapes became sharper, the world settled down, and she recognised where she was.

Please God, she was still asleep. She closed her eyes and tried to find the plane again, but this was no dream. She opened her eyes and looked around the room that she'd seen before, on one of Ash's movies.

She tried to move, but her ankles and wrists were tied; cable ties, this time, not tape that she could cut, pulled so tight they were cutting into her flesh. Perhaps it had all been a dream; the hut, the escape, Michael. Hallucinations, woven from fears and memories; perhaps she'd never left the house in Uskmouth and this was the movie studio.

A door opened and shut somewhere behind her, and

she tensed her muscles. Two sets of footsteps, one sneaker soft, the other tapping the concrete floor with the sound of expensive leather shoes. A hand rested lightly on her shoulder, almost friendly, and she heard the familiar voice of the small blonde man who had kidnapped her earlier.

'What are we going to do with you, Miss McNeil?'

He moved into her line of vision with the taller man, Mitchell, by his side.

'A small piece of information was all we needed,' he said. 'You could have told us how to find Mira, and none of this would have been necessary. Instead, we end up here. I have done my best to protect you, I really have, but I never thought you would be so stubborn.'

The video hadn't prepared her for the smell like a public toilet, all bleach and piss, and the concrete floor around the chair was patterned with dark stains. Scream down here and no one would hear you.

She kept her voice steady. 'People will already be looking for me. You should let me go, make it easier when they catch up with you.'

'No, Miss McNeil, I do not think so. You have no idea what you have interfered with.'

'Surprise me. As far as I'm concerned, you're just another bunch of sad perverts who need culling.'

'Brave words, but if your judgement is always so poor no wonder you are the one strapped into the chair, and I am standing in front of you, free to come and go as I please. I am a success, Miss McNeil, and you are not. I speak four languages fluently, I own property on three continents, the Italian government has given me an award for my charitable work. Is that the description of a sad pervert?' He reached across and stroked her hair. 'You should be flattered that I give up so much time for you. And perhaps I should not be so harsh. I know much about you, whereas you have been forced to make up your own narratives about me. So, in the best traditions of these encounters, let me introduce myself. Dr Lorenzo Bonetti, at your service. I trace my family back to the Lombards in the sixth century, a most distinguished lineage, though I say it myself.' He gave a small, Prussian bow.

'You, a doctor?'

'Clinical psychology, so valuable in this line of work. In my country we take pride in our achievements, unlike you English with your passion for the mediocre. As for my colleague here, I believe that you have already met once or twice. I might almost say that you have developed a taste for him!'

He took a step backwards and before Pav could see what was happening, Mitchell punched her face so hard she wondered if her neck had been broken.

'And now I really must insist,' said Bonetti. 'Mira is our property. She belongs with us, and we want her back. Please tell us where she has been hidden; I so hate unnecessary waste.'

In all this time he had barely stopped smiling, a mouthful of manufactured teeth.

The blood on her face was running down her cheeks like slow lava. 'Why should I tell you anything?' she said. 'There's no way I'm getting out of here. You're planning to kill me like Eva and the others. I know what happens here.'

'This is one of our creative spaces, yes. Functional, but it serves its purpose.' He frowned. 'Killing people is not so easy. What you fail to realise, detective inspector, is that the people we use are dying anyway. We offer them a mercy killing. We turn a negative into a positive, nothing more than good business sense.'

'Eva wasn't dying.'

'We are all dying, Miss McNeil, from the moment we are born. It is because of Eva that you are here today; if she had accepted her fate and not run away, we would all be going about our daily business without a care in the world.'

'And what about the girls you torture? You're mad, you must be – both of you.'

Bonetti frowned again. 'Insanity is a human construction; it is a shame that we do not have more time to share some of my theories on the matter – you might find them interesting. What you call mad, I call the single-minded pursuit of a goal. Which of us is right?'

'You don't think it's madness, raping and torturing and killing for pleasure? And what about that disease? Mira could easily be dead by now and all this has been for nothing.'

'Are the men who run the drugs trade addicted to heroin or cocaine? Of course not. How could they succeed otherwise? Drugs of any kind – I include what you call pornography – are there for the consumers, the bottom of the food chain. I, on the other hand, am at the top. What I do is purely business, not pleasure. As for the sickness...' He shrugged. 'An unfortunate by-product of a trip I made to Vietnam. We decided to widen our product offering to bring in some variety. Young people in the developing world are so compliant, so lacking in unnecessary moral scruples when the right amount of money is on offer. In my line of business, one always has to look for new products and new markets.

'When our young workers started to show symptoms, we called in a medic, one of our clients. He tried all the treatments he could think of, but nothing worked. The disease was beyond his skill, and we were running out of our product. Supply networks are so difficult to run these days, and we did our best, but when the deaths started we couldn't keep up with demand. And then I thought, there must be a way to turn the situation to our advantage. We have a wide range of customers and some of them have, how shall I put it, exotic tastes. Not everyone wants a thirteen-year-old virgin; there are always requests for girls with missing limbs, or boys who are blind – or simply very ill. Some of our customers even pay a premium for the experience – perhaps they like the spice of danger. Who knows?'

She could barely believe what she was hearing. 'You let people pay to have sex with girls who are dying?'

'The world is full of strange desires. There are certain homosexual gentlemen, free of any disease, who deliberately seek unprotected sex with partners who are HIV-positive; barebacking is the term in English, I believe. Who are we to judge their motivations? Supply and demand, Miss McNeil, that is all. Forget your high ideals and your social conscience; money, power, sex – everything else is an illusion.'

He stared at her as if she were a particularly dense schoolchild. 'The world is a cruel place. You think I am a monster, but I am not that different from you. I just see a little more clearly and I am not afraid to take my due. Look at the children you believed you were saving; how many of them were any better than cattle? The lives they led were narrow and squalid. As for these children that we help on their way to everlasting sleep, can you really tell me that the world is not better off without them? When they leave their slums and their villages, they know what is waiting for them. They come here with their eyes open. Whores, Miss McNeil, do not tell me you disagree. They deserve us, and we give them what they really want.'

There was something in his speech that sounded familiar, a memory of another conversation that she couldn't quite place. 'You know nothing about children! How dare you...'

The taller man silenced her with a blow to the face, and this time she tasted blood in her mouth. 'There is only one thing you can say of any value to us,' said Bonetti. 'Would you like me to leave you with Mitchell? Perhaps he might succeed with his fists where I have failed with my words. When he has finished with you, I know someone in the market for clean, Asian girls to work in his establishments in Lagos. Even ones as old as you. The exotic always commands a premium and, as a colleague of mine once said, why waste an asset?'

He walked around the chair, studying her from every angle. 'On the other hand, we could give you one more chance. I have, quite curiously, developed an admiration for you. What do you say, Miss McNeil? If we let you go, will you tell us where you have hidden Mira and promise to keep quiet about everything that happened today?' He sighed. 'No, of course not. You see, it is not so easy. Perhaps you know where the girl is, perhaps not, and even if you gave us information, it could be a lie. No, on balance I am persuaded that we should skin this cat in another way. You will know, Miss McNeil, that more deals are done with kidnappers than ever get reported. Money or information versus a life, an easy decision for pragmatists.'

'You want to ransom me against information about Mira – my people will never agree.'

'For your sake I hope they do, and we shall give them a little incentive.' He looked across at Mitchell. 'Let us prepare her.'

Pav watched them setting up a small video camera on a

stand. Although the room wasn't cold, her whole body had begun to shake again. How did people manage to be heroes when they were about to die?

'Why do this, Bonetti? I would tell you if I knew where Mira was, but I don't know anything. I promise. The local police handled that side of it, not me.'

Bonetti ignored her as he finished adjusting the camera and then nodded at Mitchell, who walked behind her, holding something familiar in his hand. Pav recognised it from one of the videos; a black, plastic collar with a snap clasp on the back and a small black box fixed to the front. Two metal prongs pointed inwards, not sharp, not long – less than a quarter of an inch – but long enough. She struggled, but the straps holding her to the chair were too tight, and then he'd fastened the collar around her neck, the rounded metal prongs pushing into the skin over her throat.

'Such a clever little item,' said Bonetti. 'Did you know that one used to be able to buy them freely off the Internet? People used them to train their dogs – marvellous animals, most amenable to behavioural correction. A shame that we cannot say the same about people.'

Bonetti smiled at her and then pressed a button on the small remote he was holding; she felt as if someone had stabbed her in the neck with a knife made of fire, but the pain was gone in an instant, leaving her gulping for breath like a fish drowning in air.

'We made a few changes,' said Bonetti. 'A much more powerful charge, for a start. Custom batteries, a technological marvel. Of course, they are for when our performers need to move around. For more static shows, like this, we attach the collar to the main electricity supply. I'm sure you understand the advantages that gives us.'

He held up the remote so that she could see it; the box had a dial on the top, and two red buttons. 'I have it set to minimum at the moment. And the two buttons – the top one sends a single charge through the subject. The second – as long as I hold that down, the current will flow.' He threw the remote into the air and caught it, as if it were a toy. 'Death is not guaranteed, but my colleague thinks it merely adds to the fun. Heart attacks, usually, that is what you would find written on a death certificate if we bothered ourselves with such things. Myself, I used to prefer something quicker and cleaner. A knife, for example, so much more elegant. But the customers want their money's worth and who am I to swim against the forces of the market?'

He turned back to the video camera, checked the settings, and she saw a red light flick on above the lens. 'I would suggest that you try not to struggle,' said Bonetti. 'It will not hurt so much that way. But if previous performances are anything to go by, you won't have much choice in the matter.'

And then, as if it would never stop, the flaming knife started cutting into her throat again.

CHAPTER
TWENTY-THREE

He was getting older; they just didn't make hangovers the way they used to. Finn checked the bedside clock – seven thirty in the morning, but it felt as though he'd just gone to bed.

Something had woken him although it wasn't the alarm; he'd remembered to switch that off the night before. His phone, buzzing from the pile of clothes on the chair. He swung himself slowly out of bed and found the phone in the pocket of the trousers he'd worn last night for their anniversary meal.

Sarah was still asleep on her side of the bed, curled and smiling at some private dream, which might or might not have involved her husband. Finn covered her shoulder with the duvet before he went downstairs with the phone. He needed coffee, and better to call from the kitchen if it was work; his mouth tasted as if he'd been French kissing a camel. The champagne hadn't been to blame, nor the couple of bottles of Chablis with the meal. No, he decided, downfall had come riding in with too many pints of bitter in the bar afterwards – he seemed to remember Sarah absolving herself from responsibility at that point – all smoothed down with whisky chasers. The annual Monte Cristo hadn't helped.

He put the kettle on, slumped at the kitchen table, and checked the phone. A missed call from a number he didn't recognise, but no messages. Which was good and bad; nothing gross had happened while he was enjoying himself for the first evening off in weeks, but no breakthroughs either. And still nothing from Pav, despite the message he'd left her yesterday. That had to be a first, she always got back to him. Either he'd blown it big time, or she was blaming him for Gus's decision to put him in charge. Surely she knew she couldn't carry on leading the case, not when she'd become part of it. But as she'd said to him more than once; understanding the cause doesn't cure the symptom.

He tried her again, both mobile and landline. It would be the least of his problems if she swore at him for waking her, but both calls went to voicemail. It was always possible, of course, that she was staying with her parents or a friend, with her mobile switched off. She was officially off the case, after all. And hadn't he nearly done the same thing last night?

He decided against taking a coffee up for Sarah. She had a day off too, no point in breaking into her sweet dreams. He sipped his own mug – too strong – and stirred in a spoonful of sugar. One wouldn't make any difference to his waistline, and what Sarah didn't know wouldn't hurt her.

The coffee started to work, and he took a couple of paracetamol for good measure. No point in suffering any more than he needed to. A month ago, he'd have gone back upstairs and climbed into the bed that had grown cold in the last twenty minutes, but this was today. He must have been kidding himself to think of taking a day off – thinking like a deputy, not a leader. When did Pav ever take a break?

He tried her again - still no answer - and a little bud of disquiet began to unfurl. You thought you knew how someone operated, but that was a delusion. A recent lover's suicide would be enough for most people; add that to everything Pav had been through in the past couple of weeks...

He dressed as quietly as he could, but Sarah opened her eyes as he slipped on his jacket. 'Something's come up, love. I'll call, soon as I can.' He pecked her quickly on the fore-head and ran out to the car. Pav's parents first, he thought. Old people didn't need much sleep, wasn't that what people said?

He took the upper road through the edge of the forest and found the house from memory. Pav's car was notable by its absence, and he was about to knock when the door opened.

'Finn, isn't it?' the old man's voice quavered. 'Is Parvati with you? She doesn't usually come around during the week.' His faded brown eyes blinked weakly in the early morning light.

'Sorry to bother you, Mr McNeil. I wanted a word with her, but she's not at home and her phone's switched off. I wondered if she'd popped round to see you.'

'Not since Barbs had a little excursion on Tuesday, and Parvati helped me look for her. She's a busy woman, Finn, I expect you know that.' He pulled his dressing gown around himself more tightly. 'There's nothing wrong, is there? She doesn't talk much about her job and I know she wouldn't want to worry us, but she's our daughter. She's all we have left.'

Finn forced a smile. 'Nothing's wrong, sir. I wouldn't have bothered you except that I was passing by. If you see her, ask her to give me a call.'

He started back towards Blackbrook, driving too quickly, and barely missed a tractor on a blind corner. When he got to the cottage there was no answer, not that he'd expected one with no sign of her Porsche there either.

He sat in his car, trying to think through the hammering in his skull which painkillers had done nothing to mute. A workaholic, his boss, and being sidelined wouldn't have made any difference. She'd simply take it as licence to go off-piste without needing to write up reports - or play by the rules. But he needed to start somewhere. If she wasn't with her parents, then maybe there was a friend he hadn't heard of. Blackbrook was a small enough village; someone was bound to know, and the pub was a good place to start. He drove round to the main road and knocked up Callum at the Queen Bess, interrupting the bottling up.

'Was she around last night?' Finn asked. 'She had a hard day at work. I wondered if she'd gone on the lash and couldn't be bothered to answer her phone this morning. Or maybe she's staying with a friend?'

Callum lifted another cask onto its stand. 'Try Detta. She was talking to Pav the other night, her and that new bloke.'

'New bloke? Whatever happened to her "all men are crap" line?'

'Don't ask me,' said Callum. 'Wasn't from around here, that's all I know. Pretty boy, bit soft around the gills if you get my meaning. Don't get his type in here much. They usually prefer espresso martinis in Abertrothy.'

He gave Finn the address for Detta, an old farm in the valley running back from the village. 'It's a commune these days,' Callum said, 'but they're good people. Since that woman was murdered in the house next door, Detta's been staying with her bloke in one of the caravans, the one with yellow stars painted on the side like some New Age crap. Course, it all depends what day of the week it is.'

A few years ago, when Jess was still on the scene, Finn had visited the house she shared with Pav. He hadn't believed that anyone would voluntarily live more than a mile from the nearest road, up a steep, unmade track winding through dense woods that tumbled down the side of the valley. The lane to Detta's caravan was worse. He abandoned his car halfway up just before a pothole that looked more like a sinkhole.

Sarah was always telling him to get in shape and exercise more. Perhaps she had a point. After twenty minutes on the foothills of Everest, except without snow, he arrived at the farm. The main house was unremarkable, with a few sheep absent-mindedly munching grass in one of the nearby fields. Another was like a festival site of yurts, ancient VW campers and a couple of caravans which had clearly made their last road trip.

The one with yellow stars was unmissable. Detta was sitting on the caravan steps wearing nothing but an outsize t-shirt and smoking a roll up.

'Something wrong, is it?' she asked. 'Only, she looked so happy the other night, her and that Michael. Good looking bugger, he was. Wouldn't have said no myself, not that I got the chance. Though I didn't think he was the sort of person Pav went for, if you get my meaning.'

As she said it, Finn felt a twinge of – what? Sadness, jealousy? Why should he care about Pav's love life? Maybe that was the real problem. She was probably tucked up with some new boyfriend, and what right did he have to complain?

'How about this Michael,' he said, 'can you describe him?'

'Better than that, my lovely – hold on a sec.'

She climbed inside the caravan and interrogated a sleepy male voice. An ancient Jack Russell appeared from behind a pile of wooden planks and cocked his leg with difficulty against one of the caravan wheels. Someone, somewhere, was frying bacon to perfection.

Detta reappeared, holding her phone. 'Sorry – Darren had it in the bed.' Another wink. 'It's on here some place, I never get round to deleting them. Takes cracking videos too.' She flicked through images on the screen and then handed the phone to Finn. 'It was Penny's birthday, see, we always have a competition for the worst photo.' She pointed to a dark-haired man, half turned away from the camera. 'That's him there, the soft lad next to Pav. Darren talked to him for a while, said he was a bit of a girl. But what does he know? If it don't fart on demand, it ain't a man according to him.'

Finn studied the image on the small screen. Not much to go on, but they could blow it up back at the office, see if it rang any bells. 'I'll need to take this,' he said, 'sorry.'

Detta tried to snatch it from his hands, but he held it out of reach. 'Don't worry, we won't look at any of the other artwork. What you and Darren get up to is your own affair.'

Detta snorted. 'Darren's usually too pissed to get anything up these days, more's the pity. But what do you want with the picture, anyway? Is Pav ok?'

'I just need to show the picture to a few people, see if anyone recognises Michael.'

'So why don't you send them the photo in a message,

then I can keep my phone? I got over seven hundred followers on Insta and I need to give them their daily fix of what I like to call "Country Matters". Gonna be an influencer, me. You get loadsa free stuff if you got enough followers.'

He decided not to ask.

'Here, let me,' she said. 'I'll show you.'

There was no doubt; he'd have to ask Sarah to show him how to use one of these things properly. He watched as Detta clicked a few of the keys. 'I'll send it to your number, yeah? Then it's up to you what you do with it. Come on, what is it?'

Within a few seconds, his own handset beeped. He opened the message, and the picture filled the screen.

'You can forward that on now, see? Save you darting backwards and forwards like a blue-arsed fly.'

He wished she'd stop grinning at him; one front tooth was missing, and the others were what Farrow and Ball would probably call 'Dirty Lurcher'.

'If Darren weren't here, I'd ask you in for a coffee or something,' she said, 'give you some photography practice.'

He already regretted giving her his number.

BACK AT THE CAR, he called Amir. 'Did you get that image yet? Good – get it checked out with the landlady in Wood Green. Yeah, that's the one. She had that bloke staying there, the one in the frame for the dead boy. No, nothing's wrong – don't argue man, just do it.'

He began to drive back down to the village, but before he'd gone more than a couple of hundred metres down the track, Sarah called.

'Can it wait?' he said. 'Things are hectic here, I'll explain later.'

'There was a note,' she said, 'pushed through the door this morning. I think you should come home. Now.'

He could hear the control in her voice. 'Note? What does it say?'

'Please love, just come home.'

'Tell me what the note says.'

She hesitated for a moment. 'There aren't any words, just a photo and a web address.'

He already had the car turned around and pointing back towards Gwenstow. 'C'mon, Sarah. The image, what is it.'

'It's Pav. I think something's wrong.' Her voice caught. 'What's going on Finn? Why was this put through our door?'

'I don't know – I'm on my way back. Listen sweetheart, just to be safe, lock all the doors and windows. I'll be twenty minutes.'

SARAH MUST HAVE BEEN WATCHING for him; as he put his front door key in the lock, he heard the bolts being drawn back. She hugged him, hard, as soon as the door shut behind him, and then handed him a sheet of folded A4 paper. The photo had been printed in the middle, with a shortened web address underneath. Finn studied the picture of the elderly couple, not knowing what to think. This wasn't what he was expecting. The man looked strangely familiar; of course, Pav's father. A little younger, a little stronger, and with a woman by his side – Pav's Ma, an ethereal figure draped in a pastel sari, smiling uncertainly at the camera. This must be the photograph that was taken from Pav's home the day someone murdered her neighbour.

He opened his laptop and typed in the web address.

'Looks like it's on YouTube,' Sarah said unnecessarily. 'Gonna be a video.'

Finn squeezed her arm. A good husband would ask her to leave - official business - and check this out for himself, but Sarah never needed his protection from anything.

They both stared at the screen, waiting for something to happen. 'Damned broadband,' said Finn, 'today of all days it has to be slow.'

The blurred picture suddenly clicked into high definition with a familiar scene. He'd seen a clip like this before on Ash's files. The room and the chair were the same, but this time there was only one actor. Pav, strapped down. Pav, looking towards the camera as if it were a machine gun. Pav wearing a strange, thick choker. And then Pav, screaming and jerking her body against the restraints of the straps, collapsing as the screen faded to black.

For a moment, neither of them moved. 'Jesus, Finn. What the hell have you and Pav got yourselves into this time?' said Sarah. She rested her hand on his. 'Are you sure that's even her? People mess about with these videos, don't they? Or it could be one of those deepfakes - you know, where they put one person's face on another body.' She didn't sound convinced.

Finn sat on the edge of the desk and rubbed his eyes, as if to erase what he'd just seen. He knew what this was about and what the price would be. Too high, either for ROCU or the local police.

'Why did they send this to you?' asked Sarah. 'Why not contact you at the office? More to the point, how do they know where we live?'

'This makes it personal.' He didn't need to say any more.

'So what happens now?'

'You pack a bag and pop over to your mum's. Don't argue, sweetheart. They know where we live and I can't stay here with you today.'

He heard her in the bedroom, trying not to cry. What if it were her on the video instead of Pav, he wondered. How would that feel? He walked along the landing and hugged her. 'We'll sort this out, promise.'

He called Amir on the way and told him to check Pav's phone records for the past few days. 'Look for anything unusual and get that damned YouTube clip taken down – make sure we have a copy first.'

Pav's cottage looked deserted, even from the outside, and there was still no sign of her car anywhere nearby. They hadn't taken her from here unless they'd stolen the car at the same time. He checked the front of the house, but there were no open windows to help him get in. No problem. He found the hidden back door key in the usual place, but the house was empty and untouched. Her mobile was on the floor, near the TV; that explained why she hadn't returned his calls. And on the corner of the sofa was the bag she always used. Another of Ash's presents that had stayed – Dior. Not a typical accessory for someone on her salary, but Pav was never typical. He checked inside – a dog-eared paperback, a fistful of supermarket receipts and her purse. A small world for someone who might already be dead.

He let himself out and called Amir again. 'How are you getting on with those call records?' he asked.

'We can discount most of them,' Amir said. 'She made a lot of calls on Tuesday afternoon to hospitals along the M4 corridor, and one to a Catholic seminary near Durham.'

'She was following up on the man who buried the boy in the woods near Tryleg, Sebastian Collier. Didn't get us far; we followed up with a priest at Hazelbury who showed us newspaper cuttings reporting his suicide.'

'Suicides can be faked,' said Amir. 'What else did this priest say about him?'

'He worked in Romania for a while, then he seemed to go off the rails.' He tried to remember the conversation with Father Mahoney. 'When he came back from his last trip, he was some kind of fanatic, kept blathering on about his mission.'

'What mission?'

'I don't know! He was a priest. What else do you want?'

'It may not help,' said Amir, 'but there used to be a Seamen's Mission near Uskmouth docks. I think it closed down as part of the redevelopment. There's a restaurant on the site now, Chinese, good dim sum.'

'I don't care about your fucking eating habits!' But something was scratching away inside his head, like a puppy demanding attention. 'Mission, of course! Are there any others in Uskmouth? Maybe the Seamen's Mission moved somewhere else.'

Amir muttered to someone in the background. 'Rachel's on it now... don't go away... ah, thank you Google! We have a hit, just one for now. The Forest Mission, a registered charity for rehousing asylum seekers. And you'll like this – one of the trustees is a Father Sebastian Collier. It's on Cannock Park; you know the area – bloody big houses, the sort of places where the nanny has her own four-wheel-drive. I come through there most mornings.'

'I'm on my way, meet me there. And you'd better call Jimmy Spears to organise some backup; this could end up being very messy.'

CHAPTER
TWENTY-FOUR

She came to, still strapped to the chair, but Bonetti and the other man were gone. For a moment she thought – there's no difference between life and death. We just carry on where we left off, even dying doesn't let us leave the pain behind. But this was definitely life, what little she had left of it. And someone else was in the room. She could hear him breathing behind her, just out of sight until he walked around the chair to face her.

She was in a strange dream, where all the rules were different; she wouldn't have been surprised if Ma and Pa arrived to join in the celebrations. But it was Michael standing just out of reach, looking as though he'd been tortured, not her. Her voice had stopped working, and the only sounds to come out were small, animal grunts.

Michael took a step forward and then stopped. 'I'm so sorry, Pav – I didn't know about any of this, I swear.'

The Ash defence, as unconvincing now as it had been back in her cottage.She tried again, forcing the muscles in her throat to co-operate, and this time managed a few words. 'Michael – you have to get me out of here.' His words made little sense, she couldn't understand why he was there.

'I – it's not so easy. But there was nothing I could do, they've been blackmailing me. If I'd known what was happening I would never...' His voice trailed off. 'But they promised to let you go. Bonetti took a video to prove you're here; they plan to send a copy to the police.'

Why are bodies so weak, she thought? A bit of excruciating torture and it all goes to pot. 'To prove I'm here?' she said. 'Do you know what they did to me?' Couldn't he see the choker around her neck? Not exactly a fashion accessory. And then she realised it was gone, although the skin on her neck felt thick and numb where the probes had pushed into her.

Michael turned away; a good tell for guilt or shame, or both. 'They'll give the police a choice,' he said, 'trade you for the girl they've hidden away.' His voice was quiet, and he took another step backwards as the blonde man joined them in the room.

'We can manage better than that,' Bonetti said. 'A two for one offer.' He undid her straps. 'Sebastian – help me move her. You've long since passed the point of keeping your hands clean.'

'Sebastian?' For a moment she wondered if someone else was in the room, someone she hadn't noticed.

Bonetti knelt at her feet to undo the straps around her ankles; his head brushed against her knee as he leant forward, and the muscles in her thighs clenched together in some futile attempt at bodily privacy. The Italian looked up.

'Of course, you know him as Michael – a nom de guerre. It seemed suitably angelic, even if he had long since fallen; one must keep a sense of fun. As I said earlier, we tried to make things easy for you. We gave you a priest to be your tame counsellor. We gave him a new history - a legend, isn't that what you security types call it? A perfect listener, a perfect confessor; what more could we have done? A few more hours, a night of pillow talk with an attentive lover, and we would have all we needed. Instead...' He shook his head in sadness. 'Alas, we did insufficient research - time is of the essence, after all. Perhaps a beautiful woman would have achieved what dear Sebastian failed to do.'

They pulled her out of the chair, gripping her arms, and she saw two metal dog cages pushed against the far wall. One was empty, the other contained a girl sprawled in the corner, unconscious and barely breathing. Bonetti pushed Pav to her knees and forced her to crawl into the empty cage. *Wait until I'm stronger,* she thought, *and it won't be me being treated like an animal.*

There was too little space to allow her to sit upright, and she curled up on her side, facing the girl in the other container. Bonetti padlocked the metal door. 'For your sake, I hope your policeman friend believes in the greatest good for the greatest number. Sacrifice one to save two, an excellent return on his investment.'

'I told you, my people won't give in to blackmail.'

Bonetti laughed. 'We choose our subjects carefully. I am sure your agency prides itself on being robust about these matters, at least in public, but we shared your movie debut with Finn Williams. We know about his pathetic crush on your scrawny little body. A little nudge and he'll soon become an advocate for your release.'

In spite of herself, Pav felt hope. Bonetti was right; deals were sometimes done out of the public eye, and Finn wouldn't give up easily. At the same time, she had another thought; what right do I have to live if it means someone else dies? Who am I to make that judgement?

The unconscious girl shifted slightly in her cage, but her eyes stayed shut. 'She needs treatment,' Pav said. The girl's skin had the same pallor as Mira's, and her breath carried the stale scent of death.

Bonetti didn't look at the girl, but put his arm around Sebastian and guided him out of the room. At the doorway, he stopped. 'Let me tell you something, Miss McNeil. At the beginning of my career, I was an unworldly academic. But recent events have inducted me into the world of business and I tell you this; until now, and for a while longer, you and that girl count as assets. But when we have secured Mira and her information, you will have become fully depreciated. You will be a liability.'

At least they left the lights on. Not that there was much to see, but she could do without darkness combined with this shrinking cage. Pav pushed her fingers through the solid metal rods; even a Rottweiler trapped in the cage wouldn't be able to escape.

She called to the girl, but there was no response. Still breathing, though, and from the smell that came off her body, she must have been held for a while.

She was losing all sense of time. Was it day or night? When had they brought her here, wherever 'here' was – today, yesterday, last week? Perhaps she'd always lived here, and her memories of another existence were simply dreams and fantasies.

Her body was a patchwork of bruises. Some she could see, some she could feel. But something was missing from her mind; the drugs they'd given her had a lot to answer for.

Her lips were sore from the punch in the face earlier when she was strapped to the chair. She couldn't remember when she last drank something. Her mouth was dry, her lips were cracking as she lay there, and the damage to her throat made it hard to swallow.

A shiver started in her guts and rolled out through her body; when had she last been warm? The floor of the cage was a plastic tray lying on concrete, and she was wearing nothing but the jeans and sweatshirt that Michael – Sebastian – had lent her. Perhaps she could roll the cage over, perhaps some part of it would break and she could get out. She tried rocking her body to and fro, hoping to build up momentum, but then she noticed the steel brackets fastening it to the wall. And even if she could break out of the cage, what then?

She curled up on the floor and slept the way she used to on car journeys as a child, on the border between dreams and wakefulness. The way animals slept, ready to move at the first sign of danger.

The sound of the door opening snapped her awake. She didn't stir, merely watched, as Sebastian walked across to the cage with a bottle of water and a saucer.

'They said I could give you this.'

He looked and sounded like the epitome of misery. Not that it was much comfort. The sight of the water, out of reach, was torture. She managed to sit, hunched under the metal roof.

'How am I meant to drink from that? Can't you open the cage?'

Sebastian shook his head and pushed the saucer edge-ways through the bars of the cage. 'Leave it there, at the side.' He flipped open the top of the bottle, squatted down, and squirted water into the saucer. 'Drink that, then I'll give you more.'

There was barely enough to wet her lips but it tasted

better than wine, and they repeated the process until the bottle was empty and her guts ached.

'What's your real name?' she asked. 'Michael or Sebastian?' On the basis that she was going to get out of this mess, any information could be priceless.

'Sebastian. I only used Michael when I met you.'

'Bonetti called you a priest.'

'I am... I was. I thought I was doing good.'

Vicars, priests, bishops; if she had her way, they'd all be rounded up and left to fend for themselves on a deserted island where the only people they could abuse were each other. 'Good? Fuck you, Sebastian, or whatever your name is. You stalk me, drug me and then you kidnap me and connive at my torture. And what about the murdered girls? You call that good?'

'You don't understand. I had no idea it would come to this,' he said. 'I thought I was finding jobs for asylum seekers, helping poor kids find a better life. I didn't see what else was happening.'

'You didn't want to see. Typical fucking priest.'

'They were using me.'

'For people trafficking into the sex trade. How dumb are you?'

'You think I felt good when I realised? But this...' He looked around the room. 'This I knew nothing about.' He crouched next to the door of the cage and dropped his voice. 'They were blackmailing me, then one thing led to another. I didn't know what else to do.'

'They were grooming you, but you're not a child. You could have said no.'

Sebastian shook his head. 'I could have done many things, but I didn't. You think I don't know I'm weak?'

'I still don't understand,' she said. 'You know this is

wrong, so put it right. Help me get out of here and I'll tell the police, get you a deal.' She tried to sound sincere. If it were up to her, he and his dog collar would be on that deserted island before he knew which day of the week it was.

Sebastian looked around as if worried that someone else might hear. 'I told you, it's not that easy. There's a girl...'

He stopped, looking into her eyes. 'You don't really care. What does my life matter to you?'

'You could have stopped this,' said Pav, 'but you didn't, and then you betrayed me. On the outside, you look like someone who cares, but you have no soul. I don't want to hear your justifications, you pathetic fuck.'

She shifted position in the cage, trying to massage blood back into her legs as Sebastian stood up.

'I was a priest,' he said, 'and I betrayed my trust.'

There was no point in prolonging this. 'Fuck you! Betrayed your trust? No, Sebastian, you betrayed yourself.'

Someone shouted his name from outside and he moved out of reach, as if scared she would grab him. 'I have to go,' he said. 'Forgive me.'

Pav turned away as he left. A small victory, but right now she didn't have an absolution in her. The door clicked shut behind him, and a few seconds later she heard another, heavier barrier slamming somewhere in the distance. The only sound in the bare room was the girl in the next cage, breaths bubbling in her throat; Pav pulled her knees up to her chest, closed her eyes, and tried to sleep.

TWENTY-FIVE

Amir was already parked behind Pav's empty car in a side street as Finn joined him.

'Are the locals on their way?' he asked.

'Don't hold your breath.' A tic by the corner of Amir's left eye pulled at the lid in tiny, random movements. 'You really think this is the place?'

'Give me a better option,' Finn said. 'Did Rachel kill that video on the Internet?'

'All sorted. It was definitely taken in the same room as the other movies. Have the kidnappers been back in contact?'

A teenage boy on a skateboard skidded around the corner and glided past them, knocking in the wing mirror as he went.

'Fucking wanker...'

'Leave it, Finn, he's not worth the bother.'

'I can't just sit here when Pav could be inside. She's tough, but we know what these people can do.'

'I'd bet on her any time. She thinks, that's her super power. She works things out - hate to play her at chess.'

'Let's hope you get the chance. She's my boss, but also my mate. If the roles were reversed, she'd already be wreaking bloody havoc in there.'

'We don't even know if this is the right place. And we need backup – you know what the old man's like about protocol.'

'Stay in the car if you want, but you saw the video. And statistically she's likely to be alone – kidnappers stay with their victims as little as possible, especially in these situations.'

Amir joined him on the pavement. 'If I die because of this, I'm blaming you.'

'I'll put flowers on your grave. Now give me a leg up over the fence and cover the front.'

'You don't want me to go in?'

'If anything goes wrong, you can send the flowers.'

With Amir's help, Finn scrabbled over the side wall and into the back garden. Someone else had been in this wilderness recently; the long grass had been trodden down in a single direction, towards the house. He followed the track to the overgrown patio and then levered open the French windows at the back as quietly as he could.

This was someone's study. Desk, computer, filing cabinets, a small sofa bed along one wall. The rest of the house was silent and he let himself into a hallway, standing quietly and listening. There was no sign of a cellar. Shame, he would have laid good money on a converted basement for the studio. Either the entrance was hidden or his guess was wrong.

He climbed the wide staircase, stopping when a tread creaked under his weight. There was no sign that anyone had heard him and he carried on to the first floor landing; dark oak floorboards and a worn runner faded from its original red to a dull ochre. The motions of air from his passing stirred up dust balls that skittered in excited circles before settling down to rest again.

He stopped again and listened; still nothing. Wherever Pav was, it wasn't up here, not unless she was already dead. No, dismiss that thought. He checked out the rooms with their high ceilings and pale green emulsioned walls; the place had been used as some sort of hostel with mattresses on the floor, each with a thin sheet and blanket. But there were no people, no clothes, no possessions. This was a way station; a place to pass through, not a place to stay.

He found a chair and used it to reach a trapdoor into the attic. He couldn't find a light switch, and hauled himself up into the warm darkness, breathing in air that tasted of soot. The shadows here had been undisturbed for years, if not decades. He used the torch on his phone, but his intuition had been right; the attic was empty except for an ancient mousetrap near the entrance and a dripping, metal water tank.

He lowered himself back onto the chair and closed the trap above him. If this was a mistake, then Pav was lost. Back downstairs, through the house and out from the French windows into the garden. On the other side of the patio, stuck on the rear wall of the house like an afterthought, was a small, single storey extension; flat roof, pebble-dash walls.

If you're going off-piste, might as well head for the deepest snow. He checked the padlock, then splintered the door with a couple of well-placed kicks. The barely formed hope of finding Pav alive was quickly dashed - nothing inside except for some old gardening tools and various jars and rusting tins, decades-old. Some kind of potting shed by the looks of it, although he couldn't place the unusual smell. Old compost and dead plants, probably. Gardening wasn't a strong suit. He moved a few flowerpots and plastic sacks, and then his mobile rang just as he noticed the incongruous webcam above the door.

'Is that Finn Williams?' The distorted voice was almost metallic; impossible to know if it was a man or woman. 'Listen and say nothing if you want to see your friend again. This is the deal, non-negotiable. You will give us Mira, and when we have her in our custody, Ms McNeil will be released along with another girl we are holding. Call her a bonus for good behaviour. Don't interrupt, Mr Williams; your task is to listen. You will do this thing to prove that the girl we want is alive – within two hours you will upload a clip of Mira, holding today's newspaper, on YouTube, with her name – and her name alone – as the title and as the tag. Do this now, and when we are satisfied, we shall be in contact. If you fail us, or if Mira is already dead, your friend will experience a very painful demise.'

They'd have used a burner, and he didn't have the time for forensic telephony. He ran through the house and found Amir still waiting by the front door.

'They've been in touch,' said Finn breathlessly. 'They want to swap Pav for Mira. If we don't play ball, they'll kill her.'

Amir spat a piece of gum into an overgrown rosebush. 'You have to get Gus involved. This is a hostage situation now and I know you want to be the hero, but this is way above our pay grades. And I still don't understand why they want Mira; the poor kid's barely alive as it is.'

'I know, it doesn't make sense,' said Finn. 'Getting her back would stop her talking to us, but for all they know she's already told us everything; they don't know how sick she is. Other than that, what could they possibly want with a sick teenage girl?'

'If we get Pav back, she could identify them too; their deal doesn't add up. Whatever we do, they'll never let her go free.'

'So what do you suggest? Do nothing? You really want to see another snuff movie starring our boss? For all we know, the people she's seen might be expendable. We don't want the foot soldiers, we want the generals. I admit they're holding the good cards for now, but they've made mistakes before. They left Mira alive, and Pav's their only currency if they want to buy Mira back. They have to keep her safe until they have what they want.'

'That's why Pav needs a negotiator.'

'That's why she needs a friend.' Finn rubbed his eyes, wondering why he hadn't heard from his wife yet. Pressure, always pressure. The job was ok until it got personal, like now. 'We need to put that photo of Mira online. Buys us time and doesn't commit us to anything.'

'I'll call Rachel,' said Amir. 'She'll sort it for us.'

'Just make it happen. And wait here for Spears; I'll be in touch when I'm back at base.'

THIS WAS the nightmare he thought would never happen. Taking risks was part of the job, but when people you cared about got caught up in your wake... As he drove, he thought about the dilemma. It should be simple; you don't give in to blackmail, you say no. But who would go to Pav's father and tell him, *"I could have saved your daughter but I chose not to. I chose to save a girl who might die anyway."* How do you say sorry for that?

By the time he arrived at the anonymous building on the side of the estuary, Rachel was waiting to show him a clip of Mira, unconscious in her hospital bed. He looked at the short video on Rachel's screen. The drips and oxygen were still in place; the girl was asleep or in a coma but it was recognisably her, still breathing. The camera focussed in on a copy of that day's Times newspaper, propped on the pillow beside her head.

'She looks like crap,' said Finn.

Rachel shook her head slowly. 'Multiple organ failure, according to the medics. They've started treatment with a new combination of drugs, but it might be too late. If you see me in that state, switch me off.' She paused. 'Don't wanna pry and it's not my call, but I assume Gus is on board? You're giving them Proof of Life - have they done the same for Pav? Hostage Negotiation 101 etcetera etcetera.'

Finn looked away from the screen. 'You're right, it's not your call. So what happens next?'

'I'll upload the file if you're happy - I set up a new account.'

'Glad you know what you're doing.'

Finn watched as the woman tapped at the keyboard. 'I've kept the file size small,' she said, 'that should help it transfer quickly. If there's no glitch, people should be able to search for it in the next few minutes.'

'And then what?'

'And then we wait.'

WHICH HAD NEVER BEEN one of his strengths. Ash's post-mortem report had arrived and he read it through, hoping for some new lead, but there was nothing. Cocaine and alcohol, but no signs of violence. Perhaps the man Pav knew had still been there, deep inside. Perhaps in the end he couldn't live with himself. Or perhaps he knew what life would be like in prison for someone like him and decided that death was the preferable option. Law and justice sometimes had the narrowest of intersects, but in the case of child abuse...

Finn stared at the photos of the body and wondered what it would be like to drown. He'd heard it was a peaceful way to go, but he couldn't see it. Surely your body would fight until the last moment for a single molecule of air, anything to stretch life for another second. And if somebody was holding you under against your will: he shook the thought away and closed the file. For all he knew, that's what they'd planned for Pav.

He called Amir. 'Have they found anything else yet?'

'The locals only just turned up. I checked with a couple of the neighbours; the place was owned by an old lady who'd lived here since she was a girl. She died a couple of years ago and the house was sold to the Mission. Very quiet operation, by the sounds of it. Listen – I'm going round the back, have a mosey in the garden. I'll call you if we find anything.'

Finn wandered across to Rachel's desk. 'Anything yet?'

'The clip uploaded okay. I checked ten minutes ago but so far no one's accessed it. I'll log in again now... Ah, there we go, someone's just viewed it. Might not be our targets, of course, but it's a start.'

'You can't see who it was?'

'No way, but it happened in the last few minutes.'

Finn's mobile rang as Rachel finished speaking. He took the call in Pav's shuttered, empty room and heard the same androgynous voice as before.

'Well done. Now you must do this. After this call, you will receive a text of some map coordinates. Take the girl there – you, alone – you will see a small outcrop of rock. Take Mira out of the car, leave her there and drive away.'

'Not until I know who I'm talking to. Is this Father Collier?'

The voice laughed. 'You have your instructions; follow them.'

'Why should I do that? What about Pav and this other girl you're holding? I gave you proof of life, you should do the same.' Amir had been right, a trained negotiator should be handling this. Too late now.

The voice ignored him. 'We shall tell you where they are once we have Mira.'

'I don't believe you.' He tried to keep his voice low even though no-one was listening. 'You want Mira because she can identify you but Pav could do the same. Your deal makes no sense.'

'It is the only deal you have.'

'For all I know, Pav's dead already.'

'She is not. You will have a chance to talk to her before you leave the girl – I do not expect something for nothing. Trust me, Mr Williams, you are not dealing with mindless thugs. As for identification, we have gone to great pains to prevent your friend from knowing anything worthwhile about us.'

'I still don't...'

The voice spoke over him. 'It is now two fifteen in the afternoon. At seven o'clock this evening precisely, you will be at the coordinates. You will need a four-wheel-drive; when you look at your map, you will see that you have no option but to come alone. Any attempt to deceive us – helicopters, drones, other vehicles – and you will ensure the early, and entirely unnecessary, demise of your friend.'

Within a minute, the coordinates came through in a text message. 'Somebody find me a map,' he yelled, 'tell me where this bloody place is.'

'Map of where?' asked Rachel.

'If I knew, I wouldn't be asking! Here, you see what you can do with your bloody computer.'

'You never heard of Google Maps?' She took his phone and looked at the numbers. 'Ah - this is a National Grid reference. SO - those letters at the beginning, that means it's somewhere in the South Wales area.'

'How do you know? You haven't looked anything up yet.'

'Girl Guides,' she said, as if that explained everything. A minute later, her screen filled with part of an Ordnance Survey map. 'It's the other side of the Beacons on Black Mountain,' she said. 'Very bleak – I can see why you'd need a four-wheel-drive.' She turned to Finn. 'You're not really going to do this? If you give them Mira, they'll kill her and still won't release Pav. Call Gus, he's probably still in London.'

'I tried, he's not answering. Probably in another bloody committee meeting. And what could he do? Anything we tried would be visible from miles away, and I don't think even Gus can authorise a drone strike.'

'Then we should wait.'

'Welcome to the world of moral dilemmas. Mira's sick, probably dying – there's no guarantee they started the treatment in time. And if she recovers, what sort of memories will she have? As sacrifices go, she might even thank me.'

'That's not your judgement to make.'

'So what would you do? Reject their demands when we have no other options? If we do that, two people will die instead of one. For sure, no ifs and buts. Correct me if I'm wrong, but you don't need to be a Girl Guide to reach that conclusion.'

His mobile rang again. 'Shit – what do they want now?' But it was Amir, not the anonymous voice.

'Are you still at the office? We found a fake wall at the back of the outhouse. I noticed it seemed shorter inside than it did outside, so I paced it out. A three-foot difference.'

'You can't fit much in three feet – no, don't try to explain. I'm on my way.'

WHEN HE ARRIVED at the house, a framework of wood and plaster had been exposed on the back wall. 'It didn't feel right,' said Amir. 'There was a faint smell earlier, but I couldn't place it. Then it hit me, paint. One of those new emulsions – low odour, but you can still smell when someone's been using it. Me and the missus have been decorating the spare room, that's what made me think. Then I checked the dimensions, called in the troops, and voilà! It was put up in the last day or so – quick and dirty, a few lengths of two by four and some plasterboard.'

They watched as the covering was pulled away, revealing a narrow door behind which a flight of stairs descended into the gloom. 'Light switch anywhere? Damn – somebody find a decent torch.'

Finn led the way; the wooden stairs ended in a large room stacked with cardboard boxes. No sign of Pav, no sign of another girl. Finn called her name, but the echo of his voice was the only reply.

'We found one false wall, check for others in here,' he said. 'And trapdoors, there might be a double cellar.'

In less than fifteen minutes, every section of the walls and floor and ceiling had been examined and tapped, every box moved and checked.

'I don't believe it,' said Finn. 'She has to be here – her car's outside, and this is where Collier worked.'

'There's no sign of anything except the storage boxes,' said Amir. 'And they didn't take the video of Pav here, the ceiling's much higher.'

Kicking one of the broken pieces of plasterboard helped, but not much. He felt cheated. 'I thought this was going to solve our problems.'

'I don't understand.'

'Wouldn't you sacrifice a dying girl to save a friend? And they're holding another girl as well as Pav. Two lives for the price of one death.'

'Neither you nor I get paid to make those decisions. No-one's gonna let you trade Mira for Pav and some girl who might not exist.'

Finn walked slowly over to the stairs. 'Follow orders. Is that what you're suggesting? Who said that the only thing necessary for the triumph of evil was that good men do nothing? We've let political correctness fuck with our minds so much we've forgotten that sometimes you have to break the rules to do the right thing. A friend of mine taught me that.'

FINN STOOD in the garden next to a rosebush that reminded him of the wallpaper in his grandmother's house, a miner's terrace in Merthyr. He checked his watch; just gone three thirty, barely enough time to borrow a four-wheel-drive and get to the coordinates on Black Mountain by the deadline that evening. He walked quickly through the house, reached his car, and started driving.

CHAPTER
TWENTY-SIX

The worst thing about fear was the sensation of freefall, the loss of control. From the moment Pav came to, she knew that most of her chances had evaporated. And now she was about to die. Not to be; a memory rather than a reality. She had no illusions about an afterlife, no solace in the thought of reward in heaven after hell on earth. Death had never been the worry, just the dying.

These thoughts were pointless; she might as well have never existed. Pav tried to exercise her arms and legs to keep the blood flowing, but as she squirmed around in the confined space, it felt as though her internal organs were rearranging themselves, finding new positions inside her dislocated body. The cage was too short to stretch out, too low to sit upright.

The darkness was absolute. Perhaps they'd left her alone with the dying girl. Perhaps the room was sealed, the air would run out and they would both suffocate slowly. The bubbling breaths of the girl in the next cage sounded like theft now, stealing precious oxygen. And for what? A few more minutes of a useless life; so selfish.

She noticed sounds in the room, slight movements that stopped as soon as she listened for them. A good sign; rats had to breathe. Then the sounds died away; hallucinations again, or wishful thinking? No wonder prisoners in solitary made friends with spiders and mice.

The choker they'd made her wear had surely been used, not just for torture, but to kill. Perhaps that was how Eva died; an enviably quick death, relatively speaking. A burst of pain and then oblivion; better than this abandonment. She twisted to face the wall as the noises restarted. Louder now and definitely not her imagination; a door swinging shut and then footsteps, outside the room but nearby.

A sudden, blinding light forced her eyes to scrunch shut automatically as the door flew open. She twisted around, willing her eyelids apart, and saw Bonetti standing beside the cage and smiling like an uncle.

'My apologies for leaving you so long.' He reached down to undo the padlock. 'Please, Miss McNeil, I promise you will come to no harm.'

She crawled out, giddy from moving after so long hunched in her cage. While she rested on her hands and knees, pins and needles burning through her limbs, Bonetti slipped the choker around her neck. She lifted her arms to stop him, but he brushed them aside and then pulled her upright.

'Just a precaution, you understand,' he said. 'I would hate to see you try anything stupid.'

He waited until she could walk, and then made her lead the way into a short corridor with four rooms, two on each side. The door panels were glazed with the same reinforced glass she'd seen in the windows of the fisherman's hut. Bonetti was so close behind her she felt the heat radiating from his body. She stopped suddenly and swung round to face him, but he held up the small handset with the aerial. No contest, not yet. Perhaps later, when her hands and legs weren't so cramped and she wasn't limping along like Ma on a bad day.

At the end of the corridor she stopped by a flight of steps in prefabricated metal, sprayed with a rust-coloured paint. So this was a cellar, but something didn't seem right. The stairs she'd seen at the house were solid concrete, not metal. Another entrance? A spasm of cramp clenched her calf muscle, making her stumble.

'No tricks, if you please,' said Bonetti.

When she was out of this situation, she'd glue his mouth shut to silence his smug voice, and then she'd snap him in two. Or perhaps tie him to a stake and watch him burn - anything to cause him even a hint of the misery he'd inflicted on others.

'Come along, Detective Inspector, those stairs won't climb themselves.'

She didn't have the energy to reply, and dragged herself up the stairs until she reached a metal door at the top. Bonetti told her to go through and she found herself in another room. No, not a room, a barn; a vast space with metal joists and corrugated iron walls. A piece of farm machinery was rusting in its dotage at the far end, all wheels and blades. Apart from that and the patina of grey-gold dust that might once have been wheat or straw, the space was empty. Wherever this was, it wasn't the house in Uskmouth.

Bonetti pushed past her to one of the enormous doors and swung it open; the horizontal rays of late afternoon sunlight almost blinded her again. And as she became accustomed to the glare, she looked across the courtyard at somewhere she knew well enough. This had to be another hallucination. Bonetti took her arm and led her, like an invalid, into the grounds of The Swallows.

'A rather clever idea, don't you think?' he said. 'One business covering another.' He sounded like a mother showing off her baby.

There was nothing she could say. She looked around the courtyard, blinking, not wanting to believe what her brain was telling her.

'Bella,' she said eventually, 'does she...'

'Does she what?' said a woman behind her. 'I am sorry Pav, I would have been here sooner but you know how it is – things to do, people to see.'

Pav turned as quickly as she could; the older woman had come upon them unnoticed from one of the other buildings. 'Bella – what the fuck is going on?'

'You are an intelligent woman, Pav. I thought it would be clear by now.'

Any hope left in her body drained away. Nothing mattered now.

'Please understand, this is simply business,' said Bella. 'Nothing personal, believe me. If I had my way, you would still be keeping the nation's children safe from people like me. You do not understand, of course. You think people are good, deep inside. Remember how you asked me once about my family? And I told you some fantasy about a nice middle-class upbringing in the suburbs of Barcelona. Do you want to know the truth? Do you want to know what my earliest memories are? Standing in the middle of a circle of men that my father brought home and having to take my clothes off for them. And when I cried because I was scared, because I didn't like the way they touched me, my mother would tell me to shut up and get on with it. My parents, Pav. Nice, middle-class parents in a nice, middle-class suburb. That is real life.'

No cognitive dissonance for Bella, obviously. 'You think a sob story excuses anything? said Pav. 'I've heard the same feeble reasons a hundred times, always from bastards trying to worm their way out of responsibility for the ghastly things they'd done. And if your life was so bad, why not tell someone and get help?'

'Over forty years ago in a good Catholic society? I think not. I would be the one to be blamed. But it was the best thing that could have happened to me. It taught me there is only one person I can trust – me. I had no illusions about being a nice little girl, all pink ribbons and frocks. I knew I was a slut from the very beginning; we are all sluts, Pav, all of us. Trust me, life becomes so much simpler when you stop pretending.' Bella reached over and brushed away a stray piece of hair, tucking it behind Pav's ear. 'You think you are a realist, but you wrap yourself in illusions, just like everyone else.'

The muscles in her legs were going rogue, but there was nothing to hold on to for support, only the two people studying her. 'So all of this is a front?'

'Oh no! The work we do here is genuine, and an excellent service we provide, although I say it myself. Exemplary, above suspicion. No nasty rumours about staff fiddling with the children, no exposés waiting to thrill the tabloid readers over their toast and marmalade – or their crisps and Coca-Cola. There was poor Eva, of course, but her own behaviour forced that aberration upon us. I think we constructed a charming narrative to cover her disappearance. It fooled you.'

Pav turned away, her cheeks burning. A patsy, that's all

she was. They'd played her so easily; she'd brought Eva here. She'd told the girl she was safe, then driven away and left her with a bunch of psychopaths.

'Don't be too hard on yourself,' said Bella, as if she were a mind reader. 'Her life had not been her own for years – not since she set her sights on dear Father Sebastian. Bonetti will tell you all about it; the peasant girl and the priest, the adolescent fumbling of the nymph and the celibate. Poor Sebastian thought she was still living in her Romanian hovel when all the time she was working for us. Amusing, no? Less than a couple of miles from where he existed in his own fantasy land, the acceptable face of human trafficking. I would feel sorry for him if he were not so pathetic.'

She'd raised her voice so Sebastian could hear them as he walked across from the farmhouse, flanked by Mitchell. 'Look at the way he shambles,' Bella said, quietly again, 'as if his feet are ashamed of every step they take. If he were my son, I would have strangled him at birth.'

Pav couldn't understand why they'd brought her here. If they were going to kill her, why not do it at the house? No, they still needed her for something, which meant she still had a chance. Even if she got free, though, the complex was a secure fortress. She looked around the courtyard at the high fences; another couple of minutes and the sun would disappear behind the hills.

Sebastian had reached them now, but he avoided looking at her. 'I've done everything you wanted, and more,' he said to Bella. 'I made a deal with Bonetti, now I want what he promised. He said Anca and I could disappear and leave all this behind. Tell me where she is and you'll never hear from me again.'

'Some fools are naïve, some are wilfully blind,' said Bella. 'Perhaps it is that religious background; you are so used to believing the unbelievable that you take anything as an article of faith. Your little girl, my dear, your Anca – or Eva, as we rechristened her for the paying public – I'm afraid she is no longer with us. Pleasuring the angels in heaven, that is her vocation now. Be pleased! Paradise is guaranteed after what she experienced. Unless, of course, your God judged her complicit and she is even now the plaything of some demon in hell.'

Sebastian closed his eyes for a moment, clenching and unclenching his fists, and then shrugged as though he'd been expecting this news. 'I suppose that's the real trouble with faith,' he said. 'When even God betrays you, there's no-one left to trust about anything.'

Mitchell had disappeared into the barn but now rejoined them with the unconscious girl in his arms. Each of her breaths sounded like the patter of small footsteps moving away, and Pav wondered if Bella ever felt the weight of these extinctions.

'Tell me something,' said Pav. 'Were you responsible for Ash's death or did he kill himself – I assume he was part of your organisation?'

'A minor part. His appetites were larger than his capabilities; dear Ash, so easy to manipulate. Unfortunately, he made a bid for independence and tried to set up his own distribution network for our little films. That made me very unhappy. We had a full and frank discussion about his prospects, and I believe he was minded to betray our entire operation once he had secured himself a safe haven somewhere overseas. I don't know about you, but Judas was never one of my favourite characters. Betrayal is such an ugly act.'

'Judas killed himself.'

'Sometimes people need help to do the right thing.'

Bonetti interrupted. 'Madam, the time. Our friend is due for his next check-in.'

Bella checked her phone. 'So he is.' Her mobile had a piece of tape stuck across the camera lens on the front. 'Very punctual, your colleague, so far. And to make sure that we do not have any trouble, we shall have to discommode you for a while longer. Bonetti swears by his toy collar; I prefer more visceral methods.'

Mitchell grabbed Pav from behind and held a hand over her mouth. His skin smelled of pork fat, and he pushed his groin against her like a lonely frustrate on a crowded bus. He held a knife to her throat, and any thoughts of struggling were quickly extinguished. The edge of the blade pressed against her skin, hot and cold at the same time. They didn't pay her enough for this.

Bella barely seemed to notice. 'Another few seconds or so and...'

The phone rang with an incongruous techno jingle; Bella pressed a couple of keys and showed Pav the screen. For a moment, she couldn't make any sense of the grainy video; a girl, Mira, strapped to a stretcher. As the camera panned back, the scene changed; the stretcher was in the back of a large SUV. The lens panned again to show an empty road running through moorland, and then across to a signpost.

Bella cut off the call. 'Technology, 'she said, 'such a boon. We made a personal deal with your friend Finn; he gives us Mira, we give him you and the other girl. What do you think? Is that a fair exchange?'

She nodded at Mitchell to release Pav; she spat on the ground to get rid of the taste of him.

'He wouldn't do that,' she said. 'Everyone knows we don't give in to blackmail.'

Bella laughed, soft and knowing. 'I expected this unworldliness from poor Sebastian, but not from you. Deals make the world go round, everyone does it. Your agency, the police, the so-called security services; none of them are any different. They're all just criminals in uniforms. And if you want proof about your jumped-up little agency with its pretensions to grandeur, you have just seen the evidence for yourself.'

'That means nothing. I don't know what this charade is about, but I know Finn. He'd never make a deal.'

'To be honest, I think officer Williams is playing his own hand on this one. He has a wife, and we showed him our knowledge of where she lives. A very compelling argument. When the one you love teeters on the edge of a cliff, you do anything to pull them to safety. And so, with your colleague's help, Mira is already on her way to a rendezvous; every few miles, at a specified place, Finn calls so we may see where he is – and that Mira is still with him.' She paused and smiled. 'There is another incentive, I have to confess. We let him see the home movie we made, starring the gorgeous Parvati McNeil. I cannot be sure, but I suspect it upset him a little.'

How could she, even for a millisecond, have found this woman attractive? A serious look at her judgement making was in order if she came out of this intact. On the upside, Finn was on his way. Of course he was - she'd have done the same in his shoes.

'Where's all this meant to happen?' she asked. 'He's clearly not bringing Mira here.'

'Of course not. The whole point is to neutralise the girl; she has information – experiences – we would rather she did not share and we cannot take the risk that she might recover from her unfortunate illness. Finn is taking her to a remote spot on the other side of the Beacons, a long way from any road.'

'Do you really believe they won't track him?'

'That is the exciting part – it does not matter whether or not they track him. We told your friend that we shall reveal your whereabouts when Mira is in our hands. A slight dissimulation on our part. In fact, we have left a little gift at his destination, a daisy chain of IEDs – bombs to you and me, the type used in Iraq and Afghanistan. They were Mr Mitchell's idea, not mine – two tours of duty with the upright British Army have given him quite a creative spirit. And when Finn and Mira reach the prearranged spot – and we have been very precise in our instructions – he will call a mobile phone. Not this one, but a handset attached to a detonator. When the call connects, off go the explosives. End of Mira, end of Finn. And the really elegant part is that he does it all himself.'

Mitchell was shifting his feet behind her. What would it be – a broken neck, a slow strangulation, the choker? Or would it be the knife?

Bella was talking again. 'We have an operative hidden within sight of the co-ordinates, with a sniper rifle in case anything should go amiss. Ex-SAS, I believe, one of Mitchell's old colleagues. When he sees the explosion, he will confirm to us that the business is concluded.'

'My people will find you even if you kill me,' Pav said, 'and my jumped-up little agency will show you what rules it plays by.'

'If words were deeds, beggars would be kings. I am sorry, my friend, but we hold all the best cards.'

The sun had dipped below the line of purple hills and the night shadows were growing like ivy; she'd forgotten how quickly darkness came in the mountains. She shivered in the cool evening air and looked over at Sebastian, checking his watch every couple of minutes; he would have herded people into the gas chambers as he sung hymns, passing the buck.

'This policeman is late,' said Bonetti, breaking the silence. 'Where is the confirmation?'

No one replied. Bella stared at her mobile, Sebastian stared at Pav as if he were trying to send her a message by telepathy, Bonetti lost his smile for the first time. And then the phone rang.

Bella looked at the screen, scowling. 'No, you fool – you should have called the other number!' The thin tune filled the surrounding air until she cut it off.

'We should make the call ourselves,' said Bonetti. 'He made a mistake, he is at the rendezvous now. We should act quickly.'

'And what if there has been a problem? He will hear the explosion and the entire operation will fail.' She turned to Mitchell. 'Sanitise this place. Take Pav and the girl – you know what to do. They cannot hang around our necks like albatrosses.'

Pav tensed her body for one last chance at escape, but Mitchell had already grabbed her again. And then she saw a strange play of light and shadow a few hundred metres away, in the sunken lane beyond the security gates. Car headlamps driving towards The Swallows.

Bella noticed them at the same time and smiled. 'Ah - so we have another Judas among us,' she said, looking at Sebastian. 'Why am I not surprised?'

'You called me naïve,' said the priest. 'I was, for too long, but as soon as I saw what you were doing, I knew Anca was beyond my help. I couldn't be a part of this anymore, so I told Pav's colleague what you were planning. There won't be any explosion, you won't get Mira. Don't you understand? Everything is over.'

Bella spat at him. 'I always told Bonetti you were a weak link and I was right. If your Anca were still with us, she would thank us for saving her from such an excuse for a man. Remember; because of you she lost her name, then she lost her honour, then she lost her life.'

'But whatever you do to me,' said Sebastian, 'I've regained mine.'

The car headlamps stopped by the locked security gate at the end of the drive as Bella took the knife from Mitchell. 'I would like you, Father, to kneel in front of me; you should be used to submission from all those prayers.'

Sebastian shook his head. 'I'm done with submission. You're the one who needs prayers.'

Bella nodded at Mitchell. He released Pav, strode across to the unmoving priest, and forced him to his knees. As Sebastian sank down and closed his eyes, Bella took the knife from Mitchell and ran the tip across the knelling man's eyelids, leaving a fine thread of blood in its wake. 'Do you still hanker for your God, Father? Pray that he does not exist, or this life will seem like Paradise compared to what comes next.'

Pav started forward, but a jolt through the collar made her stumble and fall. Sebastian was muttering silent words as Bella grabbed his hair, forced his head back, and sliced across his throat with all her strength. He collapsed to the ground as the blood spurted from his severed arteries, twitching impotently as his breath and blood foamed across the gravel.

Pav looked away, feeling a strange sense of relief. So that's how it would be; quick, at least.

The car headlamps in the distance were still on full

beam, blinding them to any activity by the barred gate. 'Is there another way out from here?' asked Bonetti, a tremor in his voice.

'Through the barn,' said Bella. 'Leave the girl, but bring Pav. We might need some insurance.'

Bonetti slammed the door behind them. At the far end of the barn, beside the ancient tractor, a smaller door was set next to the corner of the building.

'If we are lucky, this is a one-man show,' said Bella. 'Officer Williams riding to the rescue to save his precious boss, all without the assistance of the police. Bad form to need their help, I believe, but it gives us a chance.'

'What chance? I haven't seen another road out of here,' said Bonetti.

Bella shook her head. 'We climb into the hills. Under that tarp are a couple of quad bikes, fuelled and ready to go.'

'Hills? What do you think I am?'

'I think you are annoying me. Come or stay, it is your choice.' She hesitated by the door, turning to Pav. 'As for you, sometimes insurance can become too expensive, so please behave yourself.'

She pulled the door open. In the dusk, a shadowy figure faced them less than ten feet away. 'Hello boss,' said Finn, 'this is a fine mess you've got yourself into.'

For a couple of beats, everyone seemed frozen in a tableau. 'All alone, as I suspected,' said Bella, eventually. 'Three versus one. Why sacrifice yourself?'

'It's much too late for threats,' he said. 'Let Pav go – there's no need for more killing.'

'This is my establishment, Mr Williams. Do not tell me what I need. Get out of our way if you want Pav to live.' She grabbed the control unit from Bonetti and held it in the air. 'You know what this is. The slightest movement from you and your colleague will get an unpleasant shock. It might kill her, it might not – that is the risk you would take.'

The pain was instant, blades of fire inside Pav's body reaching for her heart. Mitchell held her in the air like a shield as she kicked and tried to scream. Then it stopped. Mitchell lowered her to the ground and she fell to her knees, retching uncontrollably.

'As you see, it was agony. She could survive many brief episodes, but I believe the nerve endings become more raw each time.'

'What's the point of torturing her?'

'Insurance,' said Bella. 'Once we are safe, we shall leave her where you can find her. Now, Mr Williams, move away.'

'I don't think so.' A different voice this time, behind them. Amir.

As they all turned to look at the new threat, momentarily diverted, Pav reached behind her neck and snapped open the buckle of the choker before Bella noticed.

'Mitchell – stop her!'

But Pav was already on her feet. It had been a while since she'd used her karate training outside a dojo, but this was as good a time as any to use her go-to sequence. She took one step backwards as Mitchell lunged forward, her eyes fixed on the man's face, and then lashed out with the side of her foot, FumiKomi, connecting with his right knee as she stepped backwards again. Another kick, Mae Geri, this time to his jaw as his leg gave way and he fell forwards. She heard a bone crack somewhere, hoping it was one of his.

Finn was already by her side, but she didn't need his help; the body on the ground wasn't moving. Pav turned to face Bella, backed against the tractor with Bonetti standing behind her.

'Drop the knife,' said Pav. 'It's over. We held all the trumps after all.'

The blade wavered. 'Over? I believe this time you are correct. To tell the truth, I have waited too long for this day.' She smiled ruefully, took the knife with both hands and thrust it under her rib cage, up towards her heart.

TWENTY-SEVEN

The hospital kept Pav in overnight for observation. She told Finn she didn't want to go, but all he said was, 'You look like shit and you smell like shit,' and he was probably right. She slept without dreams, and was dressed and waiting when Finn arrived to drive her to her cottage at lunchtime the next day.

'Gus came to see you last night, but you were away with the fairies – after effects of all those drugs. He's expecting you to call him later.'

'Bella said you were operating solo – I believed her.'

'And I thought you had more faith in me.' He drove carefully, as if Pav would break with any sudden movement. 'If you're feeling up to it, there's a celebration planned for tonight,' he said. 'I know there are a few loose ends to tie up, but Operation Hexameter came up trumps.'

'Is celebrate the right word?'

'You're here, aren't you?'

'What about Mira and the other girl?'

'Mira's still in intensive care. As for the other girl...' He shook his head. 'Poor kid was alive when we got her to hospital, but she never regained consciousness. At least she didn't know what was going on around her yesterday.'

'And the others?'

'Mitchell has a cracked vertebra in his neck – that's some right foot you have – and Bella's in hospital. They gave her a few gallons of blood last night. Waste of effort if you want my opinion, but no-one bothered to ask.'

'Will she live?'

'I'm afraid so. Stabbing yourself in the heart is apparently much harder than you think. She'll probably end up in Rampton for the rest of her life doing art therapy, and getting monthly visits from a bishop who thinks she's rehabilitated. As for Bonetti, he needs incontinence pads for his mouth. If half what he said is true, they'll need new prisons to take all the sick fucks we'll be bringing in.'

HE MADE as if to turn down towards Blackbrook as they crossed the bridge outside Abertrothy, but Pav stopped him.

'Not straight home,' she said. 'I need to see my parents first.'

They took the back road to Lydford, through the edge of the forest. Autumn had moved down from the heights; the swathes of green wore patches of russet and gold, and the stands of bracken looked dry and burned.

Ma was half-asleep in her chair when they arrived, smiling and muttering something to herself. Pav kissed her on the forehead and she shifted slightly, but didn't open her eyes.

There was a fresh bruise on her temple, purple and red. 'I should have called the doctor,' said Pa, 'but what can they do? It was the flowers. I gave her a bunch of those orange lilies, her favourites, but I no sooner put the vase on the table that she picked it up and threw it at me. I tried to calm her, but she fell and hit herself on the arm of the chair.' He finished pouring the tea. 'What about your face, pet – what happened?'

He reached out to touch the plaster stuck over a cut on Pav's cheek; when she was little, he was the one to moisten a handkerchief and wipe the dirt away from a grazed knee or elbow. 'Pa's magic spit', he called it, and it always worked.

'A silly accident,' she said. 'Nothing to worry about.' She felt as though she hadn't seen them for a year, but it was less than a week since Ma went missing, the same day that Ash disappeared.

Pa saw them to the door. 'If you're free tomorrow,' he said, 'there's a nursing home on the Gloucester Road. I drove past it a couple of days ago, looks very pretty, very peaceful. I was thinking of your Ma – maybe we could talk to them together, you and me?'

HER CAR WAS WAITING outside the cottage. 'One of the lads brought it round for you,' said Finn. 'You were almost out of petrol so he put in a full tank – don't worry, I saw him right.'

The house smelled of bleach, and the furniture was all out of place. 'Sorry about that,' said Finn, 'we've been a little busy. Housekeeping was never my thing.'

Pav watched him straighten a couple of chairs; there was something about his smile that seemed pre-packaged, and meeting her eyes was difficult.

'I've had enough of being cooped up,' she said. 'I'm going up to the Dyke. Do you fancy a walk? It's not far and the views are excellent. I used to go there with Jess, back in the day. We'd take a few tinnies or a flask of gin and some tonics, put the world to rights. Come on, has to be better than hanging around here.'

Finn looked at his feet, then at his watch, then at her. 'I would, boss, believe me. But when I got in this morning, half past four it was, Sarah was still up. She told me she did a test yesterday. Talk about good timing; we're going to have a baby.'

She could swear there were tears in his eyes as he told her. She said the right things, pecked him on the cheek, told him she'd be okay, and watched as he drove down towards the main road, leaving her with nothing but an empty house and an empty heart, and wondering if betrayal would ever end.

THE END

AFTERWORD

ABOUT THE AUTHOR

CJ Emerson was born and raised on the outskirts of London, and has an unnerving obsession with technology. After obtaining an MA In Creative Writing, her first novel, **Objects of Desire**, was shortlisted for the Crimewriters' Association New Blood Dagger Award and is the first book in the Pav McNeil series of suspense thrillers.

CJ lives in a farmhouse in the Wye Valley with her wife, two recalcitrant collies, a rescued greyhound, a noisy cat, six hens and two rescued Australian Lowline cattle (in the fields, not the farmhouse...)

ALSO BY C. J. EMERSON

www.cjemerson.com

Crime and Thrillers

Objects of Desire - Pav McNeil Book 1

Another Judas - Pav McNeil Book 2

The Seven Deaths of Quincey Radlett

Sci-Fi and Fantasy

Convergence

Short Stories

The Scent of Roses